Sorcerers of the Nightwing

"I know Rolfe can be cool," she says. "I don't hate him the way Mother does. But the fact remains that he wants to hurt my family, and there you are sneaking off to meet with him. I'm telling you, Devon, in your search for the truth, you've gone too far. Alexander's not possessed, he's just a brat. And Rolfe isn't your friend, he's just using you to get at my mother!"

"That's not true, Cecily. If you knew the stuff I've just found out—"

"I don't want to hear any more of it. It's madness!"

She turns away sharply, her hair flying, rushing to the other side of the car and sliding in beside DJ. Devon hears the engine kick in.

"Cecily!"

He runs after the car as it starts to move. DJ looks out from the driver's window.

"Hey man, she's mine now," DJ says.

The car accelerates. And in that last instant before the Camaro guns out of the parking lot, Devon sees DJ grin — shiny pointed fangs in the dark, flashing a thumbs-up sign with a hooked, yellow talon.

Other titles in the *Sorcerers of the Nightwing* series:

Demon Witch

Visit the website at www.ravenscliff.com

Hellhole

Geoffrey Huntington

SCHOLASTIC

Scholastic Children's Books,
Commonwealth House, 1–19 New Oxford Street,
London, WC1A 1NU, UK
A division of Scholastic Ltd
London ~ New York ~ Toronto ~ Sydney ~ Auckland
Mexico City ~ New Delhi ~ Hong Kong

First published in the US by HarperCollins Publishers Inc., 2002

This edition published by Scholastic Ltd, 2003

Copyright © Geoffrey Huntington, 2002

ISBN 0 439 98260 X

Printed and bound in Great Britain by Cox & Wyman Ltd, Reading, Berkshire

10 9 8 7 6 5 4 3 2 1

The right of Geoffrey Huntington to be identified respectively as the author of this work has
been asserted by him in accordance with the Copyright, Designs and Patents Act, 1988.

For T.D.H

Contents

Prologue
Monsters in the Closet

Ted March calls it the Hellhole.

It's his son's closet — a plain, ordinary little closet with sliding maple doors, where the six-year-old boy hangs his shirts and tosses his sneakers, where his stuffed animals are tumbled in a pile on the floor. A closet that, at first, seems like any other, no different from those in the rooms of the other little boys in the tidy little houses that line their street.

But in Devon March's closet, green eyes stare out at him from the darkness.

"Daddy," the boy asks, "what's in there?"

Ted March calls it the Hellhole, but not so that Devon might hear. Ted is determined that the boy he's raising as his own will grow up as normally as possible — that the truth of his past will not prevent him from living his life like any other little boy. Everyone had agreed it was best that Devon not know the truth, and so Ted had taken the child far away from the place of his birth and spared him the legacy of his birthright — and the reason why his closet is a gateway to hell.

"Daddy," Devon cries, pointing. "There are eyes in there!"

And indeed there are. Until now, Ted has managed to keep

the demons at bay. He's caught the few that have slithered out of the closet like snakes, wriggling across the boy's floor and taking up posts under his bed. He's caught them and stomped them, sending them back to where they came from. So far, they've all been small creatures – stupid, reptilian things, easily snared with the ancient skills Ted learned from his own father, in the ancient, arcane alchemy of the Guardians.

"Daddy!" Devon's crying. "Something's *moving* in there!"

Until now, the boy hadn't actually *seen* anything – but he *had* heard them, whispering and hissing at night, their nefarious scuttling about in the Hellhole awakening him from a sound sleep. He'd cry out for Ted, who has learned to sleep with one eye and ear open. Moving is pointless: the demons followed them here from Misery Point, and they'd surely track them down no matter where they fled. For Devon himself is what they seek, and seek desperately: he is a Sorcerer of the Nightwing.

He is also a six-year-old boy, with the fears of any six-year-old boy awakened in the middle of the night. And as hard as his father tries to console him, the one thing he won't do is lie. He won't tell the child the sounds are only his imagination; he won't deny the hissing and scratching in his closet are real.

"Daddy, *look*," Devon cries again, more frantic now. "The eyes are *moving*!"

And they are. Ted March stands staring into the darkness of his son's closet. He feels the stifling heat, the throbbing pressure. Green bloodshot eyes blink languidly, once, then twice, over the pile of sneakers and stuffed animals.

"They can't hurt you, Devon," Ted whispers to his son. "Remember that. No matter what. You are stronger than they are."

"But I'm scared!" the little boy cries.

Yes, that's the rub: they might not be able to hurt him, but they *can* frighten him. Frighten him badly, at least while he's still a child. Ever since the Madman opened the Hellhole at Ravenscliff, the demons have been loose, and Ted knows all too well that the sealing of the Portal six years ago didn't corral them all. They followed them here, hundreds of miles away, burrowing down deep into Devon's closet to forge a new Hellhole, taking up residence in their house like rats in a basement.

Ted watches as the eyes grow larger in the darkness. It's waking. It senses them, and its eyes narrow in contemplation. Ted can hear the demon's breath now, hissing like a faulty radiator.

"Stand back, Devon," he commands.

The little boy shrinks in terror beside his bed. His father stands facing the closet. The demon within stirs, one long arm stretching out from the dark, human except for the talons where fingers would have been.

Ted glances quickly around the room, his eyes landing on Devon's baseball bat. Grabbing it, he raises it into the air. "By the power of the Nightwing, I order you back," he yells, swinging the bat down hard on the creature's arm.

A roar of pain and anger shakes the room. Devon clutches on to his bedpost, his little eyes wide in fright. He covers his ears as the demon screams again, not retreating from his father's assault but rather pushing itself forward into the room.

Into the light.

Ted gasps in repugnance. He's seen many demons in the flesh: in his youth, on the moors of England, he battled hundreds of the tribe, stuffed dozens of the filthy brutes back down the throats of their Hellholes. But never had the sight of them not elicited repulsion. This one – tall and gaunt, dripping pus and slime, taloned and fanged – is particularly beastly.

"Get back, you hellspawn," Ted shouts, landing a savage roundhouse kick to the monster's gut. It roars, its strangely humanoid face grimacing in both pain and outrage. Its long unruly hair, growing from both its head and body, swings furiously, slapping Ted across the face and filling his nostrils with the stink of death.

"You can't touch Devon," he calls. "He's stronger than you are – and you know it!"

The thing rears back on its haunches, as if to spring. But instead, it lashes out with a sweep of its long arm, slashing Ted across the face with its talons, drawing blood.

"Daddy!" Devon screams.

Ted lunges. Gripping the creature around its middle, he topples it over, back into the closet. It roars again, the room jolted as if by an earthquake. Model dinosaurs and miniature cars rain from Devon's shelves; his bookcase tips over, spewing *Batman* videotapes across the floor. The demon, enraged, tosses Ted across the room; only the wall stops his flight. Ted thuds hard against the plaster, sliding down into a sitting position, stunned and helpless as the demon advances toward him.

"Daddy!" Devon cries.

The creature lumbers across the hardwood floor. Devon is crying, watching it approach his father, its long red tongue darting out of its mouth and licking its sharp teeth. Later, such scenes will be remembered as horrible nightmares; but in the moment, the little boy stands terrified, convinced he is about to watch his father be devoured, and that he is next.

"No!" Devon shouts.

That is all: just a simple no, and the creature turns, its eyes blazing terror.

"No!" Devon repeats, and instinctively puts out his hand.

You are stronger than they are, his father has always said.

"No!" Devon commands again.

The demon roars. Devon bites down hard on his lip and concentrates with all his might. "Go back!" he cries, and with a sweep of his arm, sends the demon flying through the air and back inside the closet. The door slides shut with a bang, and the room falls suddenly silent.

"Daddy?" Devon asks in a very small voice.

Ted March opens his eyes. The demon is gone. The heat, too. He looks up and sees his little dark-eyed son standing over him. He smiles.

Devon has yet to lose all his baby fat, but in some ways he's already a man.

"Daddy, are you OK?" Devon is asking, his little eyes welling with tears.

"I'm fine, Devon," Ted says, opening his arms. His son falls into them gratefully. "You are a strong boy, Devon. You are stronger than they are."

He holds the boy close. He can feel his heart beating wildly, his small frame trembling.

Yes, he is stronger than they are, but not nearly so cunning. They'll use that against him. This one was clumsy, ignorant — but there are others, and Ted knows they'll come too.

And the Madman — Ted doesn't believe for a second that he's really gone for good.

Father, teacher, but mostly Guardian — Ted March has pledged his life to little Devon. He vows again that no harm will come to him, that he will live as a normal boy might, that his life will be as free from the horrors of his birthright as possible.

Not an easy vow, Ted knows, when the monsters in the closet are real.

Eight Years Later

1
Misery Point

For one long moment the mournful howl of some distant animal obscures the sound of the wind. Devon March steps off the bus, one hand lugging his heavy suitcase, the other clasping the medal of St Anthony in his pocket, squeezing it so tightly that it pinches the flesh of his palms.

He feels the heat, even on this damp, windy, cold October night, the heat and the energy he's recognized ever since he was a small boy. *They're out there*, he thinks. *In the night. Watching me, as they always have.*

He heads down the steps, stepping off on to the concrete. Behind him, the bus driver yanks the doors closed and the bus screeches off into the night.

The station is left in darkness, with just an autumn moon to light his way. Only one other person had gotten off the bus with him, a man whose footsteps now echo through the empty terminal ahead of him. The rain has not yet come, but Devon can feel it already in the wind and the salty dampness blowing up from the sea. Mr McBride had said it would be this way. "Why else would they call it Misery Point?"

Devon walks out into the lot and looks around. A car had

been promised to meet him. Perhaps they were just late; perhaps the bus had been a few minutes early. But as the shadows flicker in the windy moonlight, Devon can't shake his sudden sense of foreboding. He'd expected that the creatures would follow him here, that they wouldn't allow him to simply get away. What he hadn't expected was the intensity of the heat: always the sure signal that they were close by. From the moment he'd stepped off the bus, the heat had been far more intense than it ever had been in New York.

This place holds answers, the Voice inside himself says. *That's why your father sent you here.*

In the distance, thunder rumbles.

What had the old woman said to him on the bus?

"You'll find no one there but ghosts."

"Excuse me," comes a voice, interrupting his thoughts.

Devon turns. In the empty parking lot stands a man – the same who had gotten off the bus with him a moment ago. "Are you waiting for a ride?"

"Yeah," Devon tells him. "I was supposed to be met here."

The man carries a suitcase not unlike Devon's own. He looks to be in his late thirties, tall, handsome, dark. "Well," he says, "I can't imagine a less hospitable place to be stood up. Do you need a ride into town?"

"I'm sure I'm not stood up," Devon tells him.

The man shrugs. "OK then. Just wouldn't want you to get caught in the rain."

Devon watches him. The man continues on his way to his car – a silver Porsche – parked a few yards away. It's the only car in the lot.

This man knows. This man knows what I came here to find.

The Voice comes to him as it always has: small, sure, far back in his mind. It's a voice unlike any other thought:

clear, sharp speech that Devon cannot recognize as his own.

He knows, the Voice tells him again. *Don't let him get away.*

Just what the man knows Devon isn't sure, but one thing is certain: if he hopes to find answers in this place, he needs to listen to the Voice. It's never failed him before.

"Yo!" Devon calls.

But the wind has swelled up fiercely, drowning him out.

"Hey! Mister!" he calls again, louder.

The man, oblivious, opens his car door and slides inside. Devon hears the kick of the ignition. The car's headlights switch on.

There's no time, Devon thinks. *He wouldn't see me if I try to make a run for him.*

There's only one way. He prays that it will work. He concentrates. The car begins to back out of the spot. Devon closes his eyes. He concentrates harder.

And suddenly the driver's door blows open.

"What the——?" the man shouts.

Devon grasps his suitcase tightly and begins to run toward the car.

"Hey!" he shouts.

The man leans out from the open door, finally aware of Devon. Yet he seems more concerned with checking his car door hinges than with the boy running up to him.

"Hey," Devon says, a little out of breath. "Your offer for a ride still hold?"

The man looks over at him, then quizzically back at his door. "Oh, yeah," he says. "Sure, kid. Jump in."

"You the man," Devon says, beaming.

Yes, he is, agrees the Voice. *A man with answers.*

Answers Devon has come to Misery Point to find.

* * *

11

Devon March is fourteen years old. He's not like other boys; he's known that since age four, when he made his dog Max levitate across the room. One time, running a relay race with his best friend Tommy, Devon had sprinted across the playground before any of the other kids had even left the starting point. He's stood face to face with Demons – so close he could see right up their flaring nostrils, demonic nose-hair and all. That's not something he imagines many other kids his age can claim.

No, he's not like other boys. Not at all.

"You have a gift," his father had told him, ever since he was little. "You can do things others can't. Things people wouldn't understand. Things they might fear."

"But why, Dad? *Why* can I do these things?"

"Why doesn't matter, Devon. Just know that all power ultimately comes from good, and so long as you use your power in the pursuit of the light, you will always be stronger than whatever else is out there."

So they had kept the secret between them. Devon had grown up knowing he was different, but never knowing why. His father promised him that someday he would understand his destiny. But until then, he had only to trust in the power of good.

"Call it God, as many do," his father had told him, shortly before he died. "Call it a higher force, the spirit of the universe, the power of nature. It is all of these things. It is the light within you."

Dad had started talking in these weird riddles in his last weeks, and Devon had sat there trying to make them out as best he could. But in trying to figure them out, he had gotten exactly *jack* – and then Dad had died, leaving Devon with a whole new set of mysteries to ponder.

"You're going *where?*" the old woman sitting next to him on the bus had asked.

"Misery Point," Devon repeated. "It's on the coast of Rhode Island, near Newport."

"I *know* where it is," she'd said, all eyes and shriveled mouth, "and *you'll find no one there but ghosts*."

Up until that point, the old woman had taken a liking to him. She'd asked where he was from, and he'd told her upstate New York, a little town called Coles Junction. They'd exchanged pleasantries and watched the colors of the New England foliage pass outside their window. But once he spoke the words *Misery Point*, Devon found her strange and recoiling.

"Ghosts?" Devon asked her. "Whaddya mean, *ghosts?*"

"I know these parts," she warned. "And that is not a place for a young man to go. Stay away from there."

Devon laughed. "Well, I'd take your warning under advisement, but see, my dad died, and he left guardianship to an old friend of his, who lives there. So my choices are rather limited, you understand."

She was shaking her head. "Don't get off the bus. You stay right where you are until it turns around and heads back to wherever you came from." She looked at him. Her old eyes were yellow and lined, but they glowed with a ferocity he hadn't expected to see there. "There are *legends*," she said.

His hand sought the indentation of the St Anthony medal in his pocket. "What kind of legends?" he asked.

"About the *ghosts*," the woman said, lowering her voice. "I'm telling you true, my dear boy. All you'll find there are ghosts. Oh, you young people today think nothing can harm you. You with your rap music and earphones in your ears – you've tuned out on the world around you."

But that wasn't true: at least not about Devon. He knew

that some things simply couldn't be explained, that there did exist a realm of . . . of . . . something else. When he was a boy, fearful of the monsters in his closet, his father hadn't soothed him with assurances that such things didn't exist. How could he, when Devon at six had already witnessed one try to bite off both their heads? Rather, Dad had comforted the boy by telling him he was stronger than any demon, that his powers were deep and rare.

Rare they certainly were, for they came and went with a frustrating infrequency. In times of crisis – like demon invasions of his bedroom, for example, or the time Dad nearly fell off the ladder painting the house – Devon's powers never failed. Devon always managed to save the day in those cases. But try to impress a girl by lifting a barbell with only your mind, and forget it. His powers seemed to have a will of their own, sometimes fading away, other times popping out with no warning. Like that day in Woolworth's, when he wasn't more than five, when he'd wanted that Transformer so bad – the little toy car had just risen off the shelf and floated across the aisle, dropping into Devon's bookbag. He hadn't stolen it; it had simply *followed* him. Dad was very surprised to find it when they got home, but he had accepted – he had *believed* – Devon's story of how it got there.

Then there was the time Mrs Grayson had punished him for talking in class. She was a nasty old sow, a shriveled apple of a woman everyone despised. She made Devon turn his desk around the opposite way, facing the back wall. Mortified – how he hated being singled out from the rest – Devon wished with all his might that he wasn't the only one so punished. Suddenly, every desk in the class turned around to match Devon's. Snarly old Mrs Grayson practically had a coronary up there by the chalkboard.

Yet other than the powers and the demons – not insignificant exceptions, he admits – Devon *is* like any other kid his age. At least he had been before he was sent away: hanging out with his friends, listening to music, playing computer games. He'd been a good student, with lots of friends, not the *most* popular kid in school, maybe, but certainly not *un*popular.

All that changed when his father died less than a month ago. Ted March had a heart attack in August, and was confined to his bed. "You'll get better, Dad," Devon had insisted.

His father just smiled. "I'm a very, very old man, Devon. My time grows short."

"Dad, you're only in your fifties." He looked at his father intently. "That's not so old."

His father had just smiled and closed his eyes.

Dad lingered a month. He tried to rally, but never found the strength. Devon found him one morning, just as the sun was breaking over the horizon. Dad had died quietly in his sleep, alone. Devon just sat there for an hour at the side of his father's bed, stroking his cold hand and letting the tears run down his cheeks. Only then did he telephone Mr McBride, Dad's lawyer, and give him the news.

How quickly his old life had been replaced. Practically the only thing Devon has left from that old life is Dad's St Anthony medal. It once jangled among the coins in his father's pocket, always at ready grasp. His father had called it a talisman. When Devon had asked what a talisman was, his father had smiled. "Just call it my good luck charm."

Devon holds the medal now in his palm and feels strong, feels connected to the father he misses more than he can possibly express. He still wakes up forgetting everything that's happened these past few weeks: the funeral, the lawyers, the reading of the will – especially the startling confession Dad made on his deathbed. Devon still wakes up thinking things are the way they've always been: Dad out in the kitchen frying eggs and bacon, Max panting eagerly in the hallway, his best bud Tommy and his best girl Suze waiting for him at the bus stop.

But in the second moment of wakefulness he always remembers: Dad is dead, Max has gone to live with Tommy, his old friends and old school have been left behind, and the topper of them all: *Dad wasn't even his real father.* Devon had been *adopted.* That's what Dad told him right before he died. That knowledge has been even harder to absorb than the fact that Dad is dead.

"I may not have been your blood," his father told him, in a soft, weak voice, his frail body propped up with pillows, "but always know that I loved you as my own son."

Devon had been unable to respond.

"I'm sending you to live with a family in Rhode Island. Trust me, Devon. They will know what's best for you."

"Dad, why did you never tell me before?"

His father smiled sadly. "It was for the best, Devon. I know I ask a lot when I ask you to just trust me, but you do, don't you?"

"Of course I do, Dad." Devon felt the tears push forward and drop, hot and stinging, one by one down his cheeks. "Dad, you can't die. Please. Don't leave me alone. The Demons may come back. And I still don't understand why."

"You're stronger than any of them, Devon. Remember that."

"But Dad, *why* am I this way? You said I'd understand some-day. You can't die without telling me the truth. Please Dad! Does *what* I am have something to do with *who* I am? With my real parents?"

Dad tried to answer, but found he couldn't. He just closed his eyes and settled back into his pillows. He died that night.

After the will was read, Dad's lawyer, old Mr McBride, told Devon that guardianship had been left to a woman named Mrs Amanda Muir Crandall, way out on the rocky coast of Rhode Island – in a place called Misery Point.

You'll find no one there but ghosts.

Ah – but they are your ghosts, the Voice in his head tells him.

The old woman beside him on the bus had kept her distance the rest of the way. Devon concentrated on the landscape rolling by outside his window. The day was fading. The heavy blue of the sky, threatening rain all day, blended into a wet violet, like an amateur watercolor. Mist speckled his window, and he looked out into the dampness with a growing ache of loneliness.

"You're nearly a man," Mr McBride had told him, dropping him at the bus station, not even waiting with him for the bus to arrive.

Yes, nearly a man, Devon thinks. He'd passed innocence a long time ago – the first time the eyes in his closet turned out to be real, in fact – but he still felt very young and very alone riding that bus.

Dad. . .

In the reflection of the window he tries to remember his father's face.

How can I face them without you? How can I learn everything I need to understand? How can I find out who I really am?

Thunder crackles, and suddenly the sky opens. The earth is all at once bombarded by rain. Devon slides quickly into the Porsche next to the man he's convinced holds some answers.

"The name's Rolfe Montaigne," the man says, reaching over to shake Devon's hand.

"Devon March," the boy replies.

Raindrops pound on the roof of the car like hundreds of tiny tap dancers each in a race to see who's fastest. In the dry interior, Devon finds the smell of leather soothing, the soft supple seat seeming to embrace him. The heat's gone, the pressure's lifted. He rests his head back and closes his eyes.

Montaigne flicks on the wipers and they begin swishing across the glass. He shifts into reverse, and looking over his shoulder, begins backing the car up again.

"Looks as if we made it just in time," he says. "It's supposed to get pretty bad tonight. You haven't seen a storm till you've seen one at Misery Point."

"Guess that's where the name comes from, huh?"

"That and a few other things." Montaigne heads the car out onto the road. "So where are you headed?"

Devon opens his eyes and looks over at him. "It's a house called Ravenscliff. Do you know it? Can you drop me there?"

"Do I know it?" Montaigne looks over at him sharply. "Kid, I wouldn't drive you up to Ravenscliff if I had garlic around my car windows and a crucifix on my dashboard."

Devon smiles. "So that'd be a no?"

"What are you going there for?" Montaigne asks.

Devon's not sure he should answer. "Look, if you don't want to drive up there—"

Montaigne shakes his head, a smirk creeping across his lips. "I'll take you as far as the Borgo Pass. You can get a cab there."

"Very funny," Devon says. "I get the references. I've read *Dracula*. Borgo Pass. Garlic. What — are there *vampires* at Ravenscliff? What is it about this place? Why's everyone scared of it?"

"It is Walpurgis night," Montaigne says, laughing, mock blessing himself with his free hand. He winks over at Devon. "*Nosferatu.*"

"You don't scare me, man."

"I don't?" Rolfe asks, grinning over at him, white teeth in the dark. "You sure?"

Devon turns away. Maybe he *should* be scared. Maybe this guy holds answers because he's in with the demons. But the Voice is silent, confirming nothing. Devon looks out onto the watery streets, the rain distorting the view through the glass. The street beyond is a river of blues and reds and yellows, cast in shadows, the neon of storefronts reflecting crazily.

Silence falls over the car, the only sound the swish of the wipers and the pounding rain. The highway passes over a large body of water and Devon feels the force of the high wind. They arrive onto a long narrow stretch of land. He knows from looking at a map that Misery Point sits at the end of a long rocky peninsula, jutting out from the coast into the roiling waters where Rhode Island Sound meets the Atlantic Ocean. Wind and water pelt the car windows. He hears again Mr McBride's brittle laugh. *Why do you think it's called Misery Point?*

Devon watches the swaying beams of the Porsche's head-lights as they cut into the stormy blackness of the crooked road ahead, revealing little but hostile barren branches that reach out across the road.

"Not that it's any of my business," Montaigne says, breaking the uneasy silence, "but is your business at Ravenscliff brief?"

"Not very." Devon looks over at him, deciding to try the truth. "It's only like permanent." He waits a beat. "I'm going there to live."

"Live? You're going there to *live*?"

Devon nods. "My father just died, and guardianship was left to the lady who lives at Ravenscliff. Mrs Crandall." There's no need to say more; for now, Devon withholds any further information, waiting to see what the Voice meant about the man having answers.

Montaigne looks over at him briefly, but returns his eyes to the road. The rain's coming down more furiously now. "Are you a relative?" he asks.

"Not that I'm aware. All my dad told me was that she'd know what was best for me."

"Curious." Montaigne seems to roll the information over in his mind. "Mighty curious indeed."

They come to a red light, which seems to swim in the watery darkness beyond the windshield. They pull to a stop and Montaigne looks over at the boy.

"I'm sorry about your father," he says.

Devon looks away. He can't reply.

"I know what it's like," Montaigne tells him. "I lost my father when I was eight."

The light changes. They begin driving through what appears to be the center of the village. White clapboard shops, many with their windows boarded up for the season.

"So why do you say it's curious?" Devon asks. "Do you know the people at Ravenscliff?"

Montaigne makes a small laugh. The windshield wipers screech like angry sea birds. "Oh, yes," the man tells him quietly, "I know them. *Very* well."

Devon notes the sarcasm in his voice. "Maybe you knew my father then," he inquires. "Ted March."

Montaigne considers the name. "No, sorry. I've lived here most of my life, except for a few years when I was out making my fortune. Can't say I recall that name. *Ted March*." He smiles.

"But then, Amanda Muir Crandall has *lots* of secrets. If your father said he knew her, I don't doubt him."

The man looks over at Devon again. His eyes are deeply set, and shine a brilliant green, even here in the darkened car.

He knows, the Voice tells Devon again.

But *what*? Devon doesn't think Montaigne is necessarily lying, but there's *history* behind his words, a history Devon is sure would answer many of his own questions. Who he is, where he got his powers. There's something about Rolfe Montaigne that troubles him, but he can't quite finger it. Certainly he feels none of the heat here in his car, none of the ominous pressure that signals the Demons are close.

"How do you know Mrs Crandall?" Devon asks.

"I'm an old friend," Rolfe tells him. "You make sure you give her my regards."

Devon knows that's bogus. He trusts his perceptions. Dad had called it "sensitivity," and they'd try to read each other's thoughts. Devon could sometimes manage, calling out "Chocolate cake!" and Dad would admit he was hankering for a snack.

The car splashes through a deep gut in the road, but Rolfe Montaigne doesn't seem to notice. "So you'll have to transfer to school here," he observes.

"Yeah. That's probably the worst part. I hate being the new kid."

"What year are you in?"

"I'm a sophomore."

Montaigne nods. "Did you talk with Mrs Crandall at all before coming up here?"

"No," Devon says. "My father's lawyer did. I haven't had any communication with her at all. I know she has a daughter my age."

"Oh, yes. Cecily." Montaigne smiles. "And then there's the nephew. Surely you know about Alexander."

"No," Devon admits.

"An eight year old." Montaigne looks over at him. His white teeth flash in the dark again. "You like kids?"

"Sure."

Montaigne laughs. "After you meet little Alexander, you might rethink that idea."

He turns the wheel and heads off the road, into a parking lot beside a large white house. A sign hangs out front in old Gothic lettering:

Stormy Harbor

It swings ferociously in the wind. The tires of the car crunch gravel before coming to a stop. "Here we are," Montaigne says, smiling strangely across at Devon. "The Borgo Pass. You can get a cab here to take you up to the house."

"Thanks for the ride," Devon says, turning to open the door.

"Not yet," Montaigne says, suddenly and roughly reaching across the boy to snap the car door's lock into place. "Not so fast."

Devon, startled, makes a small sound, shrinking back into his seat. Rolfe Montaigne's face is no more than four inches from his. Devon's heart echoes the rhythm of the rain pounding on the roof of the car: hard, fast, furious. He looks deep into the green eyes of this strange man, the very first man he's met since leaving the safe world of his father, his friends, his dog and his school.

"Next time," Rolfe Montaigne whispers menacingly, "you ought to think twice about who you accept rides from.

Anybody could have told you to stay away from Rolfe Montaigne. They could have told you that Rolfe Montaigne served five years in prison – for *killing* a young boy just like you."

2
The House on the Hill

"Back off," Devon says in a small, hushed voice.

Rolfe Montaigne laughs. "Sorry, kid," he says. "Didn't mean to scare you."

He leans back into his seat. Devon exhales. His hands are tightly drawn into fists, prepared to have used whatever power he might have summoned. But it doesn't appear he needs to.

"You totally *did* mean to scare me," he tells Montaigne.

The man's looking at him. "Just figured you were going to start hearing all sorts of scary stories about me, especially up there at Ravenscliff. Figured I'd let you hear it from me first."

Devon swallows. "Did you really kill——?"

"You ask Mrs Crandall to give you the whole story," Montaigne says, opening his car door and stepping outside. In seconds he's opening Devon's door, shielding him from the rain with an umbrella. "I'm sure Mrs Crandall will be only too happy to give you *all* the details."

Devon squints into the rainy darkness, trying to make sense of the place.

Montaigne gestures up at the stormclouds. "Welcome," he says, "to Misery Point."

The murky yellow light of the windows of Stormy Harbor burn through the rain. Devon and Montaigne hurry inside, where the older man shakes his umbrella and heads without any further word off toward the phone booth in back.

The place is dark, paneled in deep brown wood, hung with fishing nets and life preservers. The floorboards are uneven, warped from decades of sea air. A few tables with kerosene lamps are scattered across the floor; two craggy old men sit against a far wall drinking beer and smoking pipes.

Lining the front wall is a bar edged with stools. Devon sidles onto one, attracting the attention of the bartender. She's a plump young woman with close cut red hair, a dimple in her chin and a gold hoop through her left eyebrow. She doesn't look much older than Devon, but he figures she's got to be at least twenty-one to be working behind the bar.

"What'll it be?" she chirps.

"Do you have hot chocolate?" Devon asks.

"Sure, kid." She pours him a cup. "Here ya go. Ain't a fit night out for – ah, you know the rest."

Devon smiles. "Well, it certainly is beastly out there."

"You new in town?"

"Yes," Devon tells her, sipping the chocolate. It was good. Nice and hot. "Just arrived tonight."

"Where from?"

"New York."

"Really now?" She leans forward. "You're a big city boy."

"No," he tells her. "From upstate."

"Oh." The bartender folds her arms across her chest. "So what brings you all the way out to Misery Point, at the end of nowhere?"

"I'm going to live with a family here. At Ravenscliff. Do you know the place?"

There it is again, Devon realizes: *that look*. The same look the old woman had given him on the bus; the same that crossed Rolfe Montaigne's face in the car.

"Do I *know* the place?" The bartender laughs. "Everyone in Misery Point knows Ravenscliff. How could we not? That family owns half the town."

"They're very wealthy, I was told."

"They've got more money than *God*." She grabs a dishcloth and begins wiping down the bar. "The Muirs practically built this village. Bought the fishing fleet, started the tourist trade, everything. There was nothing here before the Muirs. Every schoolkid knows the legends of Ravenscliff – how old Horatio Muir built the house out there on the point and how all the ravens descended and came to live there."

"Ravens?"

"Yup. You know, the big black birds. My grandfather remembers when the place was covered with them. That's how it got its name. There aren't any ravens up there any more, but the place is still the creepiest thing you can imagine."

Devon laughs. "I was told all I'd find there are ghosts."

Her eyes twinkle. "You were told right. Ghosts and a few crazy real live people." She grins. "I'm Andrea, by the way. You?"

"Devon," he tells her. They shake hands.

"So you're *really* going up to that house to *live*?"

He grins. "Mrs Crandall is my guardian. My father died. I kind of got left to her in the will."

"No way," Andrea says. "That's one odd lady. Her daughter's pretty cool, though. Cecily. She comes in here to hang. She's about your age."

"Well, that's good. I was beginning to think it was going to be pretty depressing up there."

Andrea shrugs. "I don't know what the town you came from is like, but Misery Point can be pretty bleak. Especially like in January, February, March. Summertime, that's a different story. We're just under three thousand in the winter, but at the peak of the season – Fourth of July through Labor Day – we've got something like forty thousand tourists crammed in."

"Wow."

"You know, I think it's the name. You'd think it would keep people away, but no. Everybody wants to say they've been to Misery Point and back. Us poor townies – we kill ourselves in the summer trying to accommodate all of them. I suppose we should be grateful. It's their dollars that keep us all living from September to May."

"I'll be fifteen by summer," Devon tells her. "I'd like to get a job."

"There'll be plenty of them. So you're what? A sophomore?"

"Yeah. I've got to start school here in a week. Coming in mid-semester is kind of weird. I'm not looking forward to it."

"Cecily will take care of you. She's got her own little clique of friends. It's not a bad school. I graduated a few years ago. It's a regional, so that's cool. At least you meet kids from outside Misery Point." She fiddles with the ring in her eyebrow. "So you think you'll stay here for good?"

Devon looks off towards the windows. The rain continues to crash against the glass. "I don't know," he tells her. "For now, I have no choice. But later. . ."

His words fade off. He's wondered ever since the will was read how long he'd stay here. Part of him had rebelled against the idea of leaving Coles Junction and his friends. But another part of him had been compelled by the Voice: *The answers are there. Who you are. What you are.*

That night, in the hours after Dad died, the heat in his room had suddenly ratcheted up twenty degrees. Devon, in his grief, didn't think he was strong enough to withstand whatever it was that haunted him. But he *was* — just as he'd always been: with just one sharp look and a wave of his hand, his armoire had slid across his room, blocking his door. The knob turned and rattled, but nothing had gotten in.

The answers are here, the Voice is telling him.

And Devon agrees: *I knew that from the moment I stepped off the train.*

"Anybody tell you about the kid?" Andrea's asking.

Devon returns his eyes to her. "The kid? Oh, you mean the little boy at Ravenscliff."

She nods. "'Little boy' is a deceptive description. Try *monster*. Try *gremlin*. Do you know why they kicked him out of the school he was going to up in Connecticut?"

Devon grins. "I'm afraid to find out."

Andrea laughs. "He set the curtains in the cafeteria on fire. The cafeteria! Now, I could understand the headmaster's bedroom, or the math classroom — but the cafeteria!"

Devon shakes his head. "Sounds like a kid with a severe case of I-want-attention-and-I-want-it-now."

"Alexander Muir is definitely twisted. Growing up in that house, I can understand."

"Too many ghosts?" Devon smiles.

Andrea shrugs. "Hey, that's what they say." She leans in towards him. "You can still hear Emily Muir's screams at Devil's Rock. And this is first-hand information, buddy. I've heard them myself."

"Whoa," Devon says. "Screams? Devil's Rock?"

"Yeah. It's the highest point overlooking the sea, out at the end of the Muir estate, the very tip of Misery Point. Emily

Muir threw herself off the cliff forty years ago. It's said she found her husband with another woman."

Devon grins. "I see."

"Scoff if you must, but her husband is the worst ghost of all. Jackson Muir. My parents remember him from when they were kids. He terrorized the village. They say he was a warlock."

"*Warlock?* Like Uncle Arthur on *Bewitched?*"

She tosses the dishrag at him. "Hey, I'm just repeating what I've been told. Poor old Jackson. None of his spells could bring his precious Emily back, and so he died in grief."

"You're just trying to freak me out," Devon tells her, smirking.

Andrea grins. "Have I succeeded?"

"No." He takes another sip of chocolate. "I don't scare easily. Never have."

"Well, you just watch out for yourself. Mrs Crandall is just this side of Loony Toons. I'll see her driving along in that Jaguar of hers. She'll show up in some local shop all covered up with scarves so that you can hardly see her face and then she'll haggle over the price of a ten-dollar pair of sandals." She leans over the bar. "And do you know what *else* is weird about that family? They've only got one servant. *One servant!* Can you imagine? For that big house? Why, I can barely keep my little one-room apartment clean, and they've got *fifty!*"

"Fifty rooms?"

"Yup. Can you *imagine?*"

No, Devon can't. But somewhere in those fifty rooms he's convinced he'll find a clue to who he is and where his strange powers come from.

"More chocolate?" Andrea asks.

"No, thanks," Devon says, draining his cup. He looks over

his shoulder. Rolfe Montaigne is still on the pay phone. "Is there another phone I could use? I need to call a cab to get me to Ravenscliff."

"They didn't even send a car to get you?"

"They were supposed to, but no one was there." Devon takes his wallet out of his jacket pocket and withdraws two dollars, setting them on the counter. "That guy over there gave me a ride here."

Andrea looks off in Montaigne's direction and makes a face.

"You aren't messed up with Rolfe Montaigne, are you?" she asks.

"No, he just gave me a ride. Why? *Shouldn't* I be?" He looks at Andrea intently. "He told me he went to jail for murder. Is that true, or was he just trying to scare me?"

She snorts. "I've told you enough horror stories tonight. Don't get me started on Rolfe Montaigne."

She moves off to wait on a couple of new customers, an old man and a young woman. Devon watches them, waits to see if he picks anything up from them. Nothing. No voice. No heat. No energy.

But he knows there are people in this town who hold the truth he seeks. And he'll find them. Fate – or whatever – had already brought him into contact with one: the mysterious Rolfe Montaigne.

"Hey," Andrea calls to him, pointing across the bar. "Your phone's free."

Devon looks around. Rolfe has left. From outside, he can hear the engine of the Porsche kick in; the headlights cast their light through the windows behind the bar.

"Not even a goodbye," Devon murmurs.

He slides off his stool and walks across the room. Posted

above the phone are numbers for taxi companies. He calls one, gives the dispatcher his location, and is told someone will be by in about five minutes.

"You stop in here often," Andrea tells him when he returns to the bar. "I'll keep you sane."

Devon promises. When the cab honks from outside, the rain has eased up. Devon hurries outside and hops in the back seat. The driver is a squat man with leathery skin – a fisherman by day, Devon imagines – and dark eyes under a heavy brow. He too seems surprised when Devon tells him his destination is Ravenscliff, arching a furry eyebrow at him in his rearview mirror. But he says nothing and drives on.

The moon re-emerges from the dark gray clouds over-head, a shy child peeking around a corner past its bedtime. Its light is hesitant, unsure: it comes and goes, but it's bright enough to illuminate the jagged wet rocks on the side of the road and the crashing sea beyond. The white caps of the waves seem unbearably cold to Devon. He listens as they crash on the beach below.

Finally, up ahead, standing against the moonlight on the top of Devil's Rock, he sees Ravenscliff. It's little more than a shadow at first, a silhouette, as if it were a painted backdrop on a stage.

"There she is," the cab driver croaks.

"Yes," Devon replies, his eyes caught.

"I don't much say anything to the folks I drive," the man tells him, glancing sharply in the rearview mirror. "And God knows I see enough that I *could* say something. I pick up drunks and take 'em home to their wives. I pick up politicians and bring 'em to their mistresses. I don't say nothin'. Never have. But tonight, I'll give you a tip."

"What's that?" Devon asks. They round a curve on the

seaside road and begin the drive up the hill. Ravenscliff looms over them now, poised on the edge of the cliff.

"You do whatever business you have up there and leave," the cab driver tells him. "Don't ask no questions. Just do what you came to do and get out."

Devon keeps his eyes on the dark mansion. There are only two windows lit, both on the first floor. The light seems dull and uninspired, as if hesitant to disturb the shadows. A tower rises from the east end of the house into the black-violet sky.

"I'm afraid that will be difficult for me to do," Devon explains. "I'm going to live there."

The driver grunts. "Well, I feel sorry for you, my boy. I worked for Edward Muir once, on one of his boats. He thought he owned me. Don't let him do that to you."

The cab driver pulls over to the side of the road. Ravenscliff is still some yards in the distance up the hill.

"Why did you stop?" Devon asks.

"This is the end of the line for me."

Devon laughs. If anything, he isn't surprised: he might have expected such behavior, given everything else tonight. "What?" he asks. "Are you afraid the werewolves will be set loose upon you if you drive any closer?"

"Might be," the man says, and he seems utterly serious.

Devon gets out of the cab, lugging his heavy suitcase behind him. "Here," he says, thrusting three dollars through the front window. He's a little angry, tired of all these folks acting so scared, rattling his nerves. "Don't bother looking for a tip because you won't find one."

"Don't matter. Just wish you'd take mine." The driver makes a U-turn and heads back down the road, screeching his tires, leaving the boy alone in a swath of moonlight, light rain misting his face. Below, the monotonous crash of the waves drown out the sound of the speeding cab as it descends the hill back into the village.

Devon looks up at the house ahead of him. Another light has appeared: in the topmost window of the tower. "There," he says, "the place is coming to life."

Yet, trudging forward, he wishes he could believe that. Instead, he whistles in the dark, warding off evil spirits with his happy tunes, clutching his suitcase in one hand and the St Anthony's medal in his pocket in the other.

Suze had been easily frightened. Back in Coles Junction, they'd all go to the movies – Devon and Suze and Tommy and whoever else was hanging with them that day. They loved scary movies: *I Know What You Did Last Summer* and the *Screams*. Suze would get all neurotic whenever the music got creepy, and Devon would have to reach across in the darkness and take her hand, reassuring her. Once, walking home, they cut through an old churchyard corridor. The only light came from dim yellow lamps high up on the stone wall every few yards. Bats were known to get trapped in this corridor, their high-pitched cries only slightly more horrifying than the sound of their slippery wings beating against the cold stone. Suze had heard the bats and started to run, her hands covering her hair, begging for Devon to follow. But Devon was simply fascinated by the flying rodents. He caught sight of their eyes: little red embers in the shadows.

Whenever Suze got really frightened, Devon remembers, she'd start humming or whistling to herself. "She'll be comin' round the mountain when she comes, she'll be comin' round the mountain when she comes. . ." or "Jingle bells, jingle bells, jingle all the way," even in the hottest days of summer. Those little tunes: as if the bats would be lulled to sleep, the ghosts shamed into submission, the demons driven back to the depths, all because of the forced frivolity of one young girl.

Yet now Devon whistles the same little tunes himself. For the first time he admits to a little fear himself. He can feel the heat building as he approaches the great house. He can hear voices behind the wind: not the Voice that guides him, but the voices of others. The voices of the eyes that have stared out at him from the darkness of his closet since he was six.

He stops not more than two yards from the front gate and looks up. Through the rusted iron spears of the gate, he can see the house twist its way upward. The clouds are gone, and the moon, emboldened, claims the sky. There's enough light now to make out the facade of the house: rainslicked black stone worn by decades of sea wind. The wood of the house is as ebony as the stone: dark old wood, crusty with the salt of the sea. Ravens or no ravens, Devon finds the name of the house appropriate: as black as a raven's wing. Monstrous gargoyles like those on medieval French cathedrals loom out from the higher reaches of the house, hideous clawed and winged creatures Devon knows are all too real.

A wind, chill and damp, fights him as he approaches. *You can't stop me*, he thinks. *No matter how hard you try, I've come here to find out the truth. The truth that's been kept from me all my life.*

He passes through the front gate and starts up the long driveway. It curves toward the main entrance then continues out beyond the house to smaller structures. Devon walks with a briskness that belies the strength of the wind. His gait is as much to reassure him as the little tunes that still come forth from his lips: "She'll be comin' round the mountain when she comes. . ."

Someone — *something* — is watching him. He becomes convinced of it.

Be on guard, comes the Voice. He half-expects at any moment to be pounced upon by some creature from the dark bushes that line the driveway, some crazed animal with long teeth and red eyes.

But when he spots his watcher, he sees that it is decidedly human. There are indeed eyes in the darkness: there, in the moonlight on the roof of the tower, is a man — or at least, the shape of a man, intently watching Devon's arrival from an aperture in the crenellated turret.

Devon stops in his tracks, feeling the weight of his body leave him, rising from his bones and evaporating like steam. He tries to fix his gaze upon the man above, but whenever Devon's eyes settle, the man seems to vanish completely into the shadows. It's as if he can only be seen in peripheral vision, as if he exists not here but somewhere else.

Yet for the seconds that their eyes do meet, all sound ceases: the steady beating of the waves against the rocks below, the pulse of Devon's heart in his ears. It's then that the words of the old woman on the train echo in his mind, startling the stillness like the cry of a gull:

"You'll find no one there but ghosts."

3
Creatures in the Night

How long he stands there staring at the tower he isn't sure, but something rouses him from his trance, as if some unseen hypnotist had snapped his fingers. The Voice maybe — but Devon's not sure he actually heard it or what it might have said. Perhaps it was simply the light in the topmost tower room going out, leaving the upper floors of the house in complete darkness. Or maybe it was the rain, starting again, misting his features with its damp tongue.

Devon gathers his wits and takes the final steps to the house. He knocks upon the door using the tarnished brass ring that hangs there. The sound reverberates with a deep, cavernous echo, as he suspected it might.

The entrance to Ravenscliff is opened not by a servant — the lone servant Andrea had said the family employed — but by a woman Devon could not have expected. She's tall, titian-haired, and startlingly beautiful, of indeterminate age, her chin raised imperiously, with a sharp, striking profile and very long neck. Her hair is gathered in an elaborate French twist worn at the back of her head, and a single strand of pearls adorns her bare throat. Her eyes are large and set far apart, and they widen without blinking when she sees Devon standing there.

"Mrs — Crandall?" he asks.

"Yes," the woman replies, not extending her hand or asking him inside. "And you are Devon."

She says his name with a determined emphasis, and her eyes never leave his face.

"Yes, ma'am. I'm Devon March."

She smiles, finally. "Please come inside." She steps back, allowing him to enter the foyer of the great mansion. "I was looking for my daughter," she says, after she's closed the door behind him. "Isn't she with you?"

"No, ma'am. I took a cab here."

"A cab?" She seems genuinely outraged. "Why, I distinctly told Cecily this morning to arrange with Simon, our driver, to meet you at the bus station. Weren't they there?"

"No, ma'am. There was no one. It's all right, though. I was able to see a little of the village this way, and meet a few people. . ."

She looks at him hard. He suddenly has the feeling that meeting the villagers was the last thing she wanted for him on his first night in Misery Point.

And who could blame her? The stories he had heard, the legends of the ghosts, the hostility toward the Muir family. . . And now he was here, in the fabled house, standing where few had ever gained entrance.

Devon looks around him. The high cathedral ceiling of the foyer and the enormous stained glass windows — St George slaying the dragon — suggest an old church, an image aided by the presence of dozens of candles, burning atop brass and pewter candelabras. To his right the grand curved staircase is carpeted with an old Oriental runner. The floor on which it's laid is marble, a deep violet and gray stone that shines as brightly as if it had been cut and polished yesterday. Dark wood walls are hung with somber portraits of men and women Devon assumes to be Muir ancestors: which one might be Jackson, he wonders, and which the tragic Emily?

"I apologize for my daughter," Mrs Crandall is saying.

"That's all right."

"No, it's not. I don't know where she is." She glances up at the old grandfather clock that stands in the foyer. It's a quarter past ten. Mrs Crandall draws her shoulders up and walks toward a pair of closed double-doors, her dress of green velvet molded against her shapely body and reaching to the floor.

"I will speak with her," she promises Devon. "Now, put down your bag. I'll have Simon take it upstairs for you. Whenever he shows up. Come into the parlor and let's get acquainted."

She opens the doors in a manner that further solidifies her status as a great lady: with both hands on both doorknobs, sweeping into the room as the doors yield to her effort. Inside, a fire crackles in the old stone fireplace. An elegant old sofa is angled in front, watched over by a stern old man in a portrait above the mantel.

Devon can see why people whisper about Ravenscliff, why Andrea's parents might have told her old Jackson Muir was a warlock. Among the books on the shelves lining the room are several skulls, at least three shrunken heads, and a half dozen crystal balls. A suit of armor stands against the far wall. The room looks like a wizard's den.

"Wow," Devon says, looking around. "Cool room."

To the left, large glass doors draped in rich purple fabric offer a magnificent view of the coast off Devil's Rock, the moonlit stormy waters crashing against the rocks far below.

"Yes, I suppose it is," Mrs Crandall says. "Both my father

and grandfather were travelers, and quite the collectors. These trinkets come from all over the world."

"Awesome," Devon says, touching one of the skulls. His hand buzzes as if from electricity. He withdraws it quickly.

"Have a seat," Mrs Crandall tells him.

They sit in front of the fire, Devon on the sofa and Mrs Crandall in a large cushioned wing chair that the boy instinctively knows is exclusively hers. The warmth of the fire feels good to Devon, whose skin had seemed to absorb the moisture of the night. He shivers. Mrs Crandall notices, raising one eyebrow.

"Are you cold? Shall I get you some tea?"

"No, thank you. I'll be fine now that I'm finally out of the rain."

"I apologize again. Cecily will be reprimanded."

"No, please, not on my account. I wouldn't want to start off on the wrong foot with her."

She sighs. "I've tried to impose some discipline on Cecily, but it's difficult. She can be headstrong. I take it that *you* will respect the rules of the household, Devon?"

"Well, I'll do my best."

She brings the tips of her fingers against each other. The glow of the fire reflects along her face and neck. Again, Devon is struck by her beauty. He concentrates, trying to see if the Voice might tell him anything about her, but it's silent. The heat and energy he felt outside the house has subsided, too; the only warmth now comes from the fire.

"I imagine you must be anxious to resume your schooling," Mrs Crandall is saying.

He shrugs. "Well, leaving school in the middle of the semester was hard. I imagine starting up here will be even more so."

"I've arranged with a tutor at the school to help you if needed. I've spoken with the guidance counselors, and everything has been arranged for you to start on Monday. You needn't worry."

He laughs a little. "I don't worry — not about that anyway. The worst thing is just leaving my old friends behind."

Her face seems to reflect some compassion. "I was very sad to hear about your father's death, Devon," she says, softer now. "Were you very close?"

"Yes, ma'am. My mother died when I was a baby. I don't remember her. So my Dad was all the family I had."

She nods. "I see. Well, for however long you remain with us, we are glad to welcome you to ours."

"Thank you, ma'am." Devon appreciates her words, but there's little emotion behind them. "Mrs Crandall, may I ask you a question?"

"Certainly."

"Was this an agreement between you and my dad? That if anything ever happened to him, you'd take me in?"

She moves her eyes off to the fireplace. "To be frank, Devon, no. I was as surprised as you probably were when I got the call from Mr McBride telling me about the guardianship."

"Then you could've said no."

"I could have." She returns her gaze to him. "But I didn't."

"How did you know my dad? You must have been close."

"It was a very long time ago. I gather your father never spoke of Ravenscliff."

Devon shakes his head. "Never. Not until right before he died."

Mrs Crandall stands and approaches the fire, warming her hands over it. "I suppose your father felt I could offer you things he never could. That we could provide well for you here."

Devon glances around the room, at the antiques, the silver serving set, the crystal chandelier hanging from the ceiling. "Yeah, I suppose he did." His own house had been small, just four rooms: his and his dad's, a living room and kitchen. Dad had worked as a landscaper and mechanic, making what he could. He'd smelled of motor oil and cut grass, with grime permanently embedded in the pores and cracks of his hands. He'd driven an old Buick, owned just one sport jacket, and while he made sure Devon never wanted for anything – food, clothing, toys – they never took the kinds of vacations Tommy did with his folks, to Disney World or Cape Cod or up to Mount Snow for skiing.

"There are some rules, however, Devon," Mrs Crandall is saying, "and, as I said, I expect that you follow them." She draws herself up regally, like a duchess. "This is a big house, with only a few of us living here now, so we've closed the East Wing. Under no circumstances should you attempt to go into that part of the house. Is that understood?"

"Yes, ma'am."

"Also, my mother is not well. She has not left her room in years. I'd prefer for the time being you not meet her."

"All right." Devon feels a little tingle beginning in his fingertips as Mrs Crandall sets down the rules. It moves up his fingers and into his hands. Just by telling him that there are places and people in the house he was not supposed to see, she has succeeded in making him suspicious.

And he realizes that so far there's been no mention of a *Mr* Crandall, the husband to the woman standing before him. Devon wonders just how many secrets are held by this family he's suddenly found himself a part of.

"You have a nephew, too," he asks. "A little boy?"

Mrs Crandall looks down at him with some surprise. "My,

the townspeople *have* filled you in, haven't they? What else did they tell you?"

"Well, to be honest, ma'am, several warned me against coming here."

She smiles, turning around completely to face him. "I see. They warned you about the ghosts, I'm sure, and the strange, eccentric people who live in this house."

"Yes," Devon admits. "They did."

"They call me a witch down in the village. But do I look like a witch to you?"

Devon acknowledges that she does not.

"Try not to concern yourself with the petty gossips of Misery Point," Mrs Crandall tells him. She moves — it's more like gliding than walking — to the glass doors overlooking the sea. She stands there, framed in the moonlight.

She knows, says the Voice at last.

Yes, Devon agrees. *She knows more than she's saying.* His hands feel charged. He has such an urge to lift one of the crystal balls from the shelves, gaze into it. *Why not?* the Voice asks. *They belong to you.*

The thought startles him. *Belong to me? Could that be true?* He sits forward in his chair, watching Mrs Crandall. What did she know of his past? Why had she brought him here?

"This is a house with many secrets, " she says, as if responding to his unspoken questions, not turning to look back at him. "All old houses have them. Four generations of Muirs have lived in this house. Everyone who has lived here has left behind their secrets." She pauses. "We respect them. We do not pry into them. Remember that, Devon."

She turns, brightening. "But tell me about yourself. I am eager to learn more about you so that we can be friends."

"There's not much to tell beyond what you already know."

He decides against mentioning anything about his powers or the Voice. There have been too many warning signs: he's still not sure he can trust Mrs Crandall.

But he has to ask one question:

"Mrs Crandall, do you know who my real father was?"

Her face turns ashen. Her elegant eyebrows rise; her exquisite lips part. Then she recovers, a little, enough to say, "I wasn't aware that Ted wasn't your father. What makes you think that is the case?"

"He told me. Just before he died. He said I deserved to know the truth." Devon narrows his eyes at her. "I can't believe that his decision to send me here and the truth of my origins aren't connected."

She smiles. Whatever concern had flickered through her eyes is gone. "Well, I can't imagine what that connection might be."

"Are you telling me that you know nothing of who I am, or where I come from?"

She looks at him with fierce, hard eyes. "That's what I'm telling you." Then she softens, looking away. "I'm sorry that I can't be of more help."

Thunder explodes all at once, seemingly directly over the house. The rain begins again, torrentially, and the lights go out.

"Mother!"

From the foyer, a gust of wind and rain. The front doors fly open, and a pretty teenage girl with bright red hair wearing a black leather motorcycle jacket tumbles inside, a tall boy with a shaved head behind her.

If not for all the candles, the power outage would have left them all in darkness. But once Devon's eyes have adjusted to the candlelight, he's able to make out the arrival of the girl he presumes to be Cecily Crandall, his errant welcome wagon.

Mrs Crandall moves from the parlor to the foyer as quickly and as soundlessly as a cat. "Cecily!" she scolds. "Where have you been? You were supposed to go with Simon to pick up Devon at the bus station! But I haven't seen either of you all night!"

The girl's eyes peer around her mother's shoulder and spy the new boy standing awkwardly in the doorway of the parlor. Devon smiles shyly. Cecily groans.

"Oh, I'm sorry, Mother, I'm truly sorry." She turns to the boy with the shaved head. Devon can now see he has a piece of metal pierced through his nose. "Oh, DJ, I *knew* I had forgotten something! Didn't I *say* I had forgotten something?"

"Yes, Mrs Crandall, she did say that. She——"

"If you don't mind," Mrs Crandall says icily, "I'd like to speak with my daughter alone."

"Yeah, sure, no problem." The boy looks uncomfortably down at Cecily. "I'll call you tomorrow."

She nods, brushing him aside as if she's suddenly grown weary of him. She moves in for a kiss that does not quite catch her offered cheek and then marches straight past her mother into the parlor. DJ says good night to Mrs Crandall and lets himself out. His girlfriend, meanwhile, has stopped a few feet from Devon and is eying him intently.

"He's *beautiful*, Mother," she's saying, as if Devon were a puppy, or a painting, and not someone with ears and eyes to comprehend her assessment. "Just *gorgeous*."

She smiles at Devon, extending her hand in a gesture as grand as any her mother might have flourished. Devon isn't sure if he should shake her hand or kiss it. He opts for the former.

"Pleased to meet you, Cecily."

"Oh, likewise, *definitely* likewise." She shakes her hair then walks over to plop down on the sofa. "How long you think the power will be out this time? It really sucks cuz there's a concert on HBO that I wanted to—"

"Cecily," her mother says, standing over her now, "I distinctly told you to inform Simon to drive to the bus station to meet Devon. The poor boy will be lucky if he doesn't catch a cold. He took a cab here, and was nearly drenched—"

"I'm sorry, Devon," the girl says. "Really, I am. I'll make it up to you." She winks. "I promise."

"It's OK," he says. "I'm just glad to be here."

"Have you told him about Alexander?" Cecily asks suddenly, turning to her mother.

"I had just begun," Mrs Crandall says. She smiles at Devon. "Are you sure you wouldn't care for some tea?"

"I'm fine, thank you. Please. Finish telling me about the family." He smiles over at Cecily. "Since I'm going to be part of it."

The girl winks at him again and pats the place on the couch next to her. He sits down.

Mrs Crandall resumes her position beside the fire. She seems to be giving some thought to what she's about to say.

"Alexander is a . . . troubled boy," she begins. "His mother has been in a mental institution since he was four. His father travels extensively, and has not had much time to spend with the boy. We had him in a school up in Connecticut, a boys' academy. He . . . didn't do well in that environment. He withdrew, became moody. His studies went from average to failing. And last spring . . . he set a fire."

She looks over at Devon to see his reaction. He feigns surprise, raising his eyebrows.

"No one was hurt, thank God. But it did cause considerable damage. He was asked to leave, of course. And my brother has turned over guardianship of Alexander to me."

"Given that I turned out so well," Cecily says, nudging Devon.

Mrs Crandall ignores her. "It wouldn't do to send the boy away again. He's clearly crying out for help. So I decided to keep him here." She looks pointedly at Devon. "I'm hoping you might be of some help to him, Devon."

"Me?"

"Yes. Mr McBride sent me your report cards from school. You're an honors student. Perhaps you can help tutor Alexander. Not just tutor, but perhaps in some ways mentor him. Serve as an older brother, since his father is away so much. I think some male companionship might do him some good."

Devon looks over at Cecily. She shudders.

"Well, I'll give it a shot, Mrs Crandall."

"That's all I ask." She sighs. "We all have our responsibilities here. That could be part of yours. I want to make sure no harm comes to Alexander. That he is safe."

Devon picks up something in her words. "What kind of harm, Mrs Crandall?"

Cecily pipes up, "From himself. He's *crazy*. You'll see." She laughs, leaning into Devon, speaking close to his ear. "He's got little friends that only he can see."

"Most children do," Devon says.

"The *problem*," Cecily says, still leaning into Devon, "is in this *house*, you can never be sure what's his imagination and what's real."

"Now, Cecily," Mrs Crandall says.

But her daughter continues addressing Devon. "I'm sure the cabdriver warned you about our ghosts."

"Well, as a matter of fact—"

"Which ones did he tell you about?" Cecily asked. "I'm sure

he told you about old Jackson. He's our most famous ghost. A *warlock*, people say. He used to put on these really freaky magic shows for the kids in the village—"

"Cecily, stop this," her mother commands.

Her daughter ignores her. "Then there's Jackson's wife, Emily – so *tragic*." Cecily stands up, pointing to the portrait over the mantel, the solemn-looking man in gray frock coat and mutton-chop sideburns, brooding within the gilt frame. "And that's our founder, the great Horatio Muir, right there. You'll find all of them howling through the corridors on stormy nights like this!"

Mrs Crandall sighs and walks over to the window, as if giving up on Cecily, apparently having been there before and knowing it's useless to try to rein her in.

"Over there is poor Emily," Cecily says, pointing. Devon turns around. On the far wall, a portrait of a woman stares into eternity. She's a lovely, delicate creature, but there's a sadness that emanates from her large round eyes, somewhat hidden behind a white veil and pearls.

"That was painted from her wedding day photos," Mrs Crandall observes fondly. "She's always been my favorite of all the ancestors. Such a beautiful woman. And such a sad story. Falling to her death from Devil's Rock. . ."

"I was told she jumped," Devon offers.

"How the villagers like to sensationalize our family tragedies," Mrs Crandall says. It's clear she'll have nothing else to say on the subject.

"I'll give you a complete tour tomorrow," Cecily whispers. "I'll give you the full version on *all* the legends."

"I'm sure Devon would like to wash up and see his room and get some sleep," Mrs Crandall says. "We can become more acquainted in the morning."

"Actually, I *am* pretty tired," he admits.

They all move back into the foyer. Devon's bag still sits there.

"Simon didn't take your bag upstairs," Mrs Crandall says. "Where could he be?"

"I haven't seen him all day," Cecily says. "If I had, I would've remembered to tell him we needed to pick up Devon."

Mrs Crandall scowls. "Simon is our servant, Devon. He's usually very efficient. It's not like him to let a guest's bag sit unattended."

"You know," Devon says, "I think I may have seen him. I believe I saw a man standing outside on the tower when I came up the drive. Might that have been Simon?"

"That would be impossible," Mrs Crandall replies. "The tower is in the East Wing. As I told you, that part of the house has been closed off for years."

"But I'm sure I saw a man—"

"That would be *impossible*, Devon," Mrs Crandall repeats.

"Well, there was a light. I *know* I saw a light in the tower."

Her look tells him he's being absurd. She smiles. "There was lightning on the horizon," she insists. "Light can be reflected in the most uncanny ways."

Seeming to punctuate her point, lightning crackles suddenly, illuminating the room, followed by a horrible burst of thunder. Cecily laughs.

"You'll get used to the storms up here, Devon," Cecily tells him. "Sometimes they go on for *days*."

Indeed, the storm isn't yet over for that night. Devon carries his own bag upstairs, having bid good night to Mrs Crandall in the foyer. Cecily shows him to his room, a comfortable space, with large windows that look out over the sea. The four-poster bed is already turned down for him, and a candle burns beside it.

"So I'll introduce you to all my friends at school," Cecily's chatting. "Don't worry. You'll fit in fine. I've already told Ana and Marcus about you, and they can't *wait* to meet you. Oh, I am so happy to have somebody my age in this house!" She smiles over at him. "I'm sorry again for not meeting you at the bus. I totally spaced."

"That's all right," Devon replies. "I got a ride from a man who said he was a friend of the family's. Something told me I shouldn't tell your mother, though."

"Who was it?"

"Rolfe Montaigne."

Thunder crashes again, as the storm turns for a second round of attack. Cecily bursts into laughter, covering her mouth to calm herself.

"What's so funny?" Devon asks.

"Just that Rolfe *would* have the nerve to say he's a friend of the family. Your instincts were right, Devon. Don't tell Mother that Rolfe Montaigne gave you a ride."

"Why?"

"Because she'll boot you out of here, no questions asked." She smiles. "And take care who you talk to. Misery Point is a *very* small town."

With that, she leaves him alone.

Sleep does not come easily. The storm remains fierce, seeming portentous to him on his first night here – a maelstrom that seems to have descended upon the village and gotten trapped, spewing out its fury and frustration on everyone below. The shutters outside his window must have come loose, for they crash and bang; wind howls through the eaves of the old house; lightning burns through his room at regular intervals. Devon can only lie awake in his bed, the eyes of Muir ancestors looking down upon him from their portraits on the walls.

Each time he begins to doze off, a thunderclap awakens him. In one such moment, as he hovers in those tenuous seconds between sleep and wakefulness, he sees the figure of a man standing at the foot of his bed. He sits up at once, trying to focus his eyes.

"Who's there?" he asks.

There's no one. But the heat has suddenly intensified. The pressure hums in at him, a whining vibration. His sheets are drenched.

It was like this last year, he remembers. The pressure. The high-pitched whine. It was the most terrifying night of his life, a night he's been mostly successful in forgetting. But this was how it began, with the heat and the pressure: and it ended with Devon bruised and bloodied, but with a demon vanquished.

"Trust your instincts," his father had taught him. "Your body will follow."

The creature had been far more cunning than the one who had visited years before, when Devon was six. This one had arrived not through his closet, with reptilian eyes blinking in the dark, but casually instead, coming through the door of his bedroom, in the guise of Devon's father. Devon was reading a comic book on his bed and looked up to see his father walk through his door — except Devon knew his father never just walked in without knocking first, and besides, his father was at the grocery store.

"Dad?"

The thing had turned on him then: great yellow eyes and dripping fangs, Dad's form seeming to melt away in the angry rush of the demon's passion. It lunged at Devon; he fought back powered by pure instinct. The creature's talons sliced his shoulder and ripped an inch-deep gorge in his thigh, but Devon prevailed, landing a powerhouse blow in the beast's gut and sending it spiraling back into its Hellhole. It had come for him — cannier, shrewder than the others — but still Devon had won. He hadn't known he could fight like that. He just did.

It's happening again, Devon realizes now. *Another one. They've followed me here.*

Or, rather, I've found where they come from. . .

His heart begins to thud in his chest. The room seems to spin. Devon kicks off his sheets and tries to steady his vision, but he's caught in the rotation of the room. He begins to feel dizzy.

He swings his legs off the side of the bed. This is worse than last time. Far worse. It's never been this intense before. Something's happening. He can feel it. Sweat begins to pop from his forehead, running down his face. His T-shirt clings to his chest, under his pits. He forces himself to stand, but he falters, nearly losing his balance.

"I am . . . stronger . . . than . . . any . . . of it," Devon says out loud.

A dull, low roar fills the room. At first, behind the wind and rain and thunder, it's difficult to perceive, but it grows louder and more distinct. Surely the whole house can hear it. Devon grasps one of the posts of his bed, and concentrates as hard as he can. Maybe he can stop it in its tracks. He'd often done that before. Only twice has he actually come face to face with them: every other time, whenever he'd felt the pressure building or seen the eyes in the night, he'd manage to concentrate and send them away. With a raise of his hand he'd make his armoire slide across the room or his closet doors swing shut. He could make the whispering stop, the terror dissolve.

But it hadn't worked that time when the demon disguised as Dad entered his room. There had been no warning then; that creature had been far too clever for that. Devon had had to fight him, punching and kicking, throwing moves he'd never been taught to do, finding his limbs responding with a precision that both surprised and awed him.

This time, he could feel it coming – but even with a warning, he knew he couldn't send it away. He had never felt anything like this. What forces had he disturbed by coming into this house? The roar grows louder, the room keeps spinning. And suddenly his windows swing inward, the full fury of the storm invading his room.

He raises his arms, but it does no good. The windows will not shut.

All at once the room smells fetid and foul, like the stink of a swamp, like decomposing animals.

"Who's here?" Devon calls out, as the lightning flashes again.

The roar is deafening now. Devon clamps his hands over his ears to block out its noise.

From the window comes the source of the roar: a figure – a creature – something Devon could never have imagined. Small at first, but growing larger – closer – it comes from the swirling night like some prehistoric bird. Great green eyes and a sharp pointed beak filled with fangs. Its skin is scaly. Its claws reach out toward Devon, its long tongue slithering from its beak.

"No!" Devon shouts. "Back off! Get away from me!"

The demon lands. It pants hungrily, its tumor-covered tongue nearly reaching the floor.

"Go back to hell," Devon says, landing a swift kick in the creature's head. His movements always surprise him: it's as if his body responds instinctively, without any consciousness on Devon's part.

The demon roars, leaping at him, spreading its hideous wings. Devon deflects it with a thrust of his forearm, surprised again by his strength. "I *said*, go to hell!"

The thing pounces right back. Devon again slams it hard. "I am stronger than you! Get that through your ugly head!"

The demon rears up on its legs and roars in frustration. It doesn't lunge again. Instead it leaps back out into the night.

The roar subsides. The room stops spinning. The heat dies down. The night is quiet, except for the storm.

Devon lets out a long breath and can feel his body start to tremble. He approaches the window. He closes the panes, latching them together.

He turns and waits for someone to bang on his door, ask what in heaven – or hell – just went on in there. Surely Mrs Crandall will have to reveal what she knows now.

But no one comes knocking.

They didn't hear, the Voice tells him. *It came for you, and you only.*

He knows that now. It's *his* presence in this house that's caused whatever it was to leave its Hellhole. Whatever forces have haunted him since he was a boy are much stronger here.

This is where they live, the Voice tells him.

"And they don't want me to live here, too," Devon says to himself.

His heart still thudding in his chest, Devon sits down on the side of his bed.

I can't face these things without Dad. This is way too much. I can't do this alone, no matter how many answers I might find.

But how can he leave? Mrs Crandall is now his legal guardian. And where would he go? What would stop the creatures from following him?

The thought strikes him: *Dad wouldn't have sent me here if he felt I'd be in any real danger. Dad knew this was where I'd find the truth about myself.*

"Always remember, Devon," Dad had said, the first time Devon had gotten really frightened by the eyes in his closet. "No matter what happens, no matter what you see, no matter where you are. You are stronger than any of it, because you understand that all true power comes from good. Never forget that, son. Never."

"I haven't, Dad," Devon says quietly now. He lets out a long breath.

He actually feels just the slightest bit cocky. He'd fought off that thing without so much as even a cut this time. How he was able to fight like that, he's not sure – but he *is* sure of something else: *I really am stronger than any of it.*

He drifts off to sleep, and his mind will later recall a series of images: Ravenscliff etched against the night sky, the figure of the man watching him from the tower, Rolfe Montaigne's hot breath in his face saying: "I killed a young boy just like you."

In his dream, Rolfe had him backed into a corner; there was nowhere to run. He could feel the man's warm breath on his face as he had earlier in the car. His eyes, as green as those in his closet, burned into his soul.

He awakes quickly. The storm still rages, and he expects another go-round with the beast outside his window. But there's no heat, no pressure. Still, something awakened him, and he listens carefully. There it is: a soft, steady, insistent voice that seems to come from some place in his darkened room:

"Leave here. You're not wanted here. Leave here."

Devon listens intently. The constant drone of the rain and the frequent booms of thunder often obliterate it, but it's there, always underneath, over and over, like a mantra: "*Leave here. You're not wanted here. Leave here.*"

"No," he says out loud. "I will not leave."

The little voice, high and feminine, continues. Devon jumps out of bed. Standing close to his door, he can hear the voice from the other side: "*Leave here. You're not wanted here. Leave here.*"

With a sudden fierceness, Devon pulls open the door and stares into the blackness. The corridor is darker than he imagines a tomb might be, and just as cold. Still, the voice stops, replaced by the ethereal sound of wings in retreat — or else the sound of footsteps, padding away as fast as possible down the carpeted corridor.

Devon's about to close the door when he hears another sound, this one from much farther away, from deeper within the house. It appears to be the sound of someone crying. Cautiously he steps outside into the corridor. Feeling for the light switch, he pushes it up, but discovers the power is still off. He walks back to his bedside table, fumbles for the candle and matches. With his tiny, quivering flame to guide him, Devon follows the sound. It leads him down the great staircase, where strange twisting shadows dance upon the walls, into the main foyer, where every creak of the old house makes him look around, reassuring himself the demon has not followed him. Through the foyer he steps quietly, past the dining room and into a corridor.

Outside the storm thrashes against the house. For a second, Devon imagines what the house must look like to the village below, its turrets silhouetted against the sky by each flash of lightning.

There's no mistaking it now. The sound is that of a woman sobbing, crying as if the tragedy of her life is too horrible to bear any longer. It seems to come from behind a closed door at the end of the corridor. Devon's not sure, but he suspects it leads to the closed-off East Wing. This is where his memory of the house's exterior tells him the tower would be.

Under no circumstances should you attempt to go into that part of the house. Is that understood?

He hesitates, unsure about disobeying Mrs Crandall's orders the very first night he's in the house. But too many things have already happened. Something is trying to force him to leave, and he isn't going to ignore them. He came here to find the truth about himself. Even if that means confronting the demons, he'll do it. He's spent his entire life living in fear about what lurks in his closet or under his bed. He's tired of it, and Dad's death has only galvanized him to put an end to the fear.

And he has the distinct feeling that the *tower* – where, no matter *what* Mrs Crandall said, he's *sure* he saw a light – holds the answers he's looking for.

He tries the door, but it's locked. The woman continues her tears, while a crash of thunder shakes the house, the loudest yet.

Startled, Devon drops his candle, its fragile life snuffed out when it strikes the marble floor. A bolt of unnaturally brilliant lightning all at once lights up the room. He moves back into the foyer, his eyes sweeping into the parlor, coming to rest on the portrait of Emily Muir. And in the few tantalizing seconds the lightning allows him to see, he swears that the face in the portrait is contorted in sorrow, and the hands that earlier had been clasped serenely in her lap are now clawing the air in a desperate gesture of agony and despair.

4
A Strange, Precocious Child

The rest of the night is fitful, and Devon awakes early. With daylight streaming into his room, the weirdness of the previous night seems like a bad dream, already fading with the coming of the sun.

"Not bad," Devon says, stepping into his own private bathroom. "Not bad at all." There's an enormous walk-in marble shower and behind that, a jacuzzi and a sunlamp. Thick, luxurious towels have been set out for him. He and Dad had shared a cramped bathroom, with a toilet and a rusty shower stall, no tub. Now Devon steps across gleaming black-and-white tile to turn on the brass hot-water faucet in the shower.

Stripping off his T-shirt and boxers, he looks at himself in the full length mirror. Cecily had called him gorgeous. With all that happened last night, he hasn't had time to think about that fact. *She called me gorgeous.* And Cecily was certainly no slouch in the looks department herself.

He studies his reflection. Dark eyes, dark hair, a tinge of olive to his skin. Dad had been blue-eyed and pale; Devon had always just figured he took after his mother, of whom he remembers nothing. There are no pictures of her either, something Devon assumed to be part of Dad's grief at losing her. Now he wonders if his real parents were Italian – or Spanish – or something else dark and swarthy. Turks? Arabs? *Gypsies?* He laughs.

He looks again in the mirror. He thinks he's grown another inch since last week; and he was already five-eight then. He wonders if his real father was tall. He flexes his biceps quickly in the mirror, then laughs at himself. *Cecily called me gorgeous.*

He steps into the shower, wondering if it's cool to think of a girl as a babe who was now kind of your sister. "She's not *really* my sister," he assures himself. "It's cool."

He savors the warmth of the spray and the peace it permits his mind. For a moment he never wants to part the curtains and once again step out there into the world, where things came at him from his window and ghosts woke him up at night with their sobbing. Here, under the steady stream of hot water, there are no sounds, no voices – except the one in his own head.

This is a place of secrets, the Voice is telling him. *This is where you will find your secrets.*

He towels himself dry. Opening his suitcase, he withdraws a fresh pair of khakis and a flannel shirt. He combs his dark hair, letting it fall naturally across his forehead.

He determines that the most important thing – more weighty than fitting in at school, more significant than even fitting in with this family – is to discover his past. His truth. *That's why Dad sent me here. I know it.*

Downstairs he finds no one. In the daylight, with the sun filtering in through the gauzy drapes of the tall windows, Ravenscliff doesn't look nearly so ominous. The marble shines, the crystal glitters. In the dining room, a whole spread has been set out: fruit, cereal, scrambled eggs in a shiny aluminum tray over a steam heater. A pot of coffee adds its rich fragrance to the room.

He peeks into the kitchen: no one. It's just a little bit weird, as if he were the only one in the house. It's not even yet eight-thirty. Cecily and Alexander, he imagines, are already off to school — it's Friday, after all, and although he isn't scheduled to start until Monday, school hasn't stopped for the rest of the world. But where is Mrs Crandall? And Simon, the servant?

Devon shrugs, helping himself to breakfast. He eats heartily, not having had much of a dinner last night, just a burrito from Taco Bell while he waited to change buses in Hartford. He's wolfing down his food when Mrs Crandall finally arrives, in a long paisley satin robe.

"Good morning, Devon," she says. "I trust you slept well."

He looks at her. Even without the Voice to tell him, he knows it's best to reveal as little as possible for now. "Yes," he tells her. "I slept fine."

"Even with the storm?"

Is she testing me? He just smiles. "I was pretty tired."

"As I'm sure you must have been. Well, enjoy your breakfast. When you're finished, come upstairs to the playroom. I'd like you to meet Alexander."

He looks up over his forkful of eggs. "Alexander? Isn't he at school?"

Her lovely face clouds. "I'm afraid that since he's come to Ravenscliff, Alexander has not been enrolled at the public school. His father and I are still — discussing — what the best course of action should be for him."

"I assume Mr Muir is away traveling."

Mrs Crandall nods.

"When does he return?" Devon asks.

"I'm not sure." She pours herself a cup of coffee. "I'm never sure with my brother."

"Well, I look forward to meeting Alexander."

Mrs Crandall smiles. "I do so hope you become friends. He needs a solid male influence in his life. As I said last night, he's a troubled boy." She pauses. "And willful. Last night, I discovered him in the East Wing."

Devon looks up at her. "But that's locked," he says.

"A locked door has never kept Alexander Muir from where he wants to go."

Devon considers something. "Mrs Crandall, might Alexander have . . . been outside my door last night?"

"Why do you ask?"

He shakes his head. "No reason. I just thought I heard something."

"Well, if he disturbed you, I apologize." She sips her coffee, carrying it with a saucer on her palm, as she moves out of the room. "Why don't you ask him yourself? I've told him you'd come up to the playroom when you finished breakfast. He's expecting you."

Devon puts away a couple of muffins on top of his eggs and cereal. Then, not sure what to do with his plates, he decides just to leave them there for the seemingly invisible servant. He heads upstairs.

He's not quite sure where the playroom is, but continuing on down the corridor past his room, he comes upon a large door that's ajar. He can hear music inside, and the light is very bright. He peers inside. Books and toys everywhere, on the floor and on several tables: a Buzz Lightyear doll, comic books, a Gameboy, an overturned Scrabble board. He opens the door wider. At the far end of the room stands an old wooden toy horse; leaning against the wall is an ancient, over-sized Raggedy Ann doll.

But Devon doesn't see the boy.

"Alexander?" he calls.

The music comes from a television set, turned to face an empty beanbag chair. It sounds like some kids' show, with tinny voices and the repetitive crash of the laughtrack.

"Alexander?" Devon repeats. "You in here?"

Suddenly he feels something lunge at him, grab him around his shoulders. *It's back*, he thinks quickly. *I was unprepared. The thing from last night—*

Instinctively he summons all his power to thrust whatever's on his back clear across the room and into the far wall. It thuds there hard and slides down to the floor.

Devon looks.

It's a small boy.

Alexander.

The kid looks stunned as he sits against the wall. Devon realizes the boy had been up on the table, waiting for him. *He was trying to surprise me. Scare me.*

Well, it had worked all right.

"Alexander!" Devon calls, hurrying to the boy. "Are you OK?"

The boy's eyes look up at Devon in terror.

"How did you do that?" the child breathes.

"You just scared me, that's all." Devon stoops beside him. "Sure you're not hurt?"

Alexander stands up quickly. "You can't hurt me," he says, walking past Devon and brushing off his pants. It's clear he doesn't want to admit it he's hurt, even if he is, a little.

"Believe me, Alexander, I didn't mean to hurt you."

The boy turns to face him. His eyes shine malice – a

bitterness that for a fleeting second takes Devon's breath away. Everyone had warned him about the little monster, but Devon was still unprepared for the child's malevolent eyes.

"You *didn't* hurt me," the boy insists coldly.

He stands defiantly before Devon. Alexander Muir is a towheaded, chubby child with large blue eyes, as round as buttons. To see his eyes without looking into them would be to imagine Alexander Muir as a little doll. But Devon won't forget the wickedness he saw there anytime soon.

He tries to smile at the kid. "I just came up to meet you, to say hey."

Alexander grins. "Did my aunt tell you that we should be good friends?"

Devon shrugs. "Yeah, as a matter of fact, she did."

The child laughs. "And did she tell you what I did to get kicked out of school?"

Devon folds his arms across his chest. The kid seems to be trying to set up a battle. And indeed, there's *heat* in the room. Devon can feel it now, seeping in from the cracks in the walls.

"You set fire to the curtains in the cafeteria," he tells Alexander. "Isn't that it?"

The boy laughs. "I wish I'd burned the place down. I wish all the teachers and all the sniveling brats had burned with it."

"Wow, kid. You don't hold back, do you?"

Alexander sulks. He clearly isn't getting the fear out of Devon he wants. He stalks across the room and flops down into the beanbag chair in front of the TV.

Devon approaches, peering around at the television screen. "So what are you watching?"

"*Major Musick*." Alexander doesn't take his eyes off the TV. "You ever seen it?"

"No, I don't think I have."

The screen now features an obscenely tight close-up of the face of a clown. And an ugly one at that: bulbous red nose, oversized bloodshot eyes, and a thick white wig of hair. He's singing in a raspy voice, a voice so obviously phony it sounds hard, sinister.

"Is this a joke?" Devon asks. "Or a real show?"

Alexander harrumphs. "Shows how much you know. Of course it's a real show. I watch it every morning. That's Major Musick right there. Musick with a 'k.' M-U-S-I-C-K."

The clown stops singing. "Today's letter, boys and girls," he says, exposing yellow, crooked teeth, "is N. *Ennnnnnnn*. Can you say it? *Ennnnnnnn*. Hear how much it sounds like *emmmmmm*." Then he laughs.

Devon can't bear it any longer. "This is way too bizarre for me. You actually enjoy this weirdness?"

The boy smiles up at him. "I suppose my aunt has complained to you that I spend too much time in the house watching television."

"Actually, she hasn't. But I would think that a boy your age would rather be outside playing baseball and catching frogs and climbing trees. I know I did."

"I hate baseball," Alexander snarls. "Frogs are slimy. And I'm too fat to climb trees."

Devon glares down at him. "Oh, you're not so fat. I'll bet you can run pretty fast."

Alexander eyes him. "I can run faster than you."

"You can? We'll have to race sometime." Devon smiles cagily. "Of course, you might just win. You *did* run pretty fast last night."

"Last night?"

"Yes. Outside my door." Devon smiles again. He reaches over and snaps off Major Musick in mid-song. "To get all the way down the hall and then into the East Wing in such a short amount of time. . ."

Alexander looks stonily at him. "I don't know what you're talking about."

Devon has concluded one thing: whatever the reality of the demons in this house, one part of last night had been very much of this earth. The little voice telling him to leave, that he wasn't wanted here, was that of Alexander Muir. Just why Alexander didn't want him here is still a mystery — and perhaps part of the answers he sought.

"I know you were outside my door last night, Alexander. I heard you, and heard you run down the hall."

Now the boy is smiling again. "Hasn't anyone told you about the ghosts in this house?"

"Oh, yes," Devon admits. "I may have even met a few." He looms over Alexander. "But that was no ghost outside my door last night."

"Are you accusing me of something?" The young boy crosses his arms against his chest, assuming an air of precocious superiority. Alexander sure doesn't act or speak like any little boy Devon has ever known before. "Because if you *are* making an accusation," the child says, "I'd suggest you take it up with aunt. She's my guardian now, at least until my father comes back and rescues me from all of you."

Something in his words connects with Devon. Alexander Muir had been born into a world where he could expect everything and want for nothing; he did not have to struggle the way Devon and his father had. But Devon had grown up with things Alexander had not: affection, support, and understanding. Alexander's father was always traveling, his mother was institutionalized, his aunt was cold and aloof. Had anyone ever offered the child anything resembling love?

"I'm not accusing you of anything, Alexander," Devon tells him, trying a gentler approach. "Just explaining that I can't be tricked and I can't be scared away."

The boy laughs.

"In fact," Devon says, leaning down toward the child, "I want us to be friends."

"Friends?" Alexander Muir looks at him intently. There's a twinkle of something there that breaks through the ice, a flash of vulnerability. "Friends?"

"Yes, why not? Is that such a radical idea?"

His eyes harden again. "I don't need any friends."

Devon straightens up. "OK. But if you change your mind, I'm here. I'm not going to leave Ravenscliff." He starts to walk out of the room, then stops and turns back. "I came here not just because I had to, but because I'm looking for some answers. I'd like your help in finding them. We can either be friends or foes. That's up to you, Alexander."

The boy just grabs the remote and, not looking over at Devon, snaps the television back on. The voice of that repulsive clown fills the room.

The meeting with Alexander Muir had turned out to be far more than Devon had expected. The Voice is clear in telling him that the boy is key: *he holds answers, important answers.* Devon could see it in the child's eyes. It was right there, so plain and yet still so indecipherable.

Why did he jump at me? A childish prank — or something else? Devon suspects the latter, given Alexander's behavior last night outside his door. Alexander knows something — or *someone.* And that something or someone doesn't want Devon in this house. Whatever the truth is, Devon believes, little Alexander will prove essential in finding it out.

He does not see Mrs Crandall or anyone else for the rest of the morning, even into the afternoon. Devon wanders the great empty house alone, looking, seeing, ever on the alert. He won't be taken unprepared again. Every house has its secrets, Mrs Crandall had said, but this one holds *his* secrets. Had his father ever been here? What connection did Dad have with this house, with the Muirs?

The basement holds nothing more than empty boxes, crates, old locked trunks and spider webs. Piled high against one wall is a stack of old musty books. Passing them, the hair on Devon's arm suddenly stands up, attracted to them as if by electricity. He stops, lifting the first book off the pile. *The Adventures of Sargon the Great*. It's a children's picture book. He flips open to the first page. "Once upon a time," Devon reads, "many years ago, in the land of the forgotten days, lived a sorcerer named Sargon."

The drawings remind him of ones he's seen in books of Greek mythology. Sargon is wearing a tunic and has long hair and a beard. He finds a crystal ball, and then battles a two-headed dragon. On the third page he pulls his sword out of the dragon's gut, dripping blood.

"*Very* weird for a kid's book," Devon mumbles, looking quickly at the titles of some of the others. *The Mystical Journey of Diana. Vortigar and the Knights of Britain. Brutus and the Sea Monster. Wilhelm's Magical Adventures in Old Holland.*

What could a bunch of children's books tell him? Why does he feel a tingling as he flips through their pages? The Voice is silent. It could be so annoying like that.

Upon emerging from the dank darkness, Devon discovers that lunch has been mysteriously served in the dining room. The containers that this morning had steamed with eggs now bubble with macaroni and cheese, cooked apples, and beans. He eats alone, once again leaving his plates on the table.

He explores the upstairs, passing the playroom, where he can still hear the drone of the television set. He imagines Alexander sitting in there, folded into his beanbag chair, the only thing he'll let embrace him. Did Simon bring the boy's lunch to him? He must have, though it's very peculiar that Devon has yet to lay eyes upon the servant.

Down the corridor he travels, finding it turns at the far end off into a new wing. If the closed-off wing is East, this must be West. Here the windows are shuttered; deep shadows obscure the daylight. Every door is closed and locked, except the last, which stands ajar.

Devon peers within. It's a sitting room, with old furniture as if from another age: a nineteenth-century sofa, a faded gilded Victrola. Devon steps inside. The room smells old and musty. Another door stands open along the far wall. Devon begins to walk toward it when the dust of the room makes him sneeze.

"Eh? Who is that?"

It's an old voice, ragged and dry, from the room beyond.

"Is that you, Amanda?"

Devon stops in his tracks. It's the old woman. Mrs Crandall's mother — whom he's been forbidden to meet.

"Who is there?" the old woman shrills. "Who is there?"

"You are a bad boy, Devon March," comes another voice, whispering behind him.

Devon spins around. It's Cecily, home from school. She's grinning.

"Mother said you weren't to meet Grandmama yet," Cecily's saying, smirking. "You are a bad, bad boy."

"I'm sorry," he whispers. "I didn't know it was her room."

"*Who is there?*" the old voice is demanding.

"It's just me, Grandmama, Cecily," the girl calls, winking at Devon. She strides into her grandmother's room. Devon hurries back into the hallway to wait for her.

Cecily emerges in a few minutes. "She's easily rattled," she tells Devon, as they make their way down the corridor.

"I'm really sorry," he tells her. "I didn't mean to disturb her. I was just exploring the house and. . ."

"Hey, it's not a big deal," she tells him.

"Is she OK? I didn't upset her?"

"Grandmama is the craziest of us all. Rose petals falling from the bushes outside can set her off."

"Well, it's weird being in the same house as she is and her not knowing I'm here."

Cecily shrugs. "Who can understand Mother's reasons for doing anything? Not me. But she's *very* protective of Grandmama. If she knew you were in there – well, she'd have the requisite coronary, like she almost did last night when I came home with DJ."

They've reached the top of the stairs and begin the climb down. "He's your boyfriend?"

"DJ? Oh, God no. He'd like to be. We're friends. We hang out and stuff, and he does have a cool car, an old Camaro. See, DJ's sixteen and a junior. Ana and I get rides from him all the time. I've gone on a couple dates with him, but only because I get so *bored* living up here in this mausoleum."

"Bored?" Devon replies. They're standing now on the marble floor of the foyer. "You've got a tennis court, a swimming pool, the beach down the hill – not to mention all these rooms. . ."

"Everything's dead up here," she says, not without a trace of scorn. "You'll soon discover that. Oh, sure, the villagers are very curious about Ravenscliff, but try to get a decent guy to come up here. People don't like my family much."

"Why is that?"

He follows Cecily into the gleaming kitchen, where she opens the refrigerator and pulls out a carton of yogurt. "Oh, between my mother and my Uncle Edward our family owns practically every business in town, from the restaurants to the tourist boats to the fishing fleet. We provide more than half the jobs in this town, and people always hate the hand that feeds them." She spoons some of the yogurt into her mouth. "So, like, it's a gorgeous day out today. What are you doing inside?"

"As I said, exploring."

She smiles flirtatiously. "Want to explore with me outside?"

He feels his face redden. "Yeah, sure."

She motions for him to follow. They head out the back door. It is indeed a gorgeous fall day, with a bright yellow sun and clear blue sky. Warm, too – Indian summer. They stroll through the rose garden, where the roses grow in wild abandon over trellises. Most of the flowers have long since dried and withered away, but a few deep purple clusters still cling tenaciously to the vines. Devon and Cecily walk on a carpet of browned petals, remnants of a glorious summer.

"Things probably aren't as boring in the summertime," Devon suggests.

"You kidding? That's when my mother *really* keeps me chained to the pillars. All those wild degenerates from New York and Boston. . . She gave me a curfew of ten o'clock. I go, '*Mother*, I am no longer a child.' And she goes, 'I know. That's why I want you home at ten o'clock.'"

She laughs. "This past year, I did manage to get out more. I just started asserting myself. I mean, I'm *fourteen*. All my friends were dating *way* before me. My mother has kept me on a leash tighter than they keep a pit bull. I hardly *ever* went off the hill down to the village until this past year. I was cooped up here in that cold tomb."

They've wandered toward the cliffs. The waves still crash against the rocks below but the fury they'd shown the night before has ceased.

"What did you think of Alexander?" Cecily asks. "Was he everything I promised?"

"And more." Devon grins. "But I hope to make friends with him."

Cecily is walking along the edge of the cliff, the wind moving her hair. "Friends? With that little monster?"

"Well, I'm going to give it a try, anyway."

Cecily turns to face him. "So was it really hard coming here? I mean, your father dying and all, and having to move away. That must've been hard."

They sit on the grass. Devon nods. "Yeah. The worst thing – after my dad dying and all – was leaving my friends."

He pauses, looking at her.

You can tell her, says the Voice.

"Actually," he says, "there was one thing even worse."

"What's that?"

"Right before my dad died, he told me I'd been adopted."

"No *way*."

"Way." Devon sighs. "So not only does he die, but I learn he wasn't my real dad. And see, I think that's why I was sent here. I think right here in Misery Point I can find out who I really am."

"*Wowww*," Cecily says, clearly impressed. "Did you tell Mother? Do you think she knows anything?"

"I did ask her, but she says she doesn't."

Cecily snorts. "I'll bet she does. Mother keeps a lot of secrets."

"I guess *so*. Let's see: there's your grandmother, the East Wing, and – hey. Where's *your* father?"

A bitterness passes over her eyes. "Who the hell knows? And I don't really care, one way or another."

Devon smiles at her sympathetically. "How come I think that's probably not true?"

She tosses her hair over her shoulder. "Look. He left my mother when I was two. I don't remember anything about him. He's a loser. A total and complete loser."

"I'm sorry," Devon says. "I didn't mean to make you upset."

"It's not your fault. It's a logical question."

"Well, I can relate on one level. My mother died when I was a baby, and I don't remember anything about her. Not that I can exactly hold *that* against her."

Cecily narrows her eyes. "But if your father wasn't your real father, was she your real mother?"

He shrugs. "I don't know what to think any more. We never even had any pictures of her. I never even knew what her maiden name was. Dad always said it was too difficult for him to talk about. He just said she was a good woman."

"I couldn't stand not knowing who my parents were."

"Well, I've been thinking of doing my own investigation."

Cecily grins. "Awesome. Let me help. What's the first thing we should do?"

He considers. "I suppose I should go down to the town hall in the village and see if they have a birth certificate for a baby boy born in March fourteen years ago with the first name Devon," he says logically. "I guess that should be my first step."

"Then let's do it today," Cecily tells him, her eyes dancing in the afternoon sun. "I'm bored, nothing to do. And besides, there's no time like the present, right?"

"Yeah," Devon agrees.

"Come on, we'll cut through the woods to get into town. It's faster than going by the road. And I can give you the complete rundown of all our family ghosts. You've got to get to know them if you're going to live here."

They travel down a well-worn path, twigs snapping and leaves crunching under their feet, the sky above them cross-hatched by tree limbs. Cecily eagerly recounts the legends of the ghosts of Ravenscliff.

First, of course, there's Horatio, the founder of the house, and his wife Chloe. Horatio still guards the house, Cecily says, and Chloe wanders aimlessly. Chloe Muir had died giving birth to her third son, Randolph, who was Cecily's grandfather and Mrs Crandall's father. But it's Randolph's brother — Horatio and Chloe's first son — who's the fiercest legend. The notorious Jackson Muir.

"The warlock," Devon says.

"Don't laugh." They've emerged from the woods on to a wide expanse of grass. "Mother refuses to mention his name. She was just a little girl when he died, but I think he scared her. She refuses to hang any pictures of him in the house. But she loves his poor, tragic wife, Emily, who was so unhappy married to the creep that she jumped to her death from—"

"Devil's Rock," Devon finishes for her.

She nods. "She supposedly found him with another woman, and took the plunge. The old man, guilt-ridden, died from his grief."

"A very romantic tale, very *Wuthering Heights*."

She's smiling. "I *have* heard her out there, you know," she says. "Her screams on a windy night."

Devon narrows his eyes at her. "Do you really believe

them? Do you believe there are ghosts in the house? Things you can't explain?"

She considers the question. "Ever since I was a girl, I've heard things," she says finally, the frivolity gone from her voice. "Skeptics don't last long here. That's what Simon always says."

"Simon? Oh, the servant. I've yet to see him."

"He keeps to himself mostly. But he believes all the legends. Says he's seen all the ghosts."

"Have you?"

Again she considers her answer before replying. "There have been occasions when I've seen things, someone moving away at the end of the hallway when I turn on the lights quickly. And I've heard things—"

"Like sobbing?" Devon asks.

She looks at him without surprise. "So you've heard it, too."

"Yes," he tells her. "Last night. I thought it might have been Alexander, but I don't know now. I'm quite sure he was outside my door, trying to scare me, but then I heard this sound, coming from downstairs. . ."

She's nodding. "When I was a girl, my mother told me not to be frightened by anything I heard or saw in that house. 'Nothing here will hurt you,' she assured me. 'This is our house. We respect our house, and our house respects us.'" She laughs. "Strange thing for a mother to say to a little girl, huh?"

"Not if the ghosts are real," Devon says.

"I do believe they're real." She smiles again, resuming her walk along the edge of the cliff. "But they won't interfere with you. The only spook you need worry about is that very-much-alive little cousin of mine."

"I think I can handle him," Devon says.

Cecily looks up at him. "I think you can handle just about

anything you want," she says coyly, batting her long eyelashes almost comically.

Devon blushes again. She reaches up and kisses him quickly on the lips. She giggles.

"I don't know if your mother would approve," Devon says huskily.

Cecily laughs, dancing away. "Oh, Mother's never approved of *anything* I do. I wouldn't let that stop us."

She's in front of him on the path, her red hair loose and bouncing around her shoulders, its highlights reflecting the sunshine that slips through the trees.

"Cecily," Devon calls to her.

She spins around smiling, eyes closed, as if she expects him to kiss her back. But instead Devon asks: "What's the story with Rolfe Montaigne?"

She seems disappointed, then shrugs. "Rolfe owns our biggest competition in this town – our *only* competition really," she tells him, resuming her stride along the path. Tall cat tails grow like mangy children, most with their velvety hoods already turned to seed. "Ever since he's come back to Misery Point, Rolfe has been systematically buying up as much real estate in the village that's not already owned by us. His biggest catch was a restaurant called Fibber McGee's. It's the most popular place in the summer, and has practically put our restaurants out of business."

She turns around and grins at him impishly. "Don't tell Mother, but I've gone there a couple of times. It's awesome. Very artsy. That's where all the celebs hang out when they're on vacation here. I saw Julia Roberts there last summer!"

Up ahead, through a break in the yellow maples, Devon spots a graveyard, with old brownstone markers poking crookedly through the grass. He suddenly feels a chill that belies the sunshine on his face, while conversely the air around him grows warmer. And the heat is definitely not from the sun.

"So," he says, keeping his mind focused, "that's why Rolfe and your mother don't like each other."

"Well, that and—" Cecily stops in her tracks. Devon nearly runs into her. "Look, I personally don't think he was to blame, but it remains a fact—"

"That he killed a kid?"

Cecily looks at him. "Here less than a day, and already you know so much."

"He told me." Devon swallows. "I thought he was just trying to scare me."

"Well, actually it was *two* kids. A boy and a girl. He spent five years in prison. He was drunk, so he doesn't remember. But the cops pulled Rolfe's car out of the bay, and the boy was inside. The girl's body was never recovered. Washed out to sea."

Devon feels the heat intensifying. "They think he drove off the road and then left them there to drown?"

"Negligent homicide, they called it," Cecily says, sighing. "The roads along these cliffs are pretty steep and winding. It could've happened to anyone. But if Rolfe was drunk at the wheel, then I guess he deserved to go to prison."

"But it sounds as if you think maybe he wasn't?"

"Well, there are all sorts of stories. . ."

Suddenly they both fall silent. They're at the cemetery now, and the sun has disappeared behind a cloud.

"Creepy, isn't it?" Cecily asks, shivering.

"Yeah," Devon admits.

He looks around. The graveyard isn't big, with no more than a dozen stones, but it overlooks the sea, giving it an openness that makes it seem larger. The grave markers are weathered from the rain and the wind and the salt of the sea. Most are brownstone, but a number are slate. Many have fallen over into the tall grass; a white marble angel has lost her wing. Near the edge of the woods are situated three small crypts, each made of a dark red stone. The middle crypt bears the simple legend:

TOMB. 1945.

"This is our own personal graveyard," Cecily announces. "These are the first Muirs, Horatio and Chloe and their children. They didn't want to be buried in with the poor slobs down in the village, you see."

Devon has taken a few tentative steps through the wild golden grass that nearly obscures the stones. "Is Jackson buried here? And Emily?"

"Yes," Cecily says, pointing to the largest stone, closest to the cliff. It's the one with the broken angel on top. Devon approaches it with some degree of anxiety, a strange fascination he can't explain to himself. On the side of the monument that faces the woods are the words:

JACKSON MUIR. BORN 1917, DIED 1966.
MASTER OF RAVENSCLIFF.

Cecily scoffs. "Mother always bristles seeing that. Jackson was never master of the house. His brother – my grandfather – was. But Jackson always felt he was the rightful heir."

Devon takes a few steps around to the other side of the marble structure. There the stone has been coated with the whitewash of the salty sea air, but he can still make out the words engraved upon its face:

EMILY MUIR. BORN 1943. LOST TO THE SEA 1965.

Devon looks over at Cecily. "So her body was never recovered? Just like the girl in Rolfe's car."

She nods, letting out a sigh. "Ol' Jackson's all alone under there. Bitter old man."

Behind them they can hear the sea crashing on the rocks below.

Devon touches the stone. Immediately he pulls his hand back. It's burning hot. He looks down at his palm. The skin is bright red.

He looks over at Cecily. *Good*, she hadn't noticed. She's wandering off through the tall grass, heading toward what looks to Devon to be a staircase built into the side of the cliff.

"Come on, Devon," she's calling. "We need to get down to the village before the town hall closes."

But something else has now caught his eye. A large brown-stone marker in the exact center of the cemetery, an obelisk set upon an octagonal base. Even from where he's standing Devon can make out the name engraved there.

"Cecily," he says, pointing. "Look."

The name:

DEVON

He approaches it, walks all the way around it. That's all it says. No other names, nothing. Just *Devon*.

"What could this mean?" he asks. "Might this be—"

"A clue?" Cecily echoes, wide-eyed.

"A clue to what?" It's a new voice, a rough, gravelly bark that comes from the woods behind them. Devon makes a small gasp, certain that when he turns, he'll see a corpse, muddy with maggots after decades in the ground, sitting up in the tall grass and pointing a long, accusatory, bony finger at him.

But Cecily calms him. "It's only Simon," she says.

The Muir caretaker limps through the grass. He's no corpse, but he's frightening enough, Devon thinks. Small and bent, his face is drawn inwards, his eyes most of all: deep and black, and even from across the graveyard they bore into the boy.

"Simon," Cecily calls. "Who's buried here?"

"Whatchu doin' in the cemet'ry, Miss Cecily?" he growls back.

"Oh! You haven't met Devon, have you?" She giggles a little. "Devon March, this is Simon Gooch, our caretaker. And gardener. And chauffeur. And cook." She laughs. "Our everything!"

Simon has reached them now. He stands only to Devon's shoulders; surely this was not the man he had seen on the tower last night. That man had been taller, broad-shouldered. Simon is a twisted elf. His breath is foul, his hands small and scarred — short stubs of fingers, and one missing, the ring finger of his right hand.

"Pleased to meet you, Simon," Devon offers, extending his hand.

The caretaker does not accept it. He just keeps looking up into the boy's eyes. "So you've come to live at Ravenscliff, eh?"

"Yes."

Simon's face is deeply lined; Devon can't make out whether he's forty or seventy. His hair is thick and black, cut unevenly around his face.

"Simon," Cecily says, her voice reproving. "Don't be snarly now."

He grins at her, exposing perfectly shaped white teeth.

They startle Devon. "Never for you, Miss Cecily. Never for you."

"Then tell us who's buried here," she insists.

"Don't know. That ain't a Muir grave."

"But look. It reads *Devon*. And Devon here thinks he was born around here. He doesn't know who his parents were."

Simon looks back at Devon. "Only ones buried in here are Muir kin."

"Well, it just seemed such a coincidence," Devon says.

"We're going to the town hall," Cecily tells Simon. "To search for a birth record of a boy named Devon born fourteen years ago. Now we know to look under first *and* last names!"

Simon says nothing.

"Come on," Devon urges Cecily. "We should get going. It's getting late."

"All right," she says. "Simon, tell Mother we'll be back in time for supper."

They hurry through the grass back toward the cliff. Devon looks back once: Simon still stands there, waist deep in the yellow grass, still staring after him. He's several yards away, but there's something Devon can still see in his eyes. Fury. Rage. No — *fear*. But *why*?

Cecily embarks on the steep staircase cut into the side of the cliff. "Come on!" she calls.

Devon looks back again, unnerved by Simon's hostility and the energy around Jackson Muir's grave. But this time it's not Simon he sees standing in the grass. Whoever stands there now is much taller, for the grass had nearly obliterated the caretaker. Now it rises only to the man's knees.

Devon feels the heat, suddenly as intense as it was last night when the creature had come through his window.

There, in the full, bright sunshine, is the man he saw last

night on the tower, a tall man with dark eyes, dressed entirely in black, as if in mourning. And Devon now knows one thing for certain:

That man is Jackson Muir.

5
The Secret Room

"Devon!"

Cecily stands on the edge of the cliff, her red hair caught in a sudden wind. "Devon, are you all right?"

Devon turns to look at her, tearing his eyes from the thing standing only a few yards away in the swaying grass. His face is white.

"Gosh, I didn't know you were afraid of heights," Cecily says.

He can't speak. He just points behind him.

"What?" Cecily asks. "What is it, Devon?"

"Him," he manages to say.

He turns back to where he had seen the ghost – but nothing remains in the spot except for the grass, now pummeled by a wind that surprises both of them in its ferocity.

"Who? Devon, who are you talking about?"

Devon looks across the graveyard. The trees now bend in the harsh wind; crows in the trees swoop out from the branches, calling out alarms of another impending storm. But there's no man. Jackson Muir's monument stands solemnly amid the waving grass. Whatever had been there is gone.

"Nothing," Devon manages to say. "It was nothing."

"I think a storm's rolling in," Cecily says, looking up at the sky. "We should hurry."

Overhead deep purple rainclouds spread like watercolors across the pale blue sky. The wind bites at their cheeks; the bitter dampness of the sea creeps down the back of Devon's shirt like a dead hand.

He decides not to tell Cecily about the ghost. He looks up into the sky and deems they have enough time to make it into town. Seagulls circle overhead, calling out their melancholy warnings. Devon and Cecily descend the staircase along the cliff, looking over the roofs of the village. It's the first glimpse Devon has had of Misery Point in the daylight. It's a charming place, really: neat, colorful shops and boutiques along a center street, and a long narrow sandy beach beyond. At the end of the main drag the land rises sharply again into new cliffs, and there, about halfway up, Cecily points out one of the Muir family restaurants.

At the far end of town, a white square building sits very close to shore. "That's the Muir cannery," Cecily tells him. "Keeps folks employed year-round. Total gross-out stink, though. Imagine spending your day filling cans with tuna fish and crab meat."

The sky stays pregnant with rain. The day grows dark with clouds, and the wind takes on a bite. They emerge into the village behind a T-shirt and souvenir shop. A sign hanging from its front door proclaims:

THANKS FOR ANOTHER GREAT SEASON — SEE YA IN MAY!

Down the street, Devon recognizes Stormy Harbor. Across from it are more shops, most boarded up except for Adams

Pharmacy and a True Value hardware store. A few Victorian homes, all painted white, stand on well-manicured lawns. Beyond them, stretching out toward the beach, summer cottages are built up on stilts, all evenly aligned and shuttered down for the winter.

Close to the pier, Cecily points out a restaurant. "That's Fibber McGee's," she says. "Rolfe's place." It's a sprawling, California-style restaurant perched at the very edge of the land, a silver and spun-glass resort with an incredible deck overlooking the water, pink and green umbrellas dotting the veranda. Devon recognizes Rolfe's silver Porsche parked out in front.

The town hall is at the end of the road, an old brownstone structure with a clock tower. Inside, their footsteps echo down a high-ceilinged hall, and Devon feels his hopes rise. When the bespectacled woman in the clerk's office plunks a large, dusty volume on the counter in front of him, he can barely open it. *Is this it?* he thinks. *Is this the first step on my road to the truth?* But his high hopes fade to disappointment when the only Devon in the index is a Miranda Devon, born 1947, died 1966, way before Devon was born. And she was unmarried. No record of burial.

"So we'll look it up chronologically," Cecily offers, flipping the yellowed pages to the month of March fourteen years before when Devon would have been born. But the only male birth registered between January and May in the town of Misery Point is that of one Edward Stanner, whose race is listed as black.

"I think we can safely rule that one out," Devon sighs.

So the search reveals nothing. The severity of Devon's disappointment is only matched by the sudden reappearance of the rain, coming down finally as they head back up the steep cliffside stairway. They're drenched by the time they get back to Ravenscliff, but the downpour has the effect of brightening Devon's spirits rather than dampening them. He and Cecily chase each other across the yard, their clothes sticking to their bodies, laughing and carrying on for three quarters of an hour as if no ghosts intrude into their lives, no secrets hang over their heads. For that brief time, getting wild in the rain, tackling Cecily so that they fall to the ground, Devon can actually believe he's just like any other boy. They share another quick kiss, and Devon tells himself he's found at least one good thing in this freaky house.

It storms again that night, giant flashes of lightning and horrible cracks of thunder. But Devon sleeps well nonetheless: exhausted from the night before and worn out from the travel and the adventures of the day. No sounds disturb his rest, and in his dreams he sees Dad sitting on a gravestone in that windswept cemetery out on the cliff, telling him that his destiny is here.

In the morning, Cecily greets him at the breakfast table. It's Saturday, and Simon's taking her into the village to go shopping. She asks Devon if he wants to come, but he declines, saying he wants to spend some time exploring the estate. There's no sign of Mrs Crandall; he hasn't seen her since yester-day morning, in fact. She had already retired when he and Cecily returned from town yesterday. Cecily explained she did that often: either spending time with her mother or retreating into her own private suite of rooms, where sometimes she'd remain for days, Simon bringing her meals up to her.

"It's hard to imagine someone as creepy as Simon being this good of a cook," Devon says, forking a piece of Canadian bacon into his mouth.

"Oh, he's really very good," Cecily says. "He's a master chef."

Still, Devon thinks, the idea of Simon's blunt, scarred little hands touching his food is just a little revolting.

He watches as Cecily waltzes off, Simon appearing almost from nowhere to trail behind her, car keys jangling from his belt. Devon eases back a velvet curtain in the foyer to spy on the Jaguar gliding down the driveway and disappearing down the hill.

He knows he's got to try the door to the East Wing again. He's not sure what secrets this house holds – but he feels quite certain that if they're anywhere, they're in the East Wing. That's where he'd seen the man on top of the tower the night he arrived, a man he's now convinced was Jackson Muir. Seeing the spectre again yesterday in the cemetery has convinced Devon that the nefarious warlock of Ravenscliff holds some clue into his past. Mrs Crandall, he's quite confident, hadn't simply closed off the wing because there were so few people in the house. She'd closed it off because she didn't want anyone discovering what was *in there*.

Of course, the door is still locked. He tries willing it open – he could do that sometimes, like the time he'd gotten locked out of the house while Dad was still at work – but nothing happens. The knob still fails to turn. Devon sighs. He figures there must be another way into the wing from the second floor of the house. He roams up and down the corridor outside his bedroom once again; from the playroom he can hear Alexander's television set, but everything else is as quiet as a tomb.

He considers talking with the boy again, in the hopes of finding some clues. Alexander knows a way into the East Wing; Mrs Crandall had said locked doors did not stop

Alexander Muir. But he doesn't trust Alexander. Not after their first meeting. He's got to find a way in on his own.

After careful consideration of the house's structure, he determines which part of the corridor seems to be directly over the East Wing entrance downstairs. But all he finds there is a linen closet — the doorknob of which *burns* in his hand.

"Yow!" he calls out, then bites down on his lip to keep from making any more noise.

So this is it, he thinks.

He nudges the door open with his foot. Inside are deep shelves of towels and sheets, pillowcases and tablecloths. A little balsam-smelling star hangs from the center rod, scaring away moths. Devon peers into the darkness of the closet. There must be a door through here. This was likely once the upstairs entry into the East Wing, refashioned into a closet when the wing was closed down.

He decides to give up the search for the time being. He could start taking down the towels and sheets and feeling along the shelves, but Alexander could come out of the playroom at any time, or Mrs Crandall might show up behind him. It's too risky right now. But he'll be back. That's for sure.

He heads back down the stairs. He's surprised to see Mrs Crandall sitting in her chair in the parlor, sipping a cup of tea with a few crackers on a plate. A fire roars in the hearth, which feels good even out in the foyer, as the day is damp and overcast.

"Oh, Devon," Mrs Crandall calls to him. "Please join me."

He sits on the sofa opposite the fireplace. "The fire feels great," he says.

"Doesn't it? I've always been partial to fires. Oil heat alone always feels so unsatisfying." She smiles. "Are you warm enough at night?"

"Yes," he tells her. "My room is very comfortable."

"That's good," she said. "I want you to like living here."

"So far, so good," he says, pointedly looking at her.

"Is it?" Her reply seems equally pointed, as if she knows something, or suspects something.

Devon smiles. "I've encountered a few ghosts," he tells her, "but they haven't scared me away."

She lifts the dainty cup of tea to her lips. It looks fragile and ancient. Devon imagines Emily Muir drinking from that same cup, in that same chair, fifty years ago. "Well," Mrs Crandall says, after a moment's consideration, "if everyone ran from the sight of a ghost in this house, there would be no one left."

He eyes her. "You've seen your share."

"How could I not? I've spent all my life here."

"Mrs Crandall. . .?" Devon ventures suddenly.

"Yes?"

"Who is buried in the cemetery out on the cliffs under the monument marked 'Devon'?"

Her blue eyes look at him over her teacup. She seems to hesitate, with the cup not touching her lips, just hovering there in her hand. Then she carefully settles it back into the saucer.

"I don't believe I know," she says at last. "That's the center stone, isn't it?"

At least she isn't denying she knows it. "Yes," Devon says. "The obelisk."

"Curious, isn't it?" she asks. "Only Muirs are buried there . . . perhaps a few trusted friends or servants as well. . ."

"The only Devon listed in the registers for Misery Point is a Miranda Devon, who died in 1966," he tells her, somewhat despondently.

She looks at him with a tight smile. "My, two days and

you've already been busy conducting your own little investigation."

"I'm determined to find out who I am and where I come from."

"Do you think your father would want that, Devon? After all, he raised you as his own. He never told you about your birth parents. Perhaps there was a reason for that."

Devon considers this. "My father wanted me to know," he says. "I truly believe that. He could have gone to his death without telling me the truth, and I'd have never known. But he *did* tell me, Mrs Crandall, and he told me I needed to know my destiny."

Her lips tighten. She stands, walking with her teacup to the fire.

"Not only that, Mrs Crandall. He sent me *here*. He could've found another guardian. But he sent me here."

"Yes," she says, more to herself than him. "He sent you here."

Devon can't tell what inflection her words carry, if she's bitter or grateful or resentful of that fact. He continues, "I'm certain that my father sent me here because this is where I'll find the truth of my past."

She turns to face him, leveling her eyes down at him. "I told you the night you arrived here that this is a house with many secrets. I also told you we respect those secrets. We do not pry. I can offer you one piece of advice, Devon, and I hope you take it. The answers are not in the past, but in the future. If you want to be happy here, you'll look forward, not back, and not into every shadow and every closed door of this house. There are reasons that the doors are closed."

She excuses herself then, saying she has work to do, that Cecily could find her in her room if necessary. Devon nods, watching the flames crackle in the fireplace, sending shadows across the marble floor that dance with all the agility of spirits.

She definitely knows more than she's saying, he thinks. But the Voice adds that he must be on his guard around her. Whether she's friend or foe isn't yet clear, but in either scenario, asking her too much right now would be unwise. Once again, he realizes the information he seeks will need to be unearthed on his own.

That night, the first dry, peaceful night since his arrival, he takes a walk across the grounds, listening to the roar of the waves below, allowing the sound to soothe him as he makes his way along the cliffs.

The moon is bright upon the ocean. He lapses into a sort of timelessness as he watches the waves, feeling the cool October air on his face. The moonlight mesmerizes him as it flickers on the sea, a ballet of light. He finds a smooth, flat rock near the edge of the cliff and sits down, his feet dangling in the air below. It's a hundred feet or more of a sheer drop to the beach below. *This is Devil's Rock*, he realizes. Perhaps this is the very stone from which Emily Muir took her final leap. Suddenly Devon is consumed by a horrible sadness, one that settles deep into his body. He thinks of Dad then, of finding him in bed, still and cold, his eyes open as if he'd been frightened to death.

"Stop it, Devon," he whispers to himself, but it's too late. In the few weeks since his father had died, he had thought of finding his body many times, and the image was impossible to push away. Dad just lay there, staring up into the emptiness of death, his blue-veined hand over his heart. He had been in bed for several weeks, and Devon had become accustomed to their routine: sitting with him until he fell asleep, then crawling into his own bed for a few hours' sleep, only to return at dawn to be there when Dad awakened. Only that particular morning Dad never opened his eyes, and when Devon touched him, he was cold and stiff. Devon knelt beside the bed, wrapping his arms around his father's body, and cried.

"If the ghosts of Ravenscliff can come back," Devon whispers into the night, "why can't you?"

But he can, and does, comes the Voice.

I'm with you, Devon.

He reaches down into his pocket and holds the St Anthony medal in his hand.

"If you ever feel lost, St Anthony is your patron," Dad had told him, just a few days before he died, handing him the medal.

"I never knew you to be religious, Dad," Devon told him, looking down at the small, round, flat silver medal in his palm.

"All religions have insight into the truth, for religion comes from the spirit, and the power of the spirit comes from good." Dad smiled over at him. "You've promised never to forget that, Devon."

"That all power comes from good?"

"Yes," his father told him. "If you remember that, you will know why you are stronger than anything else out there."

I'm trying to remember, Dad, Devon tells his father now, *but it's hard. It's hard because I'm here all alone, in a place I don't know, with people I'm not sure I can trust. Dad, I miss you. I wish you were here so much. I'm trying to discover why you sent me here, but there are so many mysteries. And the demons, Dad — they're here, far stronger than they ever were back home. . .*

He wraps his arms around his torso, rocking himself, swaying his legs in the weightlessness below the cliff. He imagines Emily Muir standing here, her heart racing in her ears, her tears still wet in her throat, her heart broken by her savage, selfish warlock-husband — and then jumping, plunging on to the rocks below, the white water staining red, her mangled body being claimed by the sea. . .

He carefully stands and looks away from the waves. His knees suddenly feel weak, and he pushes himself up on to the grass. Away from the cliff, he feels sturdier, and he walks back across the estate, the well-manicured lawns and shrubbery a testament to Simon's skill. To his left the tennis court stands silent; to his right the gardens stretch lazily toward the sea, their flowers mostly withered, several large round pumpkins catching the moonlight. He looks up at the great house, looming in bleak silhouette against the night sky. Once again he spies the same light in the tower he had seen before, from another angle, upon his arrival.

"The tower has been locked for years," he says, as if to convince himself that the flickering yellow glow is not real.

Yet what are locks, he reasons quietly, to those who've already managed to break out of the grave?

Cecily looks at him with amusement. "I think I've told you one too many stories about our ghosts," she says.

They're at breakfast, seated at the great long polished oak table that accommodates twenty-six. They look lost and even younger than their years, huddled together at the far end, eating cereal and fresh fruit and whispering between themselves.

"No, Cecily, it was there. I'm sure of it. I saw a light in the tower."

She makes a face, clearly troubled, as if she'd prefer not to delve much deeper.

"Have you ever seen a light up there?" Devon asks her. "You admitted you've heard the sobbing."

"And maybe I shouldn't have." She frowns. "Look, Devon. I try not to see too many things in this house. I look the other way."

"But why, Cecily? You can't deny—"

"Why?" She looks at him, very upset now. "Because I'd go crazy otherwise! Imagine growing up here. Imagine what it must have been like."

"You look the other way because that's what your mother always told you to do." He levels his gaze at her. "Isn't that right?"

She pouts. Her silence tells Devon he is indeed correct.

He laughs. "Since when have you done what your mother has told you?"

Cecily's eyes flutter up to find his. Years of denial shine there – a denial of anything not easily explained. "In this one area, it's merely been easier to go along with Mother. Devon, I'd wake up at night with such nightmares as a little girl. Terrifying. Horrible. I've *had* to believe Mother when she's told me the sobbing was only the wind, that the figure in the hallway just a trick of an old house. I've *had* to believe her when she said nothing here could harm me. And I can't stop believing that now."

She pushes aside her bowl of cereal and heads upstairs.

He hadn't meant to upset her, but he needs *somebody* to confirm what he's seen and heard. After breakfast, finding Mrs Crandall in the library, he decides to confront her again.

"You are a determined young man," she says, her neck high and arch as she listens to his story. She wears a simple black dress and a single strand of pearls around her throat. In her hands are three old volumes: one is Twain's *The Adventures of Huckleberry Finn*, he can see, but the other titles are obscured. The library smells dank and dusty, but in a good way, the way old books always comforted him. Yet in this moment, he feels neither comforted nor literary. *Determined* is precisely the word he, too, would have used: determined to find out just what this family is hiding from him.

"I *know* I saw a light, both times," he insists.

"Then I'll have to check," Mrs Crandall says, idly flipping open the top book and scanning the page. "Perhaps there is a short in one of the old light fixtures up there. The wiring hasn't been updated for nearly fifty years." She closes the book. "I should thank you, Devon. You may have alerted us to a potential fire hazard."

So that's her answer. He accepts it, for now.

"By the way, Devon," she says nonchalantly. "I spoke with Alexander. He said you assaulted him."

"No, I—"

"You needn't try to explain. I understand the boy's imagination. But I suggest you try to make friends with him. Remember, I had hoped you'd provide a good influence." She hands him *Huck Finn*. "Here. Would you bring this to him? I told him I'd send him some books to read. Until we decide what to do about his schooling, I want his mind on something other than television."

She sweeps out of the library. Devon sighs, not relishing another encounter with the Bad Seed. But he trudges on upstairs anyway. Perhaps he can determine more of what the boy knows. He finds Alexander once again in the playroom, lying on his stomach in front of the television with his chin in his hands. He's watching that ugly old clown again.

"What *do* you see in that program?" Devon says.

Alexander ignores his question. He sits up and accepts the book from Devon. Behind him on the TV screen Major Musick is again comparing the letter "N" to "M": "*Listen to how they sound almost the same,*" the clown rasps.

"Is this a rerun?" Devon asks.

Alexander smiles and obligingly switches off the set. "I don't need to watch TV if you want to hang out," he says.

Devon looks at him oddly. "You want to hang out with me?"

"Sure. Why not?"

Devon grins. "You didn't seem all that willing yesterday."

"Hey, I could use an older brother." He smiles. "Did you think we wouldn't be friends?"

Devon just studies him.

The boy laughs. "I'm a tough kid to break through to," he says, and something dances in his eyes. It's that challenge – that defiance – that secret knowledge – Devon had seen the first day.

"I think you'll enjoy that book," Devon tells him, nodding down at *Huck Finn*. "It was one of my favorites when I was your age."

Alexander grins again. "I can't imagine you at my age."

"Well," Devon says, "I was."

"Did you get into trouble like I have?"

Devon considers his answer. "Well, I got into my share of troubles."

"Like what?"

"Well, there was an old corridor in this old churchyard. Sometimes we'd go there to hang out, my friends and I. We weren't supposed to go there, because it was old and the bricks were loose and there were bats that lived in the eaves. But of course, everybody liked to hang there. But one time one of the priests came out and found my friend Suze and me there—"

"What were you doing? Making out?"

"No," Devon says, struck by the child's presumption. "We were just talking."

Alexander grins deeply. "I'll *bet* you were just talking."

"We *were*." It comes out harsher than Devon had intended. "We were just talking, and squeezing vampire blood out of a tube."

"Vampire blood?"

Devon laughs. "Yeah. It's just red dye, but we were putting it on our hands and faces. The old priest thought we were sniffing glue. He called the cops. Boy were they surprised!"

Alexander grins. "It sounds like a really cool creepy old place."

"It was."

"I have a place like that where I go! Do you want to see it?"

Devon frowns. "Why do I think it's someplace you're not allowed to be?"

"Aw, come on. I thought you wanted to be my friend." The boy rests his chin in his hands, elbows on the floor.

"Where is it?"

"The East Wing."

A little bell sounds in Devon's mind. "Your aunt says you're not allowed in there."

"So don't come. I don't really care."

Of course, Devon wants into the East Wing himself – badly – but to accompany Alexander there feels doubly dangerous. Mrs Crandall had expressly forbidden it, and he's not sure he can trust the kid to keep their jaunt a secret.

Alexander looks up at him. "We could get in and out quickly," he promises, "and no one would ever know we were there."

If there are answers in this house, Devon feels quite sure they're located in the East Wing. "All right," he concedes with considerable hesitation, "but this has to *totally* be our secret."

The boy beams. "All *riiiight*," he crows, jumping to his feet. "Follow me."

Alexander runs out into the corridor as fast as his fat little legs can carry him. Devon follows the boy to his bedroom, where Alexander pulls open the top drawer of his bureau. He lifts out an old iron candlestick, a short stubby white candle and a book of matches.

"Hey," Devon says, "what do we need that stuff for?"

Alexander fits the candle into the candlestick and holds it out in front of him. "Where we're going they've shut off the electricity," he tells Devon matter-of-factly.

Devon wonders if that's the case for the tower, too, and if Mrs Crandall's line about faulty old wiring was bogus, designed to throw him off track.

"Shouldn't we use a flashlight instead of a candle?" Devon asks.

Alexander shakes his head. "This makes it spookier," he insists. "Unless you're too afraid."

"I'm not afraid," Devon tells him.

But in the hallway, the stillness of the house suddenly makes Devon apprehensive, as if they were all alone in the house. That's not the case: Mrs Crandall is somewhere, perhaps sitting with her reclusive mother, and surely that crotchety Simon is lurking around as well. Cecily, too, probably – and Devon suddenly wishes that the bright teenager was going with them on this trip.

He follows the boy as he pads down the old Oriental runner that lines the long corridor, worn a pinkish gray in some places, still brilliantly red in others. Alexander holds the candle in front of him, as if he were leading a solemn procession.

At the end of the corridor, Alexander opens the door to the linen closet. "In here," the boy whispers.

Devon can't help but smile. Just as he thought.

"Look," the boy's saying, holding his candle aloft so that its glow illuminates the back of the closet. Devon can see nothing that he hadn't seen before. Alexander brings the candle closer. Finally Devon can make out a faint rectangular shape in the plaster down below the bottom shelf.

"Watch," Alexander instructs. The boy runs his hand along the floor of the closet, his fingers gripping a section of old wood. He pushes. For a second, nothing happens: then Devon hears a soft grinding sound, like old wood against stone. The rectangular shape begins to retreat. Devon realizes it's a trapdoor, a small panel now opening inward, exposing a deep blackness within. It's only about three feet by four, just large enough for a small person to wriggle through. From it, damp air strikes Devon like a cold, musty breath.

"See?" Alexander exclaims. "A secret panel. Isn't it *cool*?"

"I don't know if it's safe to go in there, Alexander," Devon cautions.

"I do all the time!" the boy protests. "What's the matter – you *afraid*?"

No, not afraid, but suddenly aware of his responsibility with an eight-year-old boy, as part of a new family he's still unsure of. Yet his curiosity, his quest for answers, overrules any misgivings he might have about what Mrs Crandall would do if she finds out.

Alexander gets down on all fours and crawls inside. Devon takes a deep breath and follows. The fit is tighter for him, but he makes it.

The narrow passage leads between the walls of the house. On the other side, they can stand. Alexander turns around to return the panel to its place. "So no one will see we're in here," he whispers.

Ahead of them is a small passageway that veers sharply to their left. Alexander leads the way, carrying the candle, its flickering light barely allowing them to see just a few inches in front of them. Several times Devon feels the sticky kiss of a cobweb against his face; he brushes at them uselessly, convinced a large spider now crawls along his back.

At the end of the passageway, Alexander pushes at another door. It opens on to a large corridor, not unlike the one outside their bedrooms, with a similar Oriental rug that runs the length. But here everything is covered in a thick layer of dust, a heavy, bitter sediment that makes Devon cough as soon as they enter.

"We're in the East Wing," Alexander proclaims in triumph.

The wallpaper here is old silk: a faded textured blue, with a pattern of swans, Devon thinks, although it's hard to discern what's actually etched beneath the dust. On the walls, old gas lamp fixtures that have not burned in a century hang side by side with the sagging wire of old picture hooks – the portraits of dead Muir ancestors removed to livelier parts of the house. Here, sunlight barely filters through a large stained-glass window at the far end of the corridor, this one of God casting Lucifer into hell. Through the open doors that lead off the corridor, Devon peers into empty, shuttered rooms, barring the sunlight from entering except in tiny slivers. The place is so empty that their footsteps echo dully through the dust.

Alexander urges Devon to follow, beckoning him into one large room that once must have served as an upstairs parlor. A closed-off fireplace and shuttered bay windows attest to the fact that this was more than a bedroom. Devon looks up: an old, broken chandelier still hangs in the center of the room. For a second he imagines Emily Muir here, entertaining guests, laughing, the light of the chandelier reflecting on her delicate features.

"In here," Alexander says, crooking a finger at Devon to follow. They pass through an archway into a small anteroom and finally through a small door into a third room, an inner chamber with no windows. "This is it," Alexander proclaims. "This is my place."

Here the candlelight reveals some remnants of the past: a small oak bookcase filled with dusty old tomes, a roll-top desk, a broken mirror propped up against the wall. And here the heat comes at him full force, causing him to turn away from its impact. *This is the place*, Devon thinks. *The place I've been searching for.*

Why would the Muirs build an inner room? A place without windows? What secrets were kept here?

"This was a library, I think," Alexander says, and indeed, more books are piled on the floor. Suddenly there's a scampering sound: *mice*, Devon imagines. But no, not mice. Whatever's moving under the floorboards and behind the walls is heavier and faster than any mouse or rat. Once more Devon feels the heat pulsing around his face.

"And look," Alexander points out. A solitary portrait hangs on the far side of the room, the dust on its face having been brushed aside in a child's hand stroke. "Doesn't he look like you? I thought so the first time I saw you."

There's no doubt it does. The portrait is of a boy close to Devon's age, dressed in the clothing of the 1930s. Devon takes a step closer to examine it, but Alexander moves the candle, leaving the portrait in darkness.

The child sets the candle down on the roll-top desk. He looks up at Devon, the flame illuminating his features. "Do you like this place?" he asks.

Devon tries to smile. "It's very intriguing," he says, already thinking he'll come back here with a flashlight tonight without the boy. "But maybe we shouldn't stay much longer."

"We won't," Alexander says, and in that second, with the candlelight distorting his sweet childish face, Devon glimpses the creature that lurks within, and he knows he should never have trusted the boy. "But *you* will."

The candle is suddenly snuffed out, and then comes the horrible sound of footsteps running, and a door slamming. "Alexander!" Devon calls after him, as he hears an old key twist in the lock. The darkness is complete; now there is only his voice, the high, sweet voice of a demon child:

"You'll rot in there. They'll never know where you went."

"Alexander!" Devon screams.

But he's gone. In his mind, Devon follows him out through the old parlor and into the corridor, down the secret passageway, out of the closet, down the hallway, and back to his room. Later, when Mrs Crandall asks where Devon is, Alexander will reply with all the innocence with which he'd tricked him. "I don't know, Aunt Amanda," he'll say. "Perhaps he's gone for good."

For several moments, Devon does not think at all. He merely stands in the middle of the room, unable to move, immobilized by the darkness. But then he begins to concentrate, first on his heartbeat, then on his breathing, and he turns to the place where it seemed the boy had left the candle.

Or *had* he left it? Might he have snatched it from the table once he blew it out, condemning Devon here to total darkness?

But for that much at least Devon can be grateful. After fumbling through the dark and finding the roll-top desk, he places his hand around the candlestick and finds the matches nearby. Striking one and lighting the wick, he breathes a long sigh of relief.

"You didn't reckon on one thing, brat," Devon says, turning to face the door. "I have resources of my own when it comes to locked doors."

He concentrates. He wills the door to open, the way he'd flung open the doors on Rolfe's car that first night, but it doesn't budge. He grunts and puts his hands to his head. But he knows it's useless to try. The power comes at first concentration, or it doesn't come at all. It only works when it wants to work. He can never predict it, except he knows it never helps him win track meets or impress his friends. It just works when he needs something really bad, like to fight off demons. But isn't this a situation when he really needs it? If it isn't, he doesn't know what is.

Slowly a little fear begins to gather in the back of his mind. *What if I can't get the door to open? What if I scream, but no one hears me?*

I'll die here, in the darkness.

There's light for now, although the candle is short. If he needs to, he'll snuff it out and conserve it. But he leaves it burning; for now, the light gives him some comfort.

Surely Alexander will return. Devon settles himself against the wall. *If I'm raving like a child*, he thinks, *he will have won. If I remain calm, he will see that I do not frighten easily.*

But what if he meant his threat? What if he really is that disturbed? Or worse?

What if — just as one had disguised itself as Dad — Alexander Muir was in fact a demon in disguise? Or — and the possibility feels more compelling — he's in the control of one?

His eyes. His voice. Devon had recognized it from the moment he met him. There was more to little Alexander Muir than a troubled boy's mischievous behavior.

"You'll rot in there. They'll never know where you went."

"No," Devon says out loud. Surely Mrs Crandall — *and Cecily* — would know he wouldn't just disappear. They'll come searching for him.

He looks up then, toward the corners of the ceiling. Beady little eyes of bats, rose-colored and cruel, stare down at him. He is fascinated by them, as he was that day in the old corridor with Suze. He blinks, and they're gone.

Devon stands up, the candle quivering in his hand. He must occupy his thoughts or else he'll go mad. Alexander will return. He *has* to. Devon carries the candle over to the old bookcase and lifts it so he can read the titles. He's stunned by what he finds. Books on magic. Sorcery, to be exact. *The Arcane Art of the Sorcery of the Nightwing*. His hand trembles as he reaches for the book. He can feel a surge of electricity through his body. He slides the book out of the bookcase, opening it indiscriminately. With the candle he looks down at the page and reads a passage that pops out at him: "All power comes from good."

He replaces the book, and looks at the next one. This is a much thicker book, with ornate goldleaf on its binding. *The Book of Enlightenment*. Suddenly Devon is overcome with a sense of dizziness. He's forced to set the candle down on top of the bookcase and grasp a chair to support himself. Something's rushing through his brain. Words, sounds, pictures. He touches the spine of *The Book of Enlightenment*. . .

He is surrounded by blue light.

A man he does not know, a white-haired man in a flowing purple robe, studded with stars, is speaking in a deep voice that echoes through the blue nothingness:

"Of these enchanters, the most noble, powerful and feared have always been the Sorcerers of the Order of the Nightwing. Only the Nightwing have discovered the secret of how to open the Portals

between this world and the one below. For nearly three thousand years, the Nightwing have jealously guarded the secret of the Portals, which, in common parlance, have come to be known as Hellholes."

Devon staggers back a bit, breaking contact with *The Book of Enlightenment.* The blue light disappears, and he is back in the dark secret room. He attempts to catch his breath, so powerful had been the vision.

Who was that man? What did his words mean? They made no sense to Devon. *The Nightwing* — what did he mean?

But *Hellholes* Devon understands. That part he understands all too well.

He wants to touch the book again, to see what might happen, but something stops him. Part of it is fear — he can't deny that the experience freaked him out a little, especially because he had no control over it — but part of it is also because he's distracted by a third book. For the first time since he's been trapped in here, the Voice is speaking to him. *Open that one, Devon*, it's saying. It's called *Registry of the Guardians of the Portal.*

Devon slides it out, a fog of dust choking him momentarily, and flips open its musty pages. The title page indicates it was published in London in 1883. It is a compilation of Guardians — whoever they were. On its glossy pages are portraits of nineteenth-century men and women. The men are dark-eyed and somber with heavy whiskers and high collars; the women are solemn with their mouths drawn inward. One face stops him.

It's his *father*.

But it *can't* be: Dad couldn't have been alive in the nineteenth century. The name under the portrait reads:

THADDEUS UNDERWOOD.
GUARDIAN.

But it sure looks like Dad: round, pudgy face, poached egg eyes, that goofy grin Devon had loved so much. He feels the heat again then, on his back, like eyes watching him. He looks around: the little red bat eyes have returned. They blink a few times, then disappear.

He closes the book and returns it to its place.

Look around, Devon.

He follows the Voice. The secret of his past is close by. He holds the candle in front of him, squinting into the darkness.

At the far end of the room, he spies another door — metal, half-size, rising from the floor to about his chest. He hopes against hope that it isn't locked. But where might it lead? Approaching, he discovers that it is indeed locked: bolted, in fact, with a heavy iron sliding bar across the width of the door. Try as he might, he can't budge it; the bolt seems almost welded in place, as solid as the heavy door it keeps closed.

And suddenly he knows why.

"It's a Hellhole," Devon says out loud.

They're in there, the Voice confirms for him. *That's why the door is locked.*

He reaches down, places his hand against the door. Immediately he feels the throbbing heat within and withdraws his hand. He can hear them now, scuttling and squirming, agitated behind the door:

Let us out! Let us out! Open the door and let us out!

He stares down at the door, and sees it begin to pulse, as if whatever forces were imprisoned behind it were suddenly pushing against the door, begging for release.

Let us out! Let us out!

Their voices form a hideous chorus in his mind. He covers his ears.

"Never," he whispers to them.

It's like my closet, Devon realizes now. *The closet in my bed-room back home, where the green eyes stared out at me from the darkness, where the thing that had nearly killed Dad had slithered out across my floor...*

He stares at the bolted metal door. It shudders. He feels the heat emanating from it.

Who barred that door? What connection did it have to the creatures that haunted him as a boy? To the thing that assaulted him his first night in this house?

To Alexander? To Jackson Muir?

Suddenly he feels compelled to approach the portrait of the boy who looks so much like himself again. He takes a few steps and the candlelight reveals the face. *Yes, it's me — or else, it's someone who looks exactly like me...*

Devon smells the thing before he sees it. A horrible, rotting, putrefying smell. The stink of death.

"You are no match against me, you ignorant child."

Devon turns. There, behind him, breathing his rank breath down his back, is Jackson Muir. The beast smiles at him, exposing the maggots in his teeth.

Devon March screams.

The candle falls to the floor and is snuffed out.

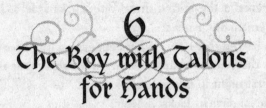

6
The Boy with Talons for Hands

Devon shouts again in the darkness and tries with all his might to fight off the ghost, but he's immobilized. His powers are gone. His father was wrong: he's *not* stronger than any of them, at least not stronger than Jackson Muir. At any moment he expects to feel the ghost's clammy hands on his throat, tightening their grip until he can no longer breathe. But all he feels is his own thudding heart, and all he hears are his own screams.

He collapses on to the floor and mercifully passes out.

When he awakes, he's alone, and Devon forgets momentarily where he is, not comprehending the darkness. Then it all comes rushing back at him: Alexander's treachery, the bolted door, his inability to fight the maggot-ridden Jackson Muir, the horrible rasp in his ear: "*You are no match against me.*"

How long has he been in here? His stomach rumbles with hunger. Surely it's now past dinner time. It may be well into the night as far as Devon can tell. Mrs Crandall must have inquired about his whereabouts by now. What had Alexander told her?

"Alexander!" he calls.

He *had* to call for help. Yet he tries, even now, to not sound frantic, to mask the terror he feels burning in his gut. He's reluctant to feel his way through the dark to find the candle he'd dropped. He's convinced that just inches away stands the moldy, rotting corpse of Jackson Muir, still smiling unseen in the darkness.

"Help!" he shouts. "Alexander! Let me out of here!"

Seconds tick into minutes in his mind. Minutes become hours, but time in a vacuum is meaningless. Now the air feels stiflingly thin. Dust seems lodged in his throat and his nostrils. His voice grows hoarse and sore from shouting. Finally he just crouches against the wall, as far away as possible from the bolted metal door, and lets sleep overtake him.

He awakes with a start some time later. Is it morning? In such total darkness one would never know. Is this how he'll die, then? Is this the destiny he had come to find? To die in this house of secrets, to discover not his past but his fate: doomed to spend eternity as one more ghost haunting the halls of Ravenscliff?

Above him, the red eyes of the bats come alive pair by pair, like horrible Christmas lights strung through the night. Something moves past him: a short rush of air. Devon swallows, staring into the dark. He hears the soft laugh of a child.

"Alexander?" he says weakly.

Devon's hands fumble across the grimy floor, searching for the candle. After much effort, his fingers close around the stubby wax. He reaches out blindly for the rolltop desk, finally feeling the book of matches. He strikes one, lighting the candle.

"Alexander!" he hollers.

He hears a noise from the outer room.

"Who is it? What is going on in there?"

A gruff, raspy voice. The low grating sound of a door being

shoved open. The beam of a flashlight, slicing through the darkness, catches him in the eye. Devon winces. In the back glow of the flashlight he sees a man approach. A short, squat man.

Simon.

"What are you doing here?" the caretaker asks, his ugly features even more hideously distorted in the darkness.

"Alexander tricked me," Devon tells him. "He locked me in."

"The boy's an imp," Simon mutters.

"Did you hear me call? Is that how you happened to come by? You heard my shouts?"

"No," the man said plainly. "If you were shouting, nobody woulda ever heard you in here. I just happened to see Mr Alexander come out of the secret door in the closet yesterday afternoon. I scolded him, but he paid me no mind. Thought I'd seal off that panel. Good thing I decided to investigate first, eh?"

"Yes." Devon just wants to get out of this place. He looks once more toward the padlocked metal door. "Please. Let's go."

Simon nods. Silently they walk out of the darkened room, through the deserted wing of the house and down the narrow passage back to the linen closet. Simon leads the way, with his flashlight. When they emerge into the warmth and light of the main part of the house, Devon blinks, his eyes not yet accustomed.

"Is it morning?" he asks Simon.

"Sure is. Monday. I'll be driving Miss Cecily to school in a half-hour. You going with her?"

School. He had forgotten. His first day at a new school. "Yeah," he says. "I mean, I was supposed to." He looks over at the stunted caretaker. "Hey, so where did everybody think I was?"

Simon shrugs. "No one noticed you were gone."

"*What?*" Devon's astounded.

"Mrs Crandall spent the evening with her mother, then went to bed early. Miss Cecily was out with that hooligan from the village. Mr Alexander told me you'd gone to bed."

"So I really *might* have rotted up there," Devon says, more to himself than Simon. "Look, I'd appreciate it if you didn't mention this episode to Mrs Crandall. I don't want Alexander getting into trouble over it. I'd like to handle it my own way with him."

Simon shrugs. "Don't make no mind to me. But I'm telling you. Stay out of that place. The East Wing was closed for a reason."

"Tell me something, Simon. Do you believe Jackson Muir's ghost haunts this house?"

"Why not? The house is rightfully his."

"Why do you say that?"

Simon looks at him. He seems defiant in a way, as if he feels the need to come to Jackson's defense. "He was the elder son. His line should've been the masters of Ravenscliff. But he had no heir. So it was his brother's family that got the estate."

Devon thinks Simon's face betrays some bitterness over the fact. "Jackson had no heir," he asks, "because his wife jumped off Devil's Rock?"

"Why are you asking all these questions?" Simon snaps, suddenly on guard.

Devon faces the caretaker. "I've seen both of them. Jackson in there, last night, and in the cemetery a few days ago. And Emily downstairs in her portrait."

Simon's beady eyes narrow further. "You'd best be careful, boy."

Devon looks back at the little man intently. "I *heard* her, too. Emily – I've heard her sobbing."

Simon's face changes, becoming suspicious. "Where? Where did you hear this sobbing?"

"Coming from the East Wing. The tower."

Simon scoffs. "It was the wind. That was no sobbing."

"What about the light in the tower room? I suppose there's nothing there, either."

Simon gives him a small, tight smile. "Mrs Crandall had me check. There was an old light fixture that had a short. It would come on and off. No ghosts involved there."

That had been Mrs Crandall's explanation earlier. Devon shakes his head. "I don't understand, Simon. At first it seems you believe there are ghosts here, then you try to offer logical explanations. What's the truth?"

"Just listen to me. I don't know what you've seen or think you've heard. Maybe you're right. Maybe there are ghosts all *through* this house. All the more reason for you to just keep your nose to your books and let it all be. The whole reason I told you about Jackson Muir is for your own good, so you won't go prowling around this house. There are secrets here, dangerous ones, that you shouldn't go messing with. The family respects the secrets of the house, just lets them lie. That's the way. Otherwise. . ."

His voice trails off. There's genuine fear in his eyes.

"I can take care of myself," Devon tells him. "Thank you, Simon. Tell Cecily I'll be down in a minute."

Devon hurriedly jumps in the shower. His hair is still damp as he bounds down the stairs to find Cecily at the breakfast table.

"Whoa, Rocky the Flying the Squirrel," she says, as Devon

hurriedly pours himself a cup of coffee and grabs a corn muffin. "You oversleep?"

"Something like that," he tells her.

"Well, let's get going. Simon's waiting." She flings her hair back, gives him a smirk. "I've told all the girls about you. Everyone can't *wait* to meet you."

"Oh, great," Devon says, rolling his eyes.

Simon doesn't speak as he drives them down the hill and through the village, out along Route 138 and into the neighboring town, past strip malls and fast food franchises. Cecily's gabbing about all her friends, trying to give Devon background on each one, but he's not listening.

I'm getting close, he's thinking. *That locked door in the East Wing . . . the portrait that looks like me . . . the picture that looks like Dad. This is my past. Somehow I'm connected to those things — but how?*

"Here we are," Cecily announces.

Devon looks up. Southeast High School. Kids hang all around the parking lot, some smoking cigarettes, most in little clusters, talking animatedly.

School. I've got to focus. I don't want everybody thinking I'm a jerk.

They bid goodbye to Simon, who grunts and drives off. Cecily takes Devon's hand and leads him toward a group of kids hanging by a bike rack. A girl and two guys; one of the guys, Devon recognizes as DJ.

"Cess," the kids say, acknowledging her. Their eyes are on Devon, though. DJ seems the most uninterested, having met him already; but the other guy and the girl watch him closely.

"Guys, this is Devon," Cecily says. "I've told you about him. He's cool."

"Hey," Devon says.

The girl, a pretty brunette with a pug nose, smiles. "You were right, Cecily. He *is* cute."

"Devon, this is Ana. Go ahead, ask her what she did on summer vacation. She'll tell you her hair and her nails."

"Run along and play in the traffic, Cess," Ana says sweetly, all smiles, moving past her to stand in front of Devon, clutching her books to her chest. She looks up into Devon's eyes. "She's just jealous cuz I made cheerleading and she didn't."

"I wouldn't be a cheerleader if I got *paid* for it," Cecily snips. "I mean, how *geeky* are those little skirts?"

"Some people are just afraid to expose their thighs, I guess," Ana coos.

"Good to meet ya," Devon says, smiling down at her, ending their banter.

She bats her eyelashes up at him. "I look forward to being *very* good friends," she says.

"You remember DJ," Cecily says, rolling her eyes, taking Devon's arm and leading him away from Ana.

"Yeah," Devon says, extending his hand. DJ looks down at it but makes no effort to take it. He barely nods, withdrawing a pack of cigarettes and popping one into his mouth.

"That is such a gross habit," Cecily scolds. "Kissing a guy who smokes is like licking the inside of an exhaust pipe."

DJ grins, the silver stud through his nostril rising and falling with every twist of his mouth. "If you promise to kiss me regular, Cess," he says, "I'll toss the Marlboros."

She just scowls, walking past him with Devon. "And, finally, last but never least," she says, "this is Marcus."

A short, dark-haired, blue-eyed guy wearing a green crewneck sweater extends his hand. Devon shakes it. "Nice to meet you," Marcus says.

"You, too," Devon says. But even as he says it, something

seems to materialize over Marcus' face. Devon can't make it out at first, but then it becomes obvious. It's a pentagram. A five-pointed star. It fades out almost as quickly as it appeared.

"Devon," Ana's saying, "how about if I show you around? You know, where your locker is and everything?"

"Thanks so much for your concern," Cecily says, gripping Devon's arm, "but I think I have everything under control."

Devon's still a little unnerved by the image he saw in front of Marcus' face, but he feels no heat, no sense of any danger. He takes out the papers Mrs Crandall gave him, looking for his locker number. "I'm 1272," he tells the girls.

"Hey," Marcus says, "I'm 1271. I can show you."

"Oh, lucky you, buddy," DJ says, laughing. "Now you got 'em *all* after you. Even Marcus."

"Yeah, whatever, DJ," Marcus snarls.

As they walk into the school, Cecily leans into Devon's ear. "Marcus is gay," she explains. "He just came out to us. I think it's great that he can be so honest, don't you?"

Devon looks back at him. There's no image on him now. What had it meant? And did it have anything to do with everything he's been finding at Ravenscliff?

The day passes in a haze. Classes, seat assignments, new books piled up in front of him. Meetings with teachers, interviews with guidance counselors, summaries of lessons. Starting in the middle of the semester is no fun; but the day does give Devon a break from the thoughts that have consumed him since his arrival at Ravenscliff. It gives him the opportunity, for a few hours at least, to be just an ordinary kid.

His mind is still swimming when the last bell rings, and Cecily meets up with him at his locker, the combination of which he's trying to commit to memory.

"Forty-five . . . fifteen. . ."

"I called Simon, told him DJ would bring us home," Cecily's gabbing at him. "This way we can hang at Gio's for a while."

"What's Gio's?"

"A pizza place," Marcus tells him, appearing suddenly at the next locker. "Everybody from Misery Point hangs there after school."

Devon watches as Cecily and Ana are suddenly *so* sweet to DJ now that they're getting a ride from him. He wonders if once they get their own licenses DJ will still be such a bud.

"Awesome car," Devon says, checking out DJ's red Camaro with a glass T-top roof.

"Thanks," DJ says, still seeming unsure of whether he likes Devon or not.

"What year is it?" Devon asks.

DJ eyes him with some distrust. "You know anything about cars?"

"A little. My father was a mechanic. He was always rebuilding engines and stuff."

"It's an eighty-five," DJ tells him. He pats the Camaro's hood. "Z28, five-point-oh. Tuned port injection. I found a rust-free drive train and restored it to show-car condition."

"Well, it looks great. And with that engine, it must be really fast."

DJ is starting to warm up. "You bet. I'll open her up sometime for you on I-195."

He slides in behind the wheel and starts the engine, the car humming to life. The music snaps on as well. Vintage Aerosmith.

"Hey," Devon says. "Aerosmith *rocks*."

DJ beams. "*Finally*," he calls over to the other kids,

climbing back out of the car. "Somebody who has some *taste* in music." He looks back at Devon. "These guys are all Backstreet and 'N Sync."

Devon shudders. DJ laughs and claps him on the back. Walking around the car, he gives Devon a detailed description of the Camaro's history of different paint jobs. Right now she's got a white stripe painted down the side, with a yellow starburst at the end. Devon learns that DJ named the car "Flo," after his grandmother, who'd bought it for him.

For the first time since leaving Coles Junction, Devon feels as if he might just fit in here. Never mind for a moment about all the creepy mysteries waiting for him back at the old house on the cliff. Just as important in some ways as finding out about his past is finding a group of friends, people he likes and can trust, people who can help him forget how much he misses old pals like Tommy and Suze. He'd already felt such a connection with Cecily, and he has to admit it's kind of sweet to have both her *and* Ana vying over him. Marcus is cool, too. Devon's never known a gay kid before, at least not one who didn't deny it and who didn't seem embarrassed to admit it. Standing at their lockers earlier, Marcus had explained he'd decided to be honest with his friends because he was tired feeling outside and "different." Devon can sure relate to that. Compared to himself – compared to the things Devon's been dealing with all his life – Marcus is just a normal kid, like any other guy in school.

Except, of course, for that pentagram that appeared over his face. Devon still wonders what *that* was all about.

He especially likes DJ. Tall and lanky, pierced and fuzzy, laidback and quiet, DJ comes alive only when something really gets him excited, like his car or the music of Aerosmith. In his black jeans and black T-shirt, he seems not to have a care in the world except for keeping his Camaro waxed and shined. Devon envies him; he can't imagine having such ordinary luxury.

They all pile into Flo: Marcus up front with DJ, Devon in back with Ana and Cecily, one on either side of him.

Ana leans into him. "It must be so creepy living up there in that old house," she whispers, shivering.

He shrugs. What can he say to that?

"If you ever want to get away," she tells him, "just call me."

Devon just smiles.

At Gio's, there are already several cars. Devon watches his new friends as they talk to the other kids. They're an odd lot, he thinks. DJ spends some time with the guys out front, smoking cigarettes. One kid, leaning against his motorcycle, DJ calls "Crispin." Ana flits over to exchange some giddy gossip with a couple other cheerleaders before sliding into a booth next to Cecily and Marcus, who speak to no one.

"So what brought you guys together?" Devon asks the group, as Gio, a barrel-chested man in a grimy apron, drops a steaming cheese pizza in the middle of their table. "How come you guys hang out with each other?"

They all look at him as if it's an odd question. Finally DJ answers: "Dunno, man. Guess we just don't pull no bull with each other."

"We just don't quite fit with any other group," Marcus tells him, lifting a slice of pizza in the air, its cheese dangling in a long string. "According to conventional wisdom, I should hang out with the *theater* crowd. But I'm not that — well, *theatrical*."

"In other words," Cecily translates, "they're all in the closet and Marcus isn't." She snorts. "Like we don't know the *real* story of the guys in the *drama club*!"

"And me," Ana says, cutting her pizza with a knife and fork.

"I could hang with the cheerleaders if I wanted. But who wants? Like I *want* to talk about shaving my legs all the time?" She pauses. "*Some* of the time, sure — but not *always*."

Devon's smiling. "And what about you, Cecily?" he asks, looking at her.

A small, sad grin plays with her lips. "Oh, I don't know. Maybe it's because these losers put up with me, and none of the others will." She looks over at DJ, then at the others. "I can be pretty demanding, can't I?"

A chorus of affirmative replies. "All right, all right," she says, laughing. "But you know what else? It's not been easy growing up at Ravenscliff, the way people talk about the place. The ghosts. The legends. The scandals. A lot of the other so-called 'rich' girls don't want anything to do with me. In some ways—"

But she's cut off by a noise. Some commotion by the front door of the pizza joint. A fight. They all look. Two boys tussling. Gio is shaking his fists at them.

"Who's fighting?" Cecily asks.

DJ bounds out over the back of the booth, landing on his feet. "Looks like Crispin," he says. Indeed, the boy being pulverized is the guy who'd earlier been leaning against his motorcycle earlier. DJ runs to help his friend.

"DJ!" Cecily calls. "Be careful!"

That's when Devon feels the heat. The vibration begins high in his ears as the pressure seems to close in on him.

That's no kid that started that fight, the Voice tells him.

He slides out of the booth and feels unsteady on feet.

"Devon?" he hears Cecily ask, but it's as if she's miles away. He begins to walk in the direction of the scuffle, the heat making him dizzy. Other kids are gathering around now. He pushes through them, wending his way to the heart of the fight.

DJ's there now, trying to lift the kid pummeling his friend by the back of his denim jacket. From here, he looks like any other kid. Blondish hair, small frame, jeans, Nike sneakers.

But when DJ manages once to pull him up by the back of his jacket, Devon sees the truth: those are *talons* instead of hands, clenched into terrible fists as they pound the boy.

"Get back to hell," Devon roars, grabbing ahold of the demon's shoulders and lifting him with strength he didn't know he had. DJ, stunned, steps backward. Holding the creature by the shoulder with one hand, Devon hauls back with his other hand and lands a punch square in the face, sending the brawling demon flying out the door.

"Duuuude," DJ breathes.

The other kids look at Devon in awe.

Outside, the demon-that-looks-like-a-boy stands and hisses.

You're the one I was looking for, he says to Devon. *Figured this would get your attention.*

Devon stares at him. He knows he's the only one to hear the creature's words.

Open that door! the demon tells him, yellow saliva dripping from its mouth. *Let them free!*

Never, Devon tells him.

The thing hisses again, then turns and runs off down the road.

"Did you see that kid's *hands*?" cries Crispin, sitting up and rubbing his face. Several girls crowd around him. Gio comes by with a cold cloth to press against his head.

"I'm going after him," DJ announces.

"No," Devon says. "He's long gone!"

"I called the police," Gio says to the assaulted kid. "They'll be here for you to file charges."

"I was just standing by my bike, doin' nothin," Crispin says. "He comes up and throws me down, starts whaling at me. *Man*. Did you see his *hands*?"

"You ever see him before?" Gio asks.

"No. Never."

The general consensus among the crowd is that he's not from around here. Devon laughs to himself. *That's for sure.*

"Hey."

He looks up. DJ is standing next to him. Behind him are Cecily, Ana and Marcus. All wide-eyed.

"Dude, how are you so strong?" DJ asks, awestruck.

Devon feels his face redden. "I don't know. Adrenaline, I guess."

"You were *awesome*," Ana gushes.

"Yeah," agrees Marcus.

Cecily sidles up next to him. "Awesome doesn't begin to describe it." She reaches up, putting her arms around his neck. "You're a superhero, Devon March."

Devon gives a statement to the police, but professes ignorance when Crispin insists his attacker had "hands like claws." Devon says in the rush to come to his aid, he never got a good look at the kid.

That's not true, of course, but he knows the creature isn't going to be caught by any police dragnet. In fact, he *did* get a good look at the thing: except for the talons, he looked like any average kid, and that's what was so scary. The dumb-ass demons like the one that came through his window the other night were not nearly so threatening as these clever ones, who could take the shape of humans. Devon realizes he's now got to be on alert twenty-four seven: at any time, those around him might not be what they seem.

Like little Alexander Muir?

Back at Ravenscliff, he takes a long shower, feeling dirty from the encounter. *Why?* he thinks. *Why is this happening so often?* Back home, the experiences with the demons were rare, and came with some degree of warning: a gradual increase in the temperature and the pressure around him. Here everything's unpredictable and far more intense. It's as if by his very arrival in Misery Point he's got them rattled and belligerent.

Devon lets the spray hit his face. *Dad sent me here to find the clues and discover my truth, a truth he apparently was not free to tell me.* He turns off the shower and steps out into the steamy bathroom. *I've got to find the answers. And soon.*

The demon at the pizza joint confirmed what he'd already believed: that bolted door must *never* be opened. Behind it lay more of the creatures that their brother demons want liberated. But what connection does Devon have to them? Why is he the only kid in the world who knows demons and monsters are real? What was all this about sorcerers and Guardians of the Portals? Who is the boy in the portrait who looks so much like him?

Devon's convinced Alexander holds some of the answer in his fat little hands.

He dresses quickly and heads down the corridor to the playroom. Once again he hears the inane laughter and sees the blue flickering light of the television before he enters.

Alexander doesn't seem surprised when Devon walks in. He just looks up at him from his beanbag chair, where he sits alternately watching the TV and reading *Huck Finn*. His eyes reflect no astonishment, no guilt, at seeing Devon. They're empty, as empty as anything Devon has ever seen.

"So," Devon says. "Tell me what you think of Huck."

"He runs around doing bad things," Alexander says,

the touch of a grin playing at the corners of his mouth.

"And what might you know of doing bad things, Alexander?"

"My teachers told me I was a bad boy."

Devon sits down on the floor beside him. "I don't think you're bad. But I do think sometimes we all do bad things, things we wish later we could take back."

The boy squints at him. "So were you scared?"

"Did you *want* me to be scared, Alexander?"

The boy shifts. Suddenly he seems uncomfortable, less calculating, even — could Devon trust it? — *sorrowful*.

"Have you ever been scared, Alexander?" Devon asks.

The boy looks at him, suddenly all bravado. "No. I've *never* been scared."

"I don't believe you."

The boy stands up abruptly. He strides over to his toy box, opening the lid, withdrawing a ball. He begins bouncing it up and down.

"I'll bet you were scared when they sent you off to that school," Devon says. "I'll bet you were scared when your father went away."

"He's coming back!" the boy says sharply, looking over at Devon.

Devon doesn't reply.

"And when he comes back, he'll make everything OK!" Alexander seems to retreat into his thoughts. "If my father were here, he wouldn't let anything bad happen to me."

Devon stands, walking over to the boy. "Do you think something bad is going to happen to you, Alexander?"

The boy seems to suddenly hear a sound far off in the distance. "It's time for *Major Musick*," he announces, almost dreamily.

"Alexander, let's talk. Are you frightened of something? Talk to me about your father. Talk to me about—"

"It's time for *Major Musick*," he repeats, enunciating each syllable, as if Devon were the foolish child, the frightened idiot. The boy lets the ball roll away and heads back over to the television set.

Devon intercepts him. He takes him by the shoulders and looks down into his round button eyes. He's startled by the raw terror he sees there, but the child does his best to keep his eyes averted. For an instant Devon wants to disbelieve what he sees, to dismiss it as Alexander's game. *Pity me, the poor innocent frightened child, abandoned by his father.* But the kid's trying too hard to disguise his fear. He doesn't want Devon to know he's scared, any more than Devon had wanted the boy to know of his own fright at being locked in that room.

But what could be frightening him? It's as if the boy acts not of his own volition, not from his own cunning. Maybe the craziness Cecily sees in her cousin, the misbehavior his schoolteachers had scorned, isn't so much the boy's doing as – *someone else's.*

"It's all right, Alexander," Devon tries. "It's OK to be frightened sometimes. We all get frightened once in a while. Tell me what's wrong. Maybe I can fix it."

"You think you could?" he asks, laughing a little, in a husky, arrogant whisper. "You really think you could?"

"I could try. At least by talking about it—"

"I can't! He won't let me!" The boy shudders against Devon. His eyes search back and forth across the room.

"Who, Alexander? Who won't let you?"

The boy is silent.

"Is it Jackson Muir, Alexander? Are you frightened of him?"

Alexander eyes him sharply. "Why would I be frightened of Jackson Muir?"

Devon looks closely at him. The boy's eyes are like burning embers. His mouth curls in a snarl that seems so alien to his smooth, childish features. It's the expression of an adult, a cynical, bitter man.

"Let me go," Alexander says calmly.

Devon complies. The boy settles back into his beanbag chair. With the remote control, he switches the channel to Major Musick. Devon walks behind him to watch.

On the screen, four rows of blank-eyed children sit on a low-rising bleacher. They're clapping, all in unison, like little robots, like those wind-up monkey bands. The camera scans past the bland gray masks of their faces. It lingers on the face of one of them: a skinny boy in a crewcut, his face a mass of brown freckles.

Major Musick comes out then, making his entrance from behind a frayed red velvet curtain. "Hello, boys and girls," he barks. "What shall we sing today?"

Just what is it about this creature that so entrances Alexander? Devon watches as the boy settles down raptly. Major Musick launches into a crazy song about big black birds circling around a house. Devon watches the painted lips, the big red nose, the little darting eyes surrounded by enormous white circles.

"He's creepy," Devon tells Alexander.

But Alexander's not paying any mind, just singing along in a low childish voice to the song about the birds.

Devon shudders, putting his questions aside for now, and leaves Alexander to his clown. More than anything else, Devon just wants to get out of that room.

"He needs a shrink," Cecily says as they walk out to the stables, the sky darkening above them. Yet another storm looms on the horizon. "His mother was loco. It must run in the family."

"Cecily, I know you think the ghosts in this house are harmless. But I'm not so sure."

"Oh, Devon, really."

She slides the bolt aside and pulls open the door. Devon inhales the thick air of the stable, heavy with straw and manure. Cecily's horse, Pearlie Mae, is a champion, a beautiful white Morgan with sharp pink ears and wide eyes.

Devon pats the side of the animal fondly. "Does Alexander ride?" he asks.

Cecily laughs. "You kidding? That little porker? He just sits in front of that damn television set and eats Hostess Twinkies all day long." She shakes her head. "I tried being friendly to him when his father first dumped him here, but he's just so miserable."

"I'm worried about him," Devon says.

"With reason. Those things can kill you!"

Devon smiles wearily. "I wasn't talking about Twinkies."

"Then what?"

"I'm not sure," he says. The horse snorts. "OK. So I think I know." He pauses. "Jackson Muir."

Cecily moves in close to him. "Oh, Devon. Maybe we've filled your head with too many of our stories. Our ghosts aren't menacing. Pretty soon you'll get used to them. They'll fade into the background, like the wallpaper." She reaches up and puts her arms around his neck, pulling him close to her. "You were just so *manly* at the pizza shop today."

They kiss. The horse whinnies and whips its tail. Devon eases Cecily back, gently removing her arms from around his neck.

"Cecily," he says, "I like you a lot. But this stuff that's been happening ever since I got here — I've got to figure out what's going on."

"What are you talking about?"

He sighs. "All right. I'm going to try something. I don't know if it'll work, but I'm going to try."

She looks at him strangely.

He closes his eyes and concentrates. Once, trying to impress Suze back home, he tried lifting the front of a Volkswagen. It didn't work. But now he isn't trying to impress Cecily as much as enlist her help; he needs an ally in fighting whatever it is that threatens him, and maybe threatens Alexander, too.

In his mind he visualizes the stable door. It's standing wide open, the way they'd left it. He concentrates as hard as he can and—

The stable door swings shut.

"Whoa!" Cecily says. "How'd you do that?"

"I can just . . . do things," he says, adding, "sometimes."

She stares at him. "Do something else."

"I don't know if I can," he tells her.

"Then how do I know that wasn't the wind?"

He sighs. He looks around. His eyes rest on Cecily's horse. He concentrates.

And within seconds Pearlie Mae levitates three feet off the straw-covered floor.

"Oh my God," Cecily breathes, her face going white.

Devon brings the horse gently back to earth.

"Oh my God," Cecily repeats. "That was *definitely* not the wind."

"Ever since I was a kid, I could do this stuff." Devon smiles awkwardly. "Sometimes. Sometimes it doesn't happen, try as I might. But see, Cecily, that's why I've got to discover the truth of who I am. Why I'm like this. And I'm certain my dad sent me here so I could find out."

"Oh my God," is all Cecily says again, sitting down on a bale of hay.

Devon sits down beside her. "Do you think I'm a freak?"

She looks up at him, and finally smiles. "I could never think that, Devon."

He sighs. "Good. Because I need your help. You've got to believe me when I tell you what I've seen in that house. What I've seen all my life."

So he tells her about the demons – the green eyes in his closet back home, his father's admonition that he was stronger than any of them. He tells her about Alexander's prank, and about what he found in the East Wing. The portrait. The door.

"It's not like I don't believe you, Devon," she tells him. "It's just that – I can't adjust to the idea that there are demons in Ravenscliff. Ghosts, sure – but Mother always told me I had nothing to fear from anything in that house. She might be odd, but I can't believe she'd let me stay here if there was any danger."

Devon considers this. "I don't think there was – not before I arrived, at least." He looks at her. "I have a theory. I think somehow my coming here has stirred things up. Gotten whatever forces are here all riled."

"But why?"

"Something about who I am. My past. Where I came from."

"Your real parents?"

He nods. "And I think Alexander knows something. Maybe not consciously even – but he's got some connection. Cecily, he locked me in that room in the East Wing for a reason."

"Yeah," she says, "to scare you. Devon, I've told you that Alexander is a screwed-up kid. Has been all his life."

"But how much now is his own screwed-up-ness and how much is Jackson Muir? I mean, it's brilliant to pick a kid like Alexander, because any weirdness won't draw suspicion."

Cecily frowns. "Devon, I can't deny something weird is going on, not after seeing you in action at Gio's and what you just did to Pearlie Mae. But why do you think Jackson Muir is involved? He's just a legend. I should never have encouraged that warlock talk—"

"I know it was him that I saw in that locked room. The Voice tells me I'm on the right track, and the Voice has never failed me yet."

She sighs. "Well, if any of our ghosts were going to go psycho on us, it would be Jackson." She looks over at Devon. "How much do you think my mother knows about all this?"

He shrugs. "I don't know. She knows *something*, I'm sure. Something about who I am."

"Do you think she knows about – what you can do?"

"I don't know." He considers it further. "No, I don't think she does. And I don't think she *should*, either, for now."

"OK," Cecily agrees.

They hear the first pitter-patter of raindrops on the stable roof. "We should get going," Devon says.

They secure the doors to the stable tightly in advance of the storm.

"Devon," Cecily says, whispering in the damp dusky air.

"Yeah?"

"Thanks for trusting me."

He grins. He reaches down, takes her hand, and they hurry back up to the main house.

The storm hits just before dinner, rocking the house like the slap of a giant hand. Great purple fingers claw across the sky, bringing darkness early to the coast. The rains pound the earth with a force strong enough to release stones from their lodgings, sending tiny avalanches of rock and soil down the steep cliffs along the roads. Deep, echoing claps of thunder set the dogs all to howling; ferocious lightning crackles against the sky, silhouetting the spires of Ravenscliff above the village below.

When Alexander fails to come down to supper — a rare gathering his aunt intended for the whole family, minus, of course, old Grandmama — Mrs Crandall sends Simon up to fetch him. When the caretaker returns to report that the boy isn't in his room, the matriarch of the house sighs. "That incorrigible child. I've told him repeatedly not to be late for supper."

Simon serves their roast turkey, carved on an enormous silver platter. Devon's famished, and he eats heartily — but something about Alexander's absence unnerves him. There's a sense of something amiss, something wrong. *There's your sensitivity again*, Dad's telling him in his mind. After supper, as Simon clears away the plates, Devon asks Cecily to accompany him through the house to search for Alexander.

"Do you think he might have snuck back into the East Wing?" she asks.

"Simon said he nailed that panel shut," Devon tells her. "But who knows if there are other ways into that place."

The thunder startles both of them then, and the lights go out. "Ever wonder why they call this Misery Point?" Cecily laughs.

"I figured it out the first night I was here," Devon replies.

They both light candles and make their way through the dark. They search every room in the main part of the house: the kitchen, the dining room, the parlor, the study, the library, the bedrooms, the playroom. But no Alexander.

"Could he be outside?" Cecily wonders, looking out the

parlor window, just as a great flash of lightning illuminates the vast stretch of the estate leading out to Devil's Rock.

Devon's looking out too. "Hey, I think I saw someone out there," he says. "When the lightning came——"

Cecily unfastens the hook and opens the panes outward. "Alexander!" she calls. "Are you out there? Are you *crazy*?" She pulls back in. "Duh. Like I don't know the answer to that question."

"Let's look in his room and see if his coat is gone."

Indeed it is. "Oh, Devon, I hope he's all right," Cecily says, finally genuinely concerned about her young cousin. She lifts a teddy bear from the boy's bed. "This storm is awfully intense."

Devon feels a shudder but suppresses it. "It's not the storm I'm worried about."

She manages a smile. "Hey, if Jackson Muir is behind this, as soon as he gets a hold of that brat, he'll send him back!"

Devon looks at her. "Stop making light of this. I believe Alexander is in danger."

She looks back squarely, suddenly terrified. "You really do, don't you?"

"Yes," he says. "At least, I believe it's worth. . ."

He pauses. Beside Alexander's bed stands a chalkboard. On it, Alexander has written:

HELP ME. HE'S COMING.

Cecily sees it too. "What do you make of that?" she asks.

It's precisely at that moment, beneath the steady pounding of the rain, just before a thunderclap shakes the very foundation of the house, that they hear the unmistakable sound of a child's scream.

7
The Woman in White

The storm rages like a lover spurned all through the night. As he searches for Alexander near the cliffs, Devon can understand why the villagers claim to hear Emily Muir on stormy nights such as this. Behind the wind the echo of her screams remains high and clear. Devon's even sure he sees her once, in that portentous second when the lightning illuminates the dark woods: a shrieking figure in long white robe, fingers clawing the night.

He fears approaching Devil's Rock any closer: what if, in his terror, Alexander had plunged from its edge?

Cecily draws closer to him. She's bundled in a bright yellow raincoat, the hood pulled tightly around her face. Wisps of her red hair poke from beneath the elastic, dripping down into her eyes. Devon carries a large flashlight. Its beam swings through the shadows, exposing tree trunks, many of their limbs now as bare as the arms of skeletons. But despite calling the boy's name over and over for the last hour, there's no sign of Alexander Muir.

"You heard the scream, too, didn't you?" Devon asks. "I'm not imagining it?"

"I heard it," Cecily admits. "Oh, Devon — where could he be? Why would he come out in a storm like this?"

Thunder rattles them both suddenly, and they pause in their steps. The flashlight sputters, then dims. Cecily makes a small cry, but Devon shakes it, bringing it back to life. Ahead of them somewhere is Simon, whose raspy voice calling after the boy has now faded into the steady beat of the rain, popping the earth with its ferocity, splashing mud up on to their shoes and pants.

Devon feels raw terror burn in his gut. Cecily's right to wonder what had possessed the boy to come outside on a night like this. Even more disturbing was the scream they'd heard. Had he fallen from Devil's Rock? Had he — Devon shudders — been led there by Jackson Muir, and then pushed?

In his mind he can't shake the image of that decomposing face, the maggots in its teeth, its rotting breath in Devon's ear. *Help me*, Alexander had written. *He's coming.*

Who else, Devon fears, but Jackson Muir?

"We've got to look down at the beach below Devil's Rock," Devon says through the driving force of the rain.

"Oh, Devon," Cecily cries.

Through the mud they push onward. They'll have to be careful themselves: here the wind rushes and swells with a force far greater than anywhere else along the coast. Cecily had told him that a tourist trespassing on the Muir estate two summers ago had been swept off the peak by a sudden and malevolent gale. His broken, mangled body had been found six miles down the coast twelve days later. His camera was still in its bag over his shoulder.

Cecily steadies herself at the brink. "Even if Alexander fell, we couldn't see from up here," she shouts into the wind. "It's too dark."

"Maybe I should go down," Devon says.

"No need," comes the deep, coarse voice of Simon. He steps out of the shadows beside them. A fog suddenly rolls off the sea; it obscures the little man's features. But his unkind eyes still bore through the night. Devon recoils.

"What do you mean, no need?" Cecily asks.

"I just been down there," Simon tells her, his unevenly cut black hair plastered down around his face and into his eyes. "There's nobody on the rocks. If the boy fell, he's washed out to sea. We'll have to wait until morning, see what turns up."

"Oh," Cecily mutters, putting her hands over her face and starting to cry.

"Come on," Devon says, placing his arm around her and leading her back across the estate.

About three o'clock in the morning, the storm finally abates. The rain is soft now, hushed and nearly invisible. Now the only sound is the mournful call of the foghorn, warning ships not to come too close to this place.

Mrs Crandall has finally called the sheriff. At first, she was uneasy about summoning the law on to the Muir estate. The Muirs regard their grounds as a private fiefdom, a sovereign state. "I don't like policemen prowling around my property," Mrs Crandall sniffed.

But she finally relented when Devon and Cecily stumbled into the foyer of the great house, drenched and dispirited. "I'm sorry, ma'am," Simon said from behind them. "I wish I could give you better news, but the boy just wasn't nowhere to be found."

In Misery Point, when Mrs Amanda Muir Crandall calls the sheriff, there's no delay. There's no paperwork to be filled out, no excuses about the lack of personnel at three in the morning. Precisely seven minutes from the time she hung up the receiver, a sheriff's deputy is knocking at the front door. Cecily lets him in, still towel-drying her hair.

"Good ev'nin', Cecily," the deputy says, smiling. He's a goodlooking youth, no more than nineteen or twenty, sandy blonde hair and a blush of acne on his chin.

Cecily sighs. "Hello, Joey."

Devon doesn't like the look the deputy gives Cecily. A little too friendly. Mrs Crandall ushers him into the parlor. He turns once more to gaze intently at Cecily, who bats her eyelashes in response.

"Devon," Mrs Crandall calls. "Please give Deputy Potts your account of last seeing Alexander."

Devon hesitates. How much should he say? *Well, Deputy, I believe the child was abducted — maybe tossed off Devil's Rock — by the avenging ghost of Jackson Muir. . .*

"I saw him last late this afternoon," Devon says. "He was getting ready to watch television. But he seemed frightened about something—"

"He scrawled a message," Cecily interrupts. "Here." She had gone up to the boy's room and retrieved the chalkboard. It now stands in the parlor. "Look, Joey. Read what he wrote."

"Help me," the deputy reads dispassionately. "He's coming."

"What could it mean?" Mrs Crandall frets.

"Well," Joey Potts says, "looks to me like he might be playing a joke on you."

"No," Devon insists. "This isn't a joke."

"Could he be hidin'? Come on, Cess, we know that kid's been in his share of trouble before. He wants ya to believe someone's after him."

"No," Devon repeats. "I think he's really in danger."

"Why do you think that?" Mrs Crandall asks, her eyebrows arching, her back going stiff.

"Because. . ." Devon pauses. He crosses the room, standing in front of the large glass doors looking down on to the now-placid sea. The moon hangs high and round and bright. The rain now comes in a leisurely silence. The night seems very still, very peaceful, and eminently rational.

"Because I believe there may be – something – that . . . wants to get to him."

He turns around to face the others. Deputy Joey Potts simply twists his eyebrows at him. Who is this punk, anyway, Potts seems to be thinking.

Mrs Crandall's lips narrow into a thin straight line. "Devon. Your talk of ghosts is becoming wearying. Please—"

"We heard him scream," Cecily insists.

The deputy shrugs. "A trick of the wind. You know how it sounds up here, Cess."

Devon leans forward. "If there's a little boy really lost out there, Deputy, you'll have to eat those words."

Joey stiffens.

"Devon, take it easy," Cecily says.

"Deputy," Mrs Crandall intones grandly, "I want you and your men to search every inch of these grounds, as well as the beach below Devil's Rock."

"Yes, ma'am."

"Meanwhile, Simon and I will search every room in this house," she says, looking over at Devon. "*Including* the East Wing."

She brushes out of the room and up the stairs.

Deputy Potts shrugs. "Guess I'll be seein' ya, Cess," he grins, tipping his hat. She gives him a wry smile. "You too, buddy," he winks at Devon. Devon doesn't respond.

Once he's gone, Devon says to Cecily, "Don't he think he's a little *old* for you?"

"Devon, it's nothing. He's just always giving me the eye whenever he sees me."

"Well, if he *tries* anything—"

Cecily grins. "Why, Mr March. I do believe you're jealous."

He snorts. He looks out the window as Misery Point's finest begin to crawl across the estate, their orange search lights casting unnatural glows through the windows of the house.

Cecily comes up behind him. "Why do you think Jackson Muir would want Alexander? I thought *you* were the one with the powers, the one who stirred all this up."

Devon shakes his head. "I don't know. I'm just convinced Alexander *knows* something. Maybe he stumbled upon something in the East Wing. Maybe—"

He thinks of something. "Maybe Jackson's trying to get Alexander to open the bolted door."

"The way you described it, no little kid could break through that."

Devon shrugs. "Well, he wants him for something. He's trying to work *through* him. I *know* that. And when the Voice tells me something, Cecily, I believe it."

"I want to believe you, Devon," Cecily tells him, but he can see she's struggling. "I really do."

Devon suddenly moves out into the foyer, fetching his still dripping raincoat from the coatrack. He pulls it on, smelling the dampness of the rubber and the clinging aroma of mud and leaves.

"Where are you going?" Cecily asks.

"I think I know where Alexander might be," he replies. Then he pushes head first into the rain.

The crooked white stones in the old Muir cemetery catch the

glare of the moon. They stand out in stark contrast to the deep purple of the night. Devon approaches the graveyard with an energy that surprises him. He feels determined, driven, and only the slightest bit fearful.

"Alexander," he calls.

The soft mist clings to his hands as he cups them around his lips. The fog has thickened, tasting of sea salt. It's low tide below the cliffs, and the tanginess of rotting crabs and seaweed reaches his nostrils. He calls the boy's name again.

His voice echoes now, bouncing off the stones. He wades into the high wet grass of the cemetery, catching a glint of moonlight from the tall obelisk in the center, the stone that bears his name. But that's not the marker he seeks tonight. Tonight, his destination is the grave of a boy he suspects might exist: a boy who should have become Master of Ravenscliff.

Why do you think Jackson Muir would want Alexander?

He can't be sure exactly, but the Voice has given him a clue. It came as clear as a bell as he stood there in the parlor with Cecily.

Jackson Muir had a child.

But somehow Jackson Muir died without an heir. Somehow the estate passed to his brother's family, from whom sprang Mrs Crandall and Cecily – and Alexander. But it was descendants of Jackson Muir – the eldest son – who should rightfully rule this house, and the secrets it held within.

He wants to reclaim what he feels is rightfully his, the Voice tells him.

Devon feels certain there must be a grave here of Jackson's child. A son who should have become Master of Ravenscliff – but through some unknown nefarious act was kept from his fate. Where exactly the pitiful remains of the young Muir rest

Devon cannot be sure, but he assumes it will not be far from the elaborate monument honoring his parents.

It's in that direction Devon heads, dangerously near the sheer drop from the cliff.

"Oh, Dad, help me now," Devon whispers.

He feels the heat. *Yes, he's here*, Devon thinks. *Alexander's here. Jackson Muir wants to use him as his own son — to replace the heir he lost — to prevent me from uncovering the truth.*

Up ahead he sees the monument with its broken angel. Devon steels himself. What if Jackson Muir deigns to show himself again? What might he do? Devon had been powerless before him in the East Wing; would he prove stronger now?

There's a stir of movement to his left. Devon pauses, straining his eyes to see through the dark. He can discern nothing, so he keeps going. A cold damp wind blows up from the sea, breaking through the heat. The fog deepens. Now he senses movement again, this time up ahead, just a yard or two to the left of Jackson's stone. There's someone there: someone moving among the shadows.

"Alexander?" Devon calls.

But the figure is garbed in white. It's kneeling in front of a flat marker. It does not appear to notice Devon's approach. Its face — hooded, Devon thinks, as he peers through the fog — is intent upon the gravestone.

"Who are you?" he calls gently.

This time the figure looks up to face him. As Devon draws closer, he has the sudden sensation of flight: as if the figure all at once transforms into a flock of white doves, flying off rapidly into the darkness. Devon can feel the cool rush of air made by their wings upon his cheeks.

Yet in that instant, too, he sees the face of a woman.

He looks down at the stone where she had knelt. Its

inscription puzzles him. All it says is:

CLARISSA

"Jackson's child?" Devon whispers, but he can't be sure. The Voice is silent.

Heading back to Ravenscliff, Devon feels chilled and discouraged. There had been no sight of Alexander in the cemetery as he had hoped. *Maybe I'm losing it. Maybe for once the Voice was wrong.*

But no. It led him to an important clue, a clue he's still puzzling over as he enters the house, takes off his raincoat, and turns to see Alexander sitting in the parlor.

"Alexander!" he shouts, rushing into the room.

Mrs Crandall is seated in her chair, hands clasped in her lap. "You were partly correct, Devon," she says. Her eyes look tired and bloodshot. "He wasn't in the house. But it wasn't a *ghost* who abducted him."

A deep, familiar voice comes from behind Devon. "I wouldn't exactly call it an abduction, Amanda," the voice says.

Devon turns around. It's Rolfe Montaigne.

"Our young friend here," Rolfe is saying, tousling Alexander's hair, "was wandering in the rain on the road back up to Ravenscliff. Seems he'd decided to run away, then thought better of it."

Alexander grins up at Rolfe. "He sure has a cool car," he says, turning to his aunt.

Mrs Crandall looks distinctly uncomfortable. Cecily is seated in front of the fireplace. "Mother, we should be grateful to Rolfe," she tells her.

"I'm not looking for gratitude," Rolfe says, and his mysterious green eyes find Devon. "I certainly couldn't have allowed the boy to walk alone in the rain in the middle of the night."

"Why did you run off, Alexander?" Devon asks, stooping down in front of the boy.

The boy looks spitefully at him. "Because of *you*."

"Me?"

"You scared me," Alexander tells him, and his round button eyes grow small, seeming to retreat into his head. Devon shudders. It's as if the boy is changing right there in front of all of them, but only he can see the transformation. Even his voice takes on a low, cold, monotonous sound: "I went looking for ghosts. You told me about the ghost of Jackson Muir."

Mrs Crandall arches an eyebrow. "Is this true?"

Devon swallows. "I just asked him what he knew—"

"You asked an *already impressionable* child about *ghosts*?" Mrs Crandall is angry. "I thought you had more common sense than that. I told you that Alexander was troubled. I asked you to have a good influence on him!"

Devon looks at the boy. Alexander's watching him, observing his every move, every reaction. This is precisely what he wanted to occur. He had manipulated the situation beautifully.

"Oh, don't be so hard on the boy," Rolfe says, and he means Devon. "He's just getting to know our young Mr Muir and his bag of tricks." He winks at Devon, who immediately turns away.

"I didn't ask for *your* opinion," Mrs Crandall sniffs. "Cecily, take Alexander up to his room. As for you, Devon, we'll discuss all this further in the morning."

Cecily takes her young cousin by the hand. Devon follows them out into the foyer. "Wait," he calls. "Alexander, tell us why you wrote what you did on the chalkboard. You wrote that *he* was coming, that you wanted someone to help you. Who, Alexander? Who was coming? Who did you need help against?"

The boy turns to face him. His plump little face is a mask of horror, like a twisted, broken doll. "*You*," he spits. "*You* were coming — to bother me and tell me scary stories. It was *you* I needed help against!"

There's silence in the great house after that. For a moment they all just stand there, looking down at the small boy.

Can't they see? Devon's thinking, and he believes suddenly that they can, even if they won't admit it. This is no innocent child. The kid's a demon as surely as the kid at the pizza joint.

Only this one's named Jackson Muir.

Cecily urges Alexander along, getting him upstairs and into bed just as the rosy glow of dawn begins to edge over the dark sea. Mrs Crandall closes the doors of the drawing room, apparently unfinished with what she has to say to Rolfe Montaigne. Devon simply wanders through the corridors, past the cavernous formal dining room, through the comfortable oak-paneled study, into the greenhouse off the kitchen, where he sits in the warmth of the orange lamps and realizes the boy has won.

This round, at least.

Alexander's possessed by Jackson Muir. If I'd been hoping to protect him, I've failed miserably. Of that much he's certain. But what did it mean? The Voice had been right after all: Devon firmly believes Jackson wants to use the boy as some kind of conduit to regain mastery of the house. And more critically, of that locked portal in the East Wing.

He's back in the foyer of the great house now, convinced that in the morning he will confront Mrs Crandall, lay all his cards on the table and demand she do the same. What could she do? Kick him out? She was now his guardian. Besides, Devon feels quite certain that she'd rather have him here than anywhere else, now that he's beginning to understand a few things about her family's secrets.

Yet what of the secrets left undiscovered? The books in the East Wing with their mysterious words and phrases? The light in the tower? The gravestone marked "Devon"? The uncanny resemblance to the portrait in the East Wing? The woman in white? Was she Emily Muir? Or the mysterious Clarissa, whoever she was?

Yes, he would demand some answers from Mrs Crandall.

"Amanda, you're as unreasonable as ever." The voice of Rolfe Montaigne startles Devon suddenly, through the closed doors of the parlor. Devon stands outside, hesitant about eavesdropping but drawn by the resonance of Rolfe's deep voice, and what secrets he might reveal.

"Unreasonable?" Mrs Crandall laughs. "I think it's *perfectly* reasonable to object to you driving a young boy along the rain-slicked streets of Misery Point." There's a calculated pause. "Remember what happened *last* time."

"You'll keep up that lie until you're cold in your grave, won't you?"

"Why did you come back to Misery Point after they let you out of jail?"

"I wanted to open a restaurant," he tells her, and Devon can hear the smile in his voice.

"To compete with me," she snaps.

"That's the American way, isn't it?"

"Didn't you already do enough damage to this family? Why come back now and try to hurt our livelihood?"

"Dear Amanda, I hardly think the livelihood of the great Muir family will be affected by one restaurant." He sighs. "Besides, I believe this family has inflicted enough damage on itself for me to have much impact."

"Get out."

"You've always been especially lovely when you're angry."

"*Get out!*"

Devon bolts when he hears the doorknob begin to turn. There's nowhere to hide in the foyer. It's a cold marble room with a great cathedral ceiling, and its only furnishings a simple coat rack and a magnificent grandfather clock. Devon has one option: to slip out the front door and hide behind the thick shrubbery. In his hurry, he leaves the door partly ajar. Just seconds after he slips behind the bushes he sees Rolfe's hand through the opening.

"Tell me," Rolfe is saying to Mrs Crandall as he leaves, "just who is this young ward you've taken in under your wing?"

"Stay away from Devon," she says, unseen. "I mean that. He's no concern of yours."

Devon can see Rolfe's face now through the bushes, lit by the pink glow of the coming dawn. "My, my, we're protective. Might I inquire as to just *who he is?*"

There seems to be something in his voice, as if Rolfe knows some secret, some tantalizing detail that unnerves Mrs Crandall. She says nothing in reply, just pushes the door shut on his face. Rolfe laughs.

Devon holds his breath in the bushes, waiting for Rolfe to pass. But instead Rolfe simply stands there, facing the rising sun. "*Oh, what a beautiful mornin'*," he sings softly. He moves out of Devon's view. "*Oh, what a beautiful day.*"

Suddenly he's on the grass behind Devon. He taps his shoulder. Devon gasps and spins around.

"Well," Rolfe says, "look who's out hiding in the bushes."

Devon feels his face flush. "I didn't want Mrs Crandall to think I was eavesdropping. . ."

"But you were," Rolfe says.

"No, no, not really. . ."

"Oh, no need to pretend with me." He smiles down at

Devon. His faced is creased from the sun, his jaw strong and hard. He puts his arm around Devon and draws him out of the bushes. "So tell me," he says, "how have you enjoyed life at Ravenscliff so far?"

"Well," Devon begins, "it's certainly been . . . exciting."

"You mean tonight's little episode?"

"That and . . . other things." Devon's anxious about Mrs Crandall catching him talking to Rolfe Montaigne. He keeps looking back toward the door.

"You mean the ghosts? The stories with which you've been filling Alexander's head?"

"I don't care if you don't believe me. I know what I've seen."

"Hey," Rolfe says. "Who said I didn't believe? I understand about ghosts. I've seen a few myself. Right here in this house."

"Really?" Devon asks. "Here?"

"I'll bet nobody's told you I lived here when I was your age," Rolfe says. "Right here. Probably in the very room you're using. Did they give you the one overlooking the garden and the cliffs?"

"Yes," Devon says.

"Figured as much."

"Why?" Devon becomes animated all at once. "Why did you live here?"

Rolfe looks at him, seeming to consider how much he should say. "My father was the caretaker here before they hired that old gnome Simon," he explains finally. "That was when Mrs Crandall's father still ruled the roost. He was a great old man."

For a moment Rolfe's eyes seem distant, lost in time, a melancholy shadow passing across his features. Then he smiles. "So I encountered my share of ghosts."

Devon looks up at him hard. "Did you ever go into the East Wing?"

Rolfe returns his look. "Have you?"

Devon nods.

"Listen, kid," Rolfe says, his voice growing serious. "You've got to be careful. I mean it. There are things—"

"Yeah, there sure *are* things. Locked behind a metal door in a closed-off room."

Rolfe looks down at him solemnly. "Come visit me at the restaurant when you get a chance. I'm there every afternoon." He pauses, studying the boy. "I think we have some things we could talk about."

Devon watches him walk off down the path. He disappears around the bend and then Devon can hear the Porsche kick into gear. The sun is edging the horizon now. Long low rays of golden sunlight reach across the estate. Devon sighs and goes inside.

He hears it then: the sobbing.

Low, sepulchral, thick: the sound rises in waves, louder now, then hushed, obscured by the increasing chatter of birds heralding the sun. The house is veiled in long shadows. Soon – in minutes, really – sunlight will spill through the windows, and Devon is certain the sobbing will not endure the harsh reality of day. But now, in the procrastination of the dark, the sound persists. It's the most wretched cry he has ever heard, the most heartsick lamentation he can possibly imagine.

It seems to seep up from the floorboards, drip down from the walls. Devon heads through the main corridor past the dining room, then through the study. He pauses at the doorway to the East Wing. There's no mistaking the fact that the sobbing is louder here. It comes from somewhere beyond this door.

Despite everything, despite all of Mrs Crandall's anger and

everything that's happened tonight, he tries the door — he *has* to know the truth — and it opens. *They were looking for Alexander in here earlier*, he thinks. *Somehow — crazily — they forgot to lock the door again.*

He pulls the door open and peers into the corridor beyond. To the right another door stands open, revealing a curved staircase leading up. *The tower*, he thinks. On the wall he flicks a light switch: a single hanging bulb pops tenuously into life. *So much for the power being shut off in here.* He makes his way up the steps one by one, pausing on each to listen. Still the sobbing comes, thicker now as he approaches its source.

At the first landing he looks around. The sobbing continues from somewhere still higher. Devon continues climbing the stairs, round and round, padding through the thick dust that's accumulated on the broken cement steps. He can see the second landing above him now, where he spots a door, ajar. A small glow from a candle flickers from within. What does he expect to find in there? Whom does he expect to confront?

The flickering candle above is his only guide now, as the light from the old bulb below doesn't make it this high. Devon keeps climbing by feeling along the cracked plaster of the wall. Across his hand scurries something soft and furry. He pulls his hand back, imagining a large spider or bat. He cringes. His heart races through his ears, but he keeps climbing.

All at once, the sobbing pitches and then stops. He's left in silence.

In the few seconds before terror overtakes his rationality, Devon tells himself that dawn's first light will soon stream in from the tower windows along the old stone walls, lighting his way. But such rationality is shattered when he smells once again the rancid breath of the demon in the dark, and feels its cold, rough fingers close around his neck.

8
The Face of the Madman

He does not surrender without a fight: Jackson Muir may be stronger, but still Devon struggles to break free of his grip, trying with all his might to scream, to summon his power. But the breath is choked out of him. He begins to feel light and heady, as if he'll lose consciousness.

Then a filter of sunlight transforms the darkness, and the first thing he notices is what's cinching his neck is no demonic hand, but rather a length of old rope. In that instant the grip is suddenly relaxed, and Devon tumbles to his knees. He coughs, spits, rubs his burning neck – and turns around to look up into the malicious face of Simon Gooch.

"You tried to kill me!" Devon gasps.

"I *will* kill ya," the ugly little man barks, "if I ever catch ya in here again."

Devon stands, clutching his chafed neck where Simon had tightened the rope. "I don't think Mrs Crandall will be too pleased to hear how you attacked me."

Simon grins. It's a horrible gesture. There's delight in the man's eyes, a sadistic pleasure gained from Devon's pain and fear. "She wouldn't be too pleased to hear you disobeyed her about comin' in here neither," he says through clenched teeth. "She's already pissed at ya enough for scarin' the boy."

Devon is silent. They stand there glaring at each other for several seconds, and then Simon laughs. "You get out of here or else I'm locking you in," he snarls, turning and clomping back down the tower steps in his heavy workboots.

Devon looks back up at the door above, then sighs, following Simon. The caretaker's sour body odor lingers in his path. When Devon reaches the last step, the little troll is waiting for him at the door back into the main house. He grunts for Devon to get moving. The boy does, taking one last look up the tower, and then walks out into the morning light.

He showers quickly and meets a groggy-eyed Cecily at the breakfast table, ready for school once again. He passes through the day in a blur: two nights of no sleep are taking their toll. He has more meetings with teachers, more classroom discussions he can't follow, more textbooks piled high on his desk. After classes the gang again piles into DJ's Camaro and heads over to Gio's, wolfing down pizza. DJ and Marcus get into a burping contest, but Devon's too tired to participate.

All day, he'd been a star. Girls gazed over at him longingly in the corridors, guys looked at him with a mixture of envy and apprehension. "You the man," Crispin told him — and if the rebels like you, you're certifiably cool.

Word travels quickly in high school, especially when a new kid exhibits nearly superhuman powers. At the pizza joint, Gio tells him their cheese-and-pepperoni is on the house. "You're welcome here any ol' time," Gio gushes. "You can protect old Gio's business from the cretins."

Yeah, Devon thinks. *Guess I might have to do exactly that.*

But thankfully, no "cretins" disrupt them this afternoon. In fact, an uneasy quiet seems to fall over Ravenscliff during the next several days. Devon's able to get to bed early, collapsing into an exhausted sleep, a pattern he follows the rest of the week. He's able to make a little headway into his studies, to finally catch up a little, to even raise his hand a couple of times in political science class and participate in the discussion.

Cecily remains as affectionate as ever, but she doesn't mention his powers, or the ghosts, or the padlocked door, or his suspicions about Jackson Muir and Alexander. It's almost as if she doesn't want to think about any of that – the way, Devon believes, she's always dealt with the unexplained and un-expected at Ravenscliff.

Mrs Crandall mentions nothing further about the incident with Alexander. Neither does the boy, who greets Devon the first time after his harrowing disappearance with a cherubic grace, a smile that belies the mystery within.

Yet whenever he encounters him, Devon just looks intently at Alexander: there's something in those round button eyes that shines like counterfeit silver. Even in the boy's most banal moments he seems to be laughing at Devon, lying in wait for the next opportunity. Devon studies the boy's every word, every glance, every movement. When might he pounce again?

"You seem fascinated by something, Devon," Alexander observes finally, a week after all the fuss.

They're both in the playroom, Alexander in his beanbag, Devon on the floor. They're watching a movie about aliens coming down to Earth, but Devon has been looking more frequently over at the younger boy than at the TV set. Alexander's eyes are on the program, but he's not really watching either: at least, not the way he watches that creepy clown.

"I am," Devon admits.

Alexander smiles. "Care to share what it is?"

"I'm fascinated by your composure, actually. Your ability to bide your time."

The little boy raises his eyebrows. "Bide my time? What do you mean?"

"I mean," Devon replies, "that I am left to wonder when next you might lock me in a room, or run off in a storm, or tell your aunt that I have filled your head with ghost stories."

"Oh," Alexander smiles, returning his gaze to the television, "is that what has gotten you so piqued? Never fear, Devon. We're friends now. All that's past. I was just testing you."

"I *want* to be your friend, Alexander. But something won't *let* us be friends." He narrows his eyes at the boy. "Tell me what it is. Do you even know?"

Alexander seems to consider his answer. He smiles, looking up innocently at Devon. "Perhaps it's the fact that I feel abandoned by my parents, and I'm desperately seeking attention." He pauses, assuming an expression of mock fear. "Or it might be Jackson Muir has come back to claim my soul. Might it be either of those scenarios?"

"You tell me."

The boy laughs. He reaches into his shirt pocket and withdraws a stick of gum. He unwraps it carefully, folding it into his mouth, and begins to chew. He turns and grins up at Devon.

"I know there are answers here," Devon whispers. "And I'm going to find them. You can tell that to him. He can't stop me. I'm going to find the truth."

"Alexander has *always* acted strange," Cecily assures him.

"I know. But there's something—" Devon searches for the

words. "I really believe Jackson Muir is working through him."

They're in the stable again, propped up against a haystack. Pearlie Mae is behind them, calmly chewing straw.

"Oh, Devon," Cecily says. "You know I trust you. You know I believe you. But it just feels *crazy*, you know. You show up here and suddenly the ghosts of our house take possession of Alexander. Come *on*. It feels like a movie on *Mystery Science Theater 3000*. All that's missing are those little robots in the first row telling us how dumb we're being."

"I know it's hard to believe, Cecily." He sighs. "But the Voice . . . I trust it. If it tells me something, I can't deny it."

She makes a face as if she's still not entirely convinced.

"Look," he tells her. "Once, when I was ten, we had this deaf kid in our class. Sammy Silbernagel. And one day, after class, I just couldn't stop looking at him. The Voice was telling me something about him, but I couldn't exactly figure out what. All I could hear was that he was in trouble. That he was going to get hurt."

Cecily blinks. "So what happened?"

"Nothing."

"So the Voice was wrong."

Devon laughs. "No. It was *right*. Because I followed Sammy out to the playground and kept watching him. He was lost in thought, just walking along towards the street. He walked *right out* into the path of a bus – and totally didn't see it coming. I was too far away to catch up with him but I yelled out for the bus to stop. And it did. Sammy just kept on walking, not knowing a thing, but the bus driver was all shook up and came out to tell me that if I hadn't yelled, he didn't think he'd have been able to stop in time."

"*You saved his life*," she breathes in awe.

"Whatever. The point is the Voice was on target. It's always been that way. Big things like that, but little things too. Like once when I couldn't find my dog, Max. The Voice told me where he was."

"That is *so* cool," Cecily says, clearly more persuaded. "Is that why you're an honors student?"

Devon shakes his head. "I once tried passing a history test without studying, thinking the Voice would tell me the answers. I failed miserably."

"I knew there had to be a catch somewhere." Cecily smiles. "So why do you think you have this Voice?"

"I don't know. The Voice, the weird powers – they're what make me so determined to find out who I am. It has to do with – those *things* – those *creatures* – that are always after me. Cecily, that guy at the pizza joint was *right*. The kid who attacked him *did* have claws. It was a demon – like the kind I've told you about."

"Get out," she says, frightened.

"It's true."

Devon stands up suddenly. He feels angry, but he's not quite sure why.

"You know what it's *like*, Cecily?" he asks. "For all your life to have this fear in the back of your mind that no one can take away? I wasn't like other kids, whose parents could come into their rooms at night and reassure them that there was no boogeyman. That there were no monsters under their bed."

He kicks the wooden planks of the straw bin. "Because there *were* monsters under my bed!" he snaps. "There *were* things crawling around in my closet! There really *were* Voices inside my head! I grew up never knowing *why* – why they picked on me but not on other kids, why I was the one who always had to be strong. I never knew why I could do these weird things with my mind – things that if anyone ever learned about would make me into a freak. Would make people scared of me."

He slumps his head against his chest.

"I just want to know *why*, finally," he says. "I want to know why I am the way I am."

Cecily's up, embracing him. "Oh, Devon. I'm sorry. It sucks. It totally sucks."

He looks into her eyes. "I've only been here a little more than a week," he tells her, "but already I know one thing for sure: this is where it originates. And there are forces that don't want me here. They don't want me to find out their secrets, because I can destroy them. My dad always said I was stronger than any of them. *Why* I don't know. But I am."

"But not Jackson Muir," Cecily reminds him. "You said he was stronger than you."

"Maybe. But if that's the case, why hasn't he just snuffed me out? Why's he playing around with Alexander?" He takes her face in his hands. "Tell me everything you know about Jackson Muir, everything you heard growing up."

"Not much," she tells him. "Mother never speaks of him except to say that he was evil. He was her father's brother and he died when she was little. He scared her, I think. He used to put on magic shows in the parlor, and really creepy things would happen. Images on the walls, things flying through the air. He'd get all dressed up like some mad magician with paint on his face and everything. Mother hated those magic shows. She said she stayed as far away from Jackson as possible. Then there was the tragedy with his wife, and there were other things, too. Simon has said some things."

"Like what?"

She makes a face as she tries to remember the exact words. "He called him a great and noble sorcerer," she says, shuddering.

Devon nods. "There are books in the East Wing on it. So how does Simon know about Jackson?'

She shrugs. "I'm not sure. Simon was only hired after my grandfather died, so he didn't know Jackson Muir. But Simon seems to know a lot of stuff about our family."

Devon considers all this information. "Rolfe Montaigne told me his father was caretaker here before Simon."

Cecily sighs. "Yeah. I guess that's when all the bad blood between Mother and Rolfe started."

"Tell me what you know," Devon says.

She looks up at him. "Let's go into the village. I feel like I'm going to go mad if we stay here. I'm feeling just a little freaked out, and seeing people will help."

"OK," he says. It *is* Saturday night, after all. They could still have *some* semblance of normal lives, he supposes. "Where do you want to go?"

"Stormy Harbor. We can get a platter of fried clams and gorge ourselves and continue talking."

He agrees. They pass across the lawn and down the cliffside staircase.

"Does Alexander know you suspect him as being in league with Jackson?" Cecily asks as they walk along the coast road, the waves crashing on the beach.

"We have these sparring matches," Devon tells her. "But I think it's Jackson I'm sparring with, not an eight-year-old boy."

She shivers. They've reached Stormy Harbor. "I can't think about any of this right now," she says, pulling open the old wooden door.

The place is packed. A heavy gray cloud of smoke hangs low around the ears of the crowd. Devon and Cecily take a table off to the side.

"Hey, if it isn't our New York boy," Andrea says, arriving with pad in hand. "With Mistress Crandall herself."

"I see the two of you already know each other," Cecily observes.

"*Old* friends." Andrea reaches down to give Devon a kiss. He blushes. "How ya doin', kid? Surviving those ghosts?"

Devon smiles over at Cecily. "What ghosts?" he says, and they both laugh.

"What'll it be, folks?" Andrea asks. "You get a Diet Coke, young lady. Don't get me in trouble again."

Cecily turns to Devon. "The manager came by and checked my ID a few weeks ago and bawled poor Andrea out for giving me a glass of wine. Can you imagine?"

"Just because you're Cecily Crandall doesn't mean you can get away with everything," Andrea quips.

"Diet Coke and an order of fried clams," Cecily says. "No bellies."

"I'll have a ginger ale," Devon says.

"Comin' up!" Andrea says, moving off among the crowd.

Devon watches the people around them. Mostly older, stocky men with heavy brows and two-days' whiskers on their faces. "Fishermen," Cecily says. "Most of whom work for my family."

During the season, she tells him, tourists hang out here too, as well as the hordes of waiters and houseboys who flock in every May looking for jobs. But now, as fall chills into winter, it's mostly the hardy natives and a scattering of teenagers.

Andrea brings their order. Cecily pops the first clam into her mouth. She eyes Devon, then asks him a question slowly, something that's apparently been on her mind:

"Devon, with all this talk about your past — your real

parents — and the connection to Jackson Muir — well, do you ever think we — you and I — might be *related*?"

"Actually," he admits, "yeah."

He dips a clam into the marinara sauce and chews it, looking over at her.

"But I can't figure out *how*," he says. "I mean, it would make sense in a way, explaining why my father sent me here. But the possibilities seem too far out."

"What do you mean?"

"Well, I wondered if maybe your uncle Edward and his crazy wife were my real parents, which would make Alexander and me brothers. But why send me away and not him?"

"Yeah," Cecily agrees. "And besides I don't think they were even married yet when you were born."

He raises his eyebrows. "So maybe I was some kid your uncle had with a girlfriend." He pauses, looking intently at her. "Then there's *your* father to consider."

"*My* father?"

Devon nods. "Maybe that's why I was sent away. Maybe that's why he left, because he got some girl pregnant and your mother wouldn't stand for it."

"That one is just *too* weird," she says. "If that were the case, why would Mother have taken you in?"

He shrugs. "Who knows?"

"Oh, Devon," she says, her eyes suddenly growing wide, "if you're my brother, then I can't *deal* with this!"

He nods. He understands. He likes Cecily — a lot. If she turns out to be his sister, well, he doesn't even want to think about it.

"But I suppose we need to consider the possibility," he says. "What else do you know about your father?"

She takes a sip of her Diet Coke. "Nothing really." Her eyes move off, as if looking at something Devon can't see. "Sometimes I think about him – wonder if he'd stayed around – if maybe I might have had a more normal life."

"Meaning?"

"Maybe Mother would have been less uptight. Maybe that house wouldn't have seemed like such a crypt. But he left her, and she's been brooding about it ever since."

She pushes the platter of clams over at Devon. "Eat some," she instructs. He obeys.

"Of course," Cecily continues, "I don't think she ever loved him. Not really." Cecily smiles. "She only married him to get back at the guy she *really* loved." She waits a beat. "Rolfe Montaigne."

Devon's eyes pop. "Rolfe Montaigne?"

Cecily laughs. "Well, I suppose if you're looking for secrets, you should also hear the ones that have nothing to do with ghosts." She finishes her soda. "Hey, Andrea, can I have another?" Andrea gives her a "comin' up" sign.

"*Tell* me."

"OK. The whole sordid story goes like this. Back when Rolfe was a teenager living at Ravenscliff, he and my mother were *real* close – *if* you know what I mean. His father was the caretaker and was the great good friend of my grandfather. So Grandpa agreed to raise Rolfe as one of the family. Rolfe got the same great education my mother and uncle did, got nearly all the same privileges."

"So when did the bad blood start?"

"Well, my mother's told me that my uncle Edward – her brother – was always envious of Rolfe, because Rolfe was bigger, faster, stronger, smarter, better looking. My grandfather even seemed to prefer Rolfe over poor Uncle Edward."

Andrea settles the Coke in front of Cecily. But she's too

engrossed in telling her story to notice. "Grandfather had always hoped Rolfe and my mother would get married, and in fact, they planned to. They were hot and heavy for a time, I take it."

The thought seems incongruous to Devon. Mrs Crandall — elegant, poised, *cold* Mrs Crandall — in the arms of Rolfe Montaigne.

"But Mother was just *devastated* to find Rolfe with another woman. I don't know who it was, but Mother was furious. She just never suspected."

"And she's still bitter at Rolfe."

Cecily takes a sip. "That's only half of it. But maybe I shouldn't—"

"You've gone this far."

She giggles. "Oh, all right. But don't breathe a word of it. You know how Rolfe went to jail?"

Devon swallows. "Yeah?"

"Of course, this was all before I was born, but the stories have become Misery Point legend. It was right after Mother found out about his affair that Rolfe drove his car off the cliff with the two kids inside. I think the girl was the one Rolfe was dallying with, but I don't know for sure. Anyway, they'd been drinking, and you know how rainslicked these roads get and how the wind gets so fierce." She gives him a little smirk. "You can do the math, I'm sure."

"They went off the road."

"Go to the head of the class." She shudders. "Oh, it was all like *really* tragic. But here's the kicker. Mother told the police that when Rolfe left Ravenscliff that night with the two others, she knew he'd been drinking. She said she tried to discourage him from driving but that he brushed her off. She swore under oath that she had seen Rolfe behind the wheel of the car just shortly before it went off the cliff. It was enough to put Rolfe away for five years for manslaughter."

"So she had her revenge."

Cecily finishes the last of the clams. "I'll say. Especially since nobody in town believes Rolfe really *was* driving that night. They think one of the two other kids was behind the wheel. Rolfe was indeed too drunk to remember much, except that he was certain *he wasn't driving*. They found him asleep in the rain the next morning at the foot of the cliffs."

"You think your mother *lied* to the police?"

"Hey, you used that word, I didn't."

"Wow." Devon takes a long sip of his ginger ale.

"Well, if isn't the Mighty Morphin Power Ranger," comes a voice. It's DJ, with Ana behind him. "Anybody giving you trouble in this joint tonight, my man?"

Devon smiles. "Not so far."

"Hey, handsome," Ana says, pulling up a chair next to him.

Cecily scowls. "Did it ever occur to you that we may have been in the middle of an important and *private* discussion?"

Ana smiles cattily at her. "You can't hog your new brother all the time, Cess."

"He's *not* my brother," she snarls.

DJ sits close to her. "Well, if he's not, I'm gonna start gettin' jealous."

"Have you been drinking?" Cecily asks him. "Your breath reeks."

"Not when I drive, Cess. You know that."

"Then you've been eating too many Cheetos. Back off a little."

DJ makes a face and slumps back in his chair.

Andrea comes by to take their orders.

"Iced latte, please," Ana says, noting the plate of fried clam crumbs in front of Cecily. "With non-fat milk. I'm watching my weight."

Cecily makes a face at her. DJ orders a Coke.

Ana gazes up at Devon. "You wanta go to a movie later? Just me and you?"

He shrugs. "Well, Cecily and I were kinda hanging out."

"Yeah, Miss Rah-Rah." Cecily's eyes widen. "Hey, Devon. Look who's just come in."

They all turn. Devon can see him, literally head and shoulders above most of the crowd, his intense green eyes looking around.

Rolfe Montaigne.

"Isn't he dreamy?" Ana says. "He is like so . . . so . . . movie idolish."

Rolfe spots them. He smiles, making his way through the crowd.

"He's coming over!" Ana gasps.

DJ snorts, "Ah, what's so great about him? He's a murderer."

"Stop that," Ana scolds.

Rolfe Montaigne arrives and smiles down at them. "Good evening, kids. Cecily."

"Hello, Rolfe," Cecily says. "How are you this evening?"

"I'm fine and dandy." He looks over at Devon. "Hope you're not filling the new boy's head with all those terrible stories of the days when I was the town drunk."

"Rolfe hasn't had a drink since he's come back," Cecily informs the group.

He winks at them. "A model citizen I've become."

"That you have," Ana gushes, sliding her chair away from Devon and gazing up at the older man. "I'm Ana Lopez."

"Pleased to meet you, Miss Lopez."

Rolfe pulls a chair over to their table and sits down. Andrea arrives and he orders them all refills plus another plate of clams. "Put it on my tab," he tells her.

"Mother would say you're trying to buy my favor," Cecily says. "Like you've bought the whole town."

He laughs. "Your mother does have a way with words. I haven't bought the whole town." He pauses, then winks over at Ana. "Yet."

Ana giggles. "How'd you get so *rich*?"

"Bet it wasn't legal, whatever it was," DJ says.

Rolfe looks mock stricken. "Young man. *Me?* Do anything contrary to the law?"

"DJ, you are so crude," Ana snarls.

"Actually," Rolfe tells them, "my wealth is all completely above-board. My books are open to anyone. After all, doesn't everyone know how I made a *killing* —" He pauses deliberately — "on the stock market?"

Cecily laughs.

"It's true," he says innocently, looking over at Devon. "I took a few risks that paid off. Do *you* take risks, Mr March?"

"Only calculated ones," Devon tells him.

"Ah," Rolfe scoffs. "Playing it safe never made anyone rich. When I got out of prison, do you know what I did?"

"Tell us," Ana gushes.

"I got a job on an oil rig in Saudi Arabia. That's where my fortune began. From there it was an easy hop to Egypt, where I had the good fortune to hitch my wagon to an archaeological dig. And guess what we found?"

"A mummy's tomb!" Ana exclaims.

Rolfe's grinning. "You are one clever girl. That's absolutely right. King Rootintutin. Ever hear of him?"

"I think we studied about him in Western Civ," Ana says.

Cecily laughs out loud. "Ana, you are a three-way light bulb set permanently on dim."

Rolfe smirks. "Lots of gold. Lots of it."

Cecily shakes her head. "Aren't you going to regale us with tales of the mummy's curse?"

Rolfe's standing. "Another time. Don't want to use up all my stories in one sitting."

Ana stares up at the older man in awe. "Can you imagine? A mummy's tomb!"

But Rolfe's not paying her any more attention. He's looking at Devon again. "So," he asks, a trifle more serious. "Any more ghosts?"

Devon holds his gaze. "Maybe a few," he says.

"Keep me informed." Rolfe's voice is steady now, firm. Devon's eyes flutter up to meet his gaze. He can tell Rolfe means what he says. "You know where to find me."

He gives the table a little salute and moves off.

He knows, the Voice tells Devon again. *He knows things you need to find out.*

"He seems awfully interested in you," Cecily says. "I wonder why."

Devon doesn't know either. But he aims to discover just what Rolfe Montaigne knows. And soon.

On the way home, the night is cool and crisp. The leaves on the trees are mostly gone. The air is pungent with the sweet fragrance of the harvest: freshly scythed hay, overturned soil. Crickets keep up their monotonous chorus, and the moon shines high in the clear sky.

They left DJ and Ana at Stormy Harbor, preferring to wander along the beach and then back up the cliffs by themselves. Devon had reached down and taken Cecily's hand. At one point he'd kissed her – the first time on his own initiative. She smelled so great, felt so soft. He wouldn't think about what they'd talked about. It couldn't be true.

Inside the great house, the old grandfather clock in the foyer strikes midnight. Twelve resounding chimes echo across the cold marble. Long purple shadows stretch lazily along the floor, and the movements of the bare trees outside cast weird dancing shapes on the walls.

Cecily goes off to bed, and Devon stands in the parlor watching through the windows as the white capped waves crash against the rocks far below. Their sound lulls him, and he wonders what Mrs Crandall would say if she knew about his budding romance with Cecily. He has a feeling she wouldn't approve.

Then, startling him, it comes.

The Voice.

The boy's in danger.

Devon turns, knowing exactly what it means, and bounds quickly up the stairs. He finds Alexander in his room awake, sitting on his bed, his back against the headboard, his hands folded in his lap. As if he were just waiting for something.

For *Devon*, perhaps.

"What are you doing up, Alexander? It's past midnight."

"I was watching the moon."

"The moon?"

"To think. Men have walked there. Isn't that extraordinary?"

Devon has never really thought of it. The first moon walk had taken place years before he was born, and he'd grown up with space shuttles and satellites as commonplace as bicycles and trains. "I suppose it is," Devon acknowledges. "When you think about it."

The boy laughs sharply. "Do you know what *this* is?" he asks suddenly, sliding a cordless telephone from under his pillow.

"That's the telephone from the kitchen. What are you doing with it up here?"

"Isn't it astounding?" Alexander looks at the phone in his hand as if he's never seen anything like it before. "I can carry it with me wherever I go and still it will ring, still it will find me."

Devon sits down on the edge of the boy's bed. Something's going on. The boy – or Jackson – is playing with him again.

"Of *course* cordless phones will ring if you carry them around," Devon says. "That's what they're *for*."

The boy is admiring the phone in his hand as if it were a rare find. He stretches the antenna out as far as it will go, then pushes it back in. He punches four numbers. They make little musical beep sounds.

"Alexander, what are you doing?"

"I'm calling my father," he says simply, holding the phone to his ear.

"Your father's in Europe. You only punched four—"

"Hello, Father?" Alexander asks cheerily. "How are you?"

Devon feels his shoulders stiffen. The boy's face brightens. His greeting sounded authentic. Could he really have called Edward Muir in London – or was it Paris? But it's midnight here; it would be five in the morning in Europe.

"Alexander," Devon says.

The boy glares at him over the phone. "I'm *talking to my father*," he whispers, his teeth suddenly clenched, anger glowing in his eyes.

Tightness clutches Devon's throat. He stands up, looking down at the child.

"It's just *Devon*," Alexander is saying into the phone, spitting the name with horrible malice. "Do you want to talk with him?" he asks. The boy nods then, handing the phone over to Devon. "He wants to talk with you."

"Alexander, is that really your fath—"

"*He wants to talk with you!*"

The boy's eyes now blaze with such fury that his face contorts into a nearly unrecognizable shape. Devon recoils, making a small sound. Alexander thrusts the receiver violently toward him. Devon has no option but to accept it.

"Mr . . . Muir. . .?"

Of course there's no answer. Not for a second had Devon really believed that Alexander had so effortlessly punched in four numbers and called Europe.

But there *is* someone on the other end of the line. Someone is breathing, short and raspy, the labored breath of a very old man. Devon hits the off button with a forceful thrust of his index finger.

"What did he say?" the boy asks innocently, now calm and smiling.

"Who *was* that, Alexander?"

"My father. What did he say?"

"You – you just woke someone up. That's what you did. You hit some random numbers and woke some poor old man out of a sound sleep."

Alexander shrugs. "Maybe it was a bad connection." He reaches behind him and pulls out another device from his pillow. "And this. Do you know what *this* does?"

It's the remote control for the television.

Devon studies the boy. He sits back down on the bed. "No," he says cagily. "Why don't you explain it to me?"

"If I push this button like this," Alexander says, holding the remote in his right hand and pressing a knob with his thumb, "the TV comes on." The set at the foot of his bed pops into life.

The sound jars the silence of the dark room, sending shivers of blue light across the floorboards. "Isn't it a marvelous invention?"

But what chills Devon far more than the boy's strange attitude, far more than the breathing on the other end of the phone, is the program that is suddenly playing on Alexander's television set. *The Major Musick Show*, with its gravelly-voiced host and rows of vacant-eyed children, singing a song about a big dark house on the top of a hill.

"Alexander," Devon whispers, "it's the *middle of the night*. Why is this *on*?"

But the boy is watching raptly. Major Musick dances in a sinewy rhythm in front of the tattered red velvet drapes. His garish outfit sparkles in the bright lights of the camera: reds and blues and big pink fuzzy buttons down his ruffled shirt.

Devon draws closer to the set to stare at the show. The camera moves in now for a hideous close-up of the clown. The putty on his red nose is cracked and caked, the white make-up on his face is pasty and thick.

"How was that, boys and girls?" Major Musick rasps. "Did you like that song?"

But the camera keeps moving in closer, closer, closer — until only one yellow bloodshot eye of the beast fills the screen. Major Musick's laughter fills the room, and for a moment Devon is as entranced by its spell as Alexander. It's easy to get lost in the sound, to allow it to turn you over and over and over again, to carry you up and out the window, to get inside your head and stay there.

But Devon forces himself finally to blink. The camera has pulled back again, and now Major Musick is in front of a chalkboard, writing with long, unnerving squeaks. "The letter for the day, boys and girls, is N," he's saying.

"*Ennnnnn*," Alexander enunciates from behind Devon.

"Listen to how much it sounds like *emmmmm*," the clown says.

"*Emmmm*," Alexander repeats.

The camera frames the clown's face. Devon stands in front of the TV set. Major Musick: Devon recognizes him. He's seen him before, in a moment of terror, in the last seconds of consciousness. He's seen him — in the darkness of the closed-off room in the East Wing.

Major Musick smiles then, and there are maggots in his teeth.

Devon knows the truth at last: beneath the chalky white make-up of the television clown lurks the diabolical face of Jackson Muir.

9
The Corpse Walks

Devon switches off the TV.

"Don't you *like* Major Musick?" Alexander asks angelically behind him.

The eerie silence that overtakes the room is only slightly less unnerving than the clown's hideous laughter. Devon says nothing, just turns and stares at the boy.

Cecily comes in behind him. "What's going on in here? It's pretty late for Alexander to still be awake."

Devon grabs the remote control. "Cecily, look at this," he says, switching the TV back on. It's Jay Leno interviewing Gwyneth Paltrow. "Wait," Devon says, switching channels. Grace Kelly and Gary Cooper in an old western. He presses the next channel. Some girl modeling a bathing suit on the Home Shopping Channel. Then Janet Jackson on VH-1.

"He was *there*," Devon says.

"*Who* was there?" Cecily asks.

He keeps flicking through the channels until he's done one complete cycle. He snaps off the TV, looking back at Alexander. "How did you do that? How did you get that show on the screen?"

"Devon, what are you talking about?" Cecily demands.

"Can I go to sleep please?" Alexander asks sweetly.

"No! Tell me who you are!" Devon shouts. "What do you want from me?"

"Hey," Cecily says, putting her hand on Devon's arm. "Take it easy. Let's go."

Alexander just smiles. Devon feels an overwhelming urge to slap him, to shake him, to force the truth from his smug little throat. But instead he allows Cecily to guide him from the room and out into the hallway. He hears her tell her young cousin to go to sleep, that as usual he's caused enough trouble. Then she switches off the light and closes the boy's door.

"Devon," Cecily whispers, as they walk down the corridor, careful not to wake her mother, "what did you see on the TV?"

"If I needed any proof that Alexander's in Jackson Muir's power, I got it."

He leads her into the playroom. On top of the television he finds that week's *TV Guide*. He flips through the listings. There's no program called *Major Musick*.

Musick. With a *K*.

His eyes land on a stack of board games in the corner. He lunges for them.

"Devon, what's going *on*?"

He pulls the Scrabble box out of the pile.

"What are you *doing*?" Cecily asks. "Suddenly you want to play *games*?"

Devon ignores her. He removes the lid of the box and shakes the little squares of the alphabet on to the table. He begins going through them. Cecily stands over him, watching. He spells out, one letter at a time:

MAJOR MUSICK

"I don't understand," Cecily says. "Who is Major Musick?"

"Hang on," Devon tells her, as he begins sliding the letters around. First the J, then the A. . .

And he spells out:

JACKSOM MUIR

"Jack-*som?*" Cecily says, totally confused.

Devon's body tingles.

"The letter for today, boys and girls," he says softly, "is N." He looks over at Cecily. "Listen to how much it sounds like M. *Ennn.*"

"Devon, you are freaking me out!"

"Replace the M with N and it's *right there.* It's spelled out as plain as day. He *wanted* me to figure this out. He was giving me clues."

"Figure *what* out? *Who* wanted you to?" Cecily sounds desperate.

He takes her by the shoulders. "That show Alexander is always watching. That's how Jackson Muir got him. How he hooked him."

"Devon, I'm not following."

"That's all right. I'm not sure yet what it all means myself, but I'm now *absolutely* convinced that Alexander is the key to finding out what I need to know."

"You're telling me the ghost of Jackson Muir was on a *TV show?*"

Devon smiles. "He seems fascinated with modern technology. What was his death date on the tombstone?"

"I don't remember."

"It was 1966. Before the moon walk. Before cordless phones. Before everybody had remote controls."

"I *guess*," Cecily says, still not getting it all.

Devon kisses her quickly. "Let's get some sleep. I have a feeling tomorrow's going to be a big day."

"Wait, Devon."

He looks at her. "What is it?"

"This is going way too far. I mean, you move around a few letters and get Jackson's name. Except not even totally. And that's enough to convince you that his ghost has got Alexander under his control."

"I *saw* Jackson, Cecily. Behind the clown's make-up."

She closes her eyes. "You saw a dead man on a kids' TV show?"

"It's not a real show! It only exists in this house! There's no TV show by that name listed."

She seems at a loss. "All I know is Alexander's a very clever little kid. The stories his headmaster told — he used to trick them all the time."

"Cecily, you didn't see him in there. How he was acting—"

"No, but I've seen him plenty of other times. He can be devious. Even running away the other night. You saw how he manipulated the whole situation."

"It wasn't *him*, Cecily! It was Jackson Muir!"

She sighs, makes a face, runs her hand through her hair. "Devon, has it ever occurred to you that in your fever to find out the truth about yourself and your abilities you may have begun seeing things that *aren't really there?*"

He looks at her hard. "I know it's all weird to you. I know I've arrived here with stories about ghosts and goblins and you don't know what to believe." He pauses. "And I can find the answers on my own, Cecily. If you don't want to be involved, I can't blame you."

She seems near tears. "It's not that I don't want to be involved," she says. "It's just that . . . I was always taught not to question. Not to look too deeply into the rooms of this old house, or the motives of anyone who lived here. You're asking me to go against everything my mother has told me, Devon. I'm frightened of what you might find out."

He nods. He can understand. They head off to their rooms without further conversation. He, too, is frightened by what all this might be leading to: not only the truth about himself, but of his father as well. What had Dad been involved with? What was his connection to this house, to its secrets?

And if Dad wasn't his real father, who was?

Mrs Crandall is present at breakfast the next morning, bright and smiling and full of good cheer. "Simon's brought in the pumpkins from the garden," she announces. "That always makes me glad."

She pours herself some coffee from the silver urn that Simon had placed on the table. Devon notices that Cecily's not here: she's already had breakfast, her bowl of unfinished Special K remaining at her place, a few slices of banana growing soggy in the skim milk.

"Cecily's taking her morning exercise regimen quite seriously," Mrs Crandall comments. She reveals her daughter just breezed past her this morning in running shoes and sweat pants, out to circle the grounds a couple of times. "I wonder how long this phase will last."

Devon suspects Cecily's avoiding him after their confrontation last night. He concentrates on his orange juice, preferring not to dwell on the fact that Simon's malformed little hands squeeze it fresh every morning.

Mrs Crandall is watching him. She raises her chin, displaying her long neck, adorned by a single strand of pearls. Her dress this morning is scarlet red, striking against her pale skin and upswept golden hair. No lipstick or mascara mar her features. They are delicate but solid, soft yet firm. Her chin has not yet begun to sag; few wrinkles line her eyes. Devon imagines her as a young girl Cecily's age; he can understand how Rolfe Montaigne could have found her lovely.

"I wasn't always such a dowager," Mrs Crandall smiles, as if reading Devon's thoughts. "Once I was as young and carefree as Cecily, running out to jog around the estate. I don't suppose you can imagine that."

"Oh, but I can." Devon smiles at her. "I'm sure there are many sides of you I don't know."

Her smiles fades a little. "A curious remark, Devon."

"Mrs Crandall," he says, changing the subject, "Alexander claims to have telephoned his father in Europe last night. Is that possible?"

Mrs Crandall sighs. "I hardly think so. Even I have trouble tracking that man's whereabouts."

Devon takes a bite of his Belgian waffle. "I thought perhaps Alexander had entered a code on the phone or something. He only pressed a few numbers."

"Well, that just shows you he was playing with you. Where Edward is at the moment is a mystery. Paris, possibly. Or Amsterdam. Or Helsinki. My brother has never stayed in one place for very long."

Devon looks at her. "Mrs Crandall, we've never talked about the other night. The night Alexander disappeared—"

She silences him with her hand. "Don't bring it up. It's forgotten. I know what this house can do to those who are new here. It can play all sorts of tricks with one's mind. My own mother, God bless her, still talks to everyone who's ever lived here."

"But there are *questions* I have, Mrs Crandall. And I think you might know something that might—"

She stands up. "Devon, I want so much for this to work out. I want very much for you to be a part of this family." She walks over behind Devon's chair, placing her hands on his shoulders. "But you must do your part as well. I told you that you shouldn't go looking for answers. I wish I could help you, but I can't. Is it not possible for you to just look forward, to a bright and shining future, instead of looking only to the past?"

He steels himself, and imagines she can feel his shoulders tense. "Mrs Crandall, until I can understand my past, I can't see any future." Her hands lift from his shoulders. She walks away, pouring herself another cup of coffee, preparing to disappear back into the house.

"Mrs Crandall, I'm worried about Alexander. I think – no matter what you say – he's in danger."

"The child is in no danger," she says, dismissing him impatiently.

"How can you be so sure?"

"Because I *am*." She glares at him. "Because I vowed *no one in this family* would ever be in danger again. And I've taken measures to ensure that. Do you understand, Devon? *There is no danger here!* So don't go looking for any!"

Then she's gone. Devon sighs. What is she hiding? Why is she so certain there's no danger? He realizes now he can't confront her in the hope of discovering anything. He's still on his own – maybe even without Cecily.

He resumes his breakfast. When he looks up he sees Alexander, standing in the archway between the dining room and the kitchen.

"How long have you been standing there?" Devon asks.

"Long enough." The boy sits down opposite Devon. He looks very small in the tall chair, his shoulders barely clearing the table.

"Want to watch some TV?" Alexander grins impishly.

"Maybe." Devon stares over at the child. "Maybe it's time you told me about Major Musick."

"He's *on*, right now."

"He's *always* on, isn't he?"

Alexander smiles.

"Who is he, Alexander?"

The boy's eyes dance. "Have you been to the tower, Devon?"

"Why should I go to the tower?" Devon decides to play along with him to see where he's heading with this. "What's there for me to see?"

"Oh, I don't know. I've never been there myself. But maybe tonight – maybe tonight you'll be able to get in."

"What game are you planning, Alexander? Are you planning to lock me in there the moment my back is turned?"

Alexander just laughs. He gets down off the chair and scampers back upstairs. Devon listens as his footsteps against the marble fade off into the house.

Devon determines that he's not going to get much more out of Alexander either; he's too far gone into Jackson Muir's power. Somehow, however, he's got to find out why the demon has appeared in the form of the television clown, and what he hopes to gain by it, besides control over Alexander. It's not so much that Jackson is trying to *prevent* him from finding out the secrets; in fact, he almost seems to be *egging him on* to try.

Devon resolves that his next step will be twofold. First, he'll find out all he can about Jackson Muir and his black magic. Then, after school tomorrow, he'll make a visit to Rolfe Montaigne to discuss the "business" Rolfe had offered to talk about.

The first part of Devon's plan doesn't take long. Cecily is nowhere to be found, Alexander is ensconced in front of the TV in the playroom, Simon is outside raking leaves, and Mrs Crandall is cloistered with her mother. Devon has the library all to himself, a blazing fire in the fireplace. He begins leafing through books on the Muir family history.

Of course, the books he *really* needs are in that inner chamber of the East Wing. Devon knows he's got to find a way back in there, even if he dreads the proximity to that bolted door. But for now he contents himself with what he might discover from these more standard accounts, the first of which is called simply, *A History of Ravenscliff*.

The publication date is 1970, and it seems to have been put together by a local historian at the request of Randolph Muir, Mrs Crandall's father. Devon flips open to the first page:

DEDICATED TO OUR FOUNDER
HORATIO MUIR

There's a photograph of him: an old man with heavy sideburns and thick brow, stern and solemn. *But not evil*, Devon thinks. *Horatio Muir was not an evil man. Not like his first-born son.* He reads on:

Horatio Muir was born in London in 1882, scion of a long and distinguished heritage. He came to America in 1900 and settled at Misery Point, Rhode Island, commencing upon a structure that would rival the mansions of nearby Newport. A powerful businessman,

Horatio was also a judicious man, believing that with great power came great responsibility. His wealth would be shared with the village, bringing jobs and prosperity.

Ravenscliff was completed in 1902, and it drew the curious and awestruck from around the nation. A sprawling mansion of fifty rooms, it comprised not only two wings but also a tower, from which Horatio Muir often viewed the surrounding estate reaching off to the sea.

The house was so named for its black stone and ebony wood, and also for the birds that took up roost there, eliciting wondrous comment from the village. The ravens became Horatio Muir's constant companions among the battlements of the house; they could be seen for miles swooping around the tower and alighting upon the gargoyles on the facade of the mansion.

So it was true. There *were* once ravens at Ravenscliff. Devon wonders why the birds had left, and where they had gone.

There are photographs of Horatio and his wife, and then others with Randolph Muir, Mrs Crandall's father, but none with Jackson, Horatio's first-born. Devon flips ahead several pages but finds nothing.

"Not one picture of Jackson," he murmurs. "Not one."

Devon recalls Jackson's tombstone, with "Master of Ravenscliff" etched into the granite.

There must have been some rivalry between the brothers, Devon surmises. *But why would Randolph allow Jackson to construct a monument to himself proclaiming himself master of the house? Just what happened between them, and what relevance does that rivalry have for me?*

He's not surprised that an "official" history, apparently commissioned by Randolph Muir, leaves out any mention of magic or demons. But somehow, at some point, Jackson had achieved knowledge of the black arts. Devon recalls Mrs Crandall on his first night here telling him that both her father and grandfather had been "world-travelers." The skulls and shrunken heads and crystal balls in the parlor were their "trinkets," she said. Was this, then, a *family* of warlocks?

Or, rather, as the books in the East Wing had suggested, *sorcerers?*

What had been the exact wording? Sorcerers of the Order of the Nightwing.

The Nightwing.

Devon feels a sudden surge of electricity run through his body. What did that word mean?

Finally, from a book on the great whaling ships of Misery Point, slips a faded, yellowed newspaper clipping. It's undated. Devon holds it up to the light to read:

ELDEST MUIR SON, RETURNED FROM EUROPE, DELIGHTS CHILDREN WITH FANTASTIC SHOW

Jackson Muir, elder brother of Randolph Muir of Ravenscliff, entertained his niece and nephew and several of the village children with a magic show yesterday on the estate, exhibiting tricks and sleights-of-hand he'd learned while on an extended tour of European cities. Dressed as a clown in white face and bright red nose, he delighted the boys and girls with such fantastic feats as pulling a rabbit from a hat, summoning a dragon from its lair, and making one little boy seem to disappear.

Devon's blood runs cold. Jackson Muir, dressed as a *clown*.

Yet the image of a kindly Jackson entertaining children just doesn't cut it. Devon knows what kind of a clown he was, and he bets the kids were more frightened than delighted. He doesn't need the Voice to tell him that Jackson's "dragon" was no sleight-of-hand, and Devon can't help but wonder what *really* happened to the little boy Jackson "seemed" to make disappear.

Returning the clipping to the book, he chances upon another notice tucked among the pages. On this one, the headline reads:

MRS EMILY MUIR FALLS TO DEATH FROM DEVIL'S ROCK

Dated November 1, 1965, it reads:

Police are investigating eyewitness accounts that Mrs Emily Muir, 22-year-old wife of Jackson Muir of Ravenscliff, fell from the cliff at Devil's Rock last night. Both her husband and Muir family caretaker Jean-Michel Montaigne told investigators they followed Mrs Muir on to the estate grounds at the height of last night's thunder storm. Distraught and confused, Mrs Muir apparently fell from the rock around midnight. She is presumed dead, although her body has not been recovered.

Mrs Muir is the former Emily Day. She and her husband were married four years ago, shortly after Mr Muir's return from Europe. They have no children.

Devon stares down at the clipping. Jean-Michel Montaigne must have been Rolfe's father, but another fact intrigues Devon more. *Emily killed herself on Halloween*, he thinks — not far from today's date. The clipping trembles in his hand, close to crumbling. "They have no children," Devon reads aloud.

But the Voice told him otherwise, that Jackson *did* have a child.

Clarissa? The stone where he'd seen the figure of the woman in white?

Who, by rights, should have inherited this house.

But the name "Clarissa" doesn't appear in any of the books on the shelves. Devon goes through each of them, one by one. Most are general texts on fishing or whaling or the New England coast. There are a few old picture books of ravens; in one, he finds a black-and-white photograph of Ravenscliff with dozens of the birds perched atop the parapet and nestled among the heads of gargoyles. He thinks again: *Where did all the ravens go?*

He's about to end his search when he hears a sound. The rustling of fabric. He turns. There, in the corner, he can see a figure.

He gasps. The glow from the fireplace illuminates the figure in the corner briefly. It's a woman — horribly mangled, deformed. Her head is crushed, one eye dangling from the socket. Her shoulders are twisted, her hands broken. She walks slowly toward Devon, reaching out her hands.

It's Emily Muir.

Devon covers his mouth with his hands to avoid shouting out. *Emily Muir — or rather, her corpse. How she looked after the fall from Devil's Rock.*

Her broken hands beseech him. She tries to speak, but makes no sound. Then she disappears.

She wants me to find out the truth, Devon thinks.

The fire is dying in the fireplace. Devon lets out a long

breath and makes his way upstairs. He sees no one else that night. It takes a long time to clear his mind of thoughts of Emily's mangled hands reaching out to him, but finally sleep overcomes him.

He begins to dream: he's outside, near Devil's Rock, staring up at the light in the tower room. Behind him stands Rolfe — but it isn't Rolfe as he knows him now, but the Rolfe of twenty years before, when he was Devon's age and slept in Devon's very room.

"Don't you want to know who's up there?" this teenaged Rolfe asks.

"I do," Devon says dreamily, and all at once he's wandering down long and twisting corridors of the dark, dusty house. He quickly becomes lost: every new turn thrusts him deeper into the maze of the house. He has the sense of climbing, and now he stands at the door of the tower room, and he can hear the sobbing coming from within. He reaches out his hand to turn the knob—

"Don't go in there," comes a voice from behind him. He turns. It's Dad. "Not unless you really want to know, Devon."

"I do," Devon says, close to tears now. "Dad, you sent me here to find out. I've got to know who I am."

His father looks at him sadly. "Then go ahead, son."

He turns back and throws open the door. There, in the candlelit darkness, is the rotting, white-caked skull of Major Musick, who's pulling a rabbit out of a hat. He laughs horribly when he spots Devon, his laughter filling the room.

Devon awakes with a start. He sits up in his bed, listening to the crickets chirping in the still night air. A window has blown open, and a cool October breeze fills the room. Devon shivers, trying to shake off the anarchy of the dream. He throws back his sheet and stands to refasten the window. He glances up at the tower, standing bleakly against the deep blue sky.

Of course, there's a light there. He closes the window, hooking it tightly.

Without making a conscious decision, Devon pulls on his jeans and slips a T-shirt over his head. He steps out into the shadowy corridor, hearing his own heart in the hushed stillness of the house. He first makes a deliberate stop at Alexander's room — the boy is fast asleep — and then continues on his mission.

He could not have expected to find the door to the East Wing unlocked once again, but it is — of course, just as Alexander had said it would be. It stands ajar, a strange golden light flickering from beyond.

What secret does this place hold? Devon steadies himself, casting off the lingering miasma of the dream. He's fired by a will not entirely recognizable as his own, and he does not challenge it. The door creaks as it opens, sending a shiver all through the house. Upstairs, Devon is sure, Mrs Crandall turns restlessly in her sleep, Cecily sits up in sudden alarm. And of course Alexander is now awake, wide-eyed and knowing.

Devon steps into the small round room behind the door. It's the same as before, except this time he doesn't pull the string for the overhead bulb. He begins his ascent up the bare concrete steps. The light comes from above, a candle as before, sending quivering glimmers down the steps that make the shadows dance. Devon moves forward.

He's stopped by the sense of someone else's motion. Someone — *something* — is descending the steps toward him. Devon can see its shadow take on contours along the curved wall as the light comes closer. It's the figure of a person — no, *two* people. He can now clearly make out their shadows cast by the candle one of them carries. He stops in his tracks as he hears his name – "Devon!" – exclaimed by a woman – but then the candle that had offered their only light is snuffed out and they're all left in darkness.

"Who's there?" he calls, and his voice echoes against the marble and concrete.

There's only a rustle of fabric in response, and perhaps the muffled whisper of the woman who had called his name. But then nothing, and Devon, unnerved yet determined, places one foot in front of the other and begins ascending the stairs once more.

"I thought I warned you not to go prowling around in here," comes the voice of Simon. New light strikes him: the harsh golden beam of Simon's flashlight.

"Someone just called my name," Devon insists.

"Maybe it was a ghost," Simon snarls. "Whatcha doin' in here in the first place?"

"The door was ajar."

"Don't give you no right to go where you're not allowed."

"I'm surprised you didn't try to strangle me again," Devon says belligerently.

"Didn't have no rope." Simon glares up at him. Devon believes that was indeed the only reason the caretaker hadn't again assaulted him. "Now, g'wan. Get outta here."

"What's up there?"

"Nothin' but ghosts."

"Then what are *you* doing in here?"

"Checking on that light fixture. Making sure it wasn't shortin' out again."

"Simon, it's the middle of the night."

"I keep odd hours."

Devon knows he's lying. But he's not going to tangle with Simon again. He turns and heads back down the stairs, back out into the great hall. He looks up at the grandfather clock. It chimes three. He doesn't sleep the rest of the night, but instead just lies there, listening to every sound, every creak of the old house in the wind.

All the next day Devon drags through his classes. Exhausted, frustrated, itching for a showdown — any kind of showdown — he keeps looking at the clock, anxious for the last bell. When it finally comes, he throws his books into his locker and seeks out DJ.

He finds him leaning up against Flo in the parking lot. "Will you do me a huge favor?" Devon asks.

"Name it, my man."

"Will you give me a ride to Rolfe Montaigne's restaurant?"

His friend makes a face, then nods for Devon to get into the car. DJ slides in behind the wheel and cranks Aerosmith on the CD player. *Dream on . . . dream on . . . dream onnn. . .*

"So what you got goin' with that jailbird?" he asks Devon.

"I can't tell you just yet. I'm sorry, I just can't."

"Ask no questions and you tell me no lies, huh?" DJ says over the music, as they peel out of the parking lot.

"Something like that," Devon says.

"You are one mysterious dude," DJ tells him as they glide on to Route 138. "It's like you're a superhero or something. Devon's just your mild-mannered secret identity."

Devon grins. "I'm not feeling very heroic. I'm just looking for some answers, DJ. And I think Rolfe Montaigne may know what went down here fourteen years ago."

"Fourteen years ago? Like the time you were born."

"Bingo."

DJ turns off toward Misery Point and soon the white clap-board of the village comes into view. He pulls the car up in front of Fibber McGee's. Devon just looks over at the restaurant, not moving or opening the door.

"For a man looking for answers," DJ observes, "you don't seem to be in much of a hurry."

Devon sighs. "Thanks for the ride, man."

"No prob." DJ reaches over and slaps his back. "March on, Dick Tracy."

Devon gets out of the car.

"You want me to wait?" DJ calls.

"Naw. Thanks anyway. I can walk back up to Ravenscliff from here."

He watches as the Camaro burns out down the road. He drops his hand into his pocket and cups the St Anthony medal. He wishes he was still in the car with DJ, just two ordinary kids hanging out, listening to music, eating pizza. Devon doesn't know why he feels so unnerved by this visit to Rolfe. Maybe because he feels he's going behind Mrs Crandall's back. If she'd be pissed about his exploration of the tower, she'd go ballistic if she knew about this, given her hatred of Rolfe. But she's forced him to do it: by stonewalling him, by refusing to give him answers, she's driven him as surely as if she'd dropped him off here herself.

He walks up the sidewalk to Fibber McGee's. It'll be a few hours before the restaurant opens for dinner, but already Rolfe's Porsche is parked out front. Through the large glass windows Devon can see the waiters, dressed in white shirts and black bow ties, setting out vases of chrysanthemums on the tables. Others are folding napkins and arranging silverware. Devon takes a deep breath and pushes open the door. He's struck by the thick, wheaty aroma of bread baking in the kitchen. He realizes he's hungry.

He doesn't have to ask for Rolfe. It's almost as if he'd been waiting for Devon. The man appears in an archway leading into a backroom, and he's smiling, arms crossed.

"Well, if it isn't the young ward of Ravenscliff," he says.

"Can I talk with you?" Devon asks.

"I was wondering when you'd show up."

Rolfe looks over at one of the waiters, probably the maitre d'. "I'll be back in a few," he says, striding quickly towards Devon, snatching a long black leather coat from the rack.

He slips the coat on and opens the door outside. "Come along," he says to Devon, nodding for him to follow.

Devon's confused. "Where are we going?"

"For a little ride."

Devon has no choice but to follow him. Rolfe's already in his car, revving the motor. Devon opens the passenger-side door and slides in. He's hit by the memory of the first time he'd been in this car: his first night in Misery Point, not even a month ago but already seeming an eternity.

Rolfe backs out of the lot and heads on to the coast road. "We can talk better at my house," he says. "Not so many ears."

Devon says nothing. He just looks out the window. The day has become very gray; a slight mist speckles the windshield. He looks anxiously over the rocks of the sea. Suddenly he feels as if he's blundered into a trap, turning to this man for help – this *murderer*? What if, out of some blind hatred toward the Muir family, Rolfe sees Devon as his means for revenge?

The car accelerates, picking up speed as it rounds the sharp, twisting curves of the road. Devon pushes his head back into the leather seat, feeling his blood begin to race.

"Whatsa matter?" Rolfe grins over at him. "Don't you like fast cars?"

"I like them just fine," Devon tells him. "It's the drivers I worry about."

Rolfe laughs. "What? Afraid we'll have an accident? Maybe go off the side?"

Just then two headlights like eyes burning holes in the mist suddenly appear in front of them. Devon gasps. The oncoming car heads straight for them, as if to force them off the cliff. Rolfe lays on the horn but to no avail: the car keeps coming, and in an instant Devon knows — *sees* in his mind — the sharp fangs of the opposing driver, its talons gripped around the wheel.

10
The Nightwing

Rolfe expertly swerves around the oncoming car, which passes them at breakneck speed, and Devon can hear manic laughter in its wake.

"Damn idiots," Rolfe mutters, looking suspiciously in his rearview mirror at the car. "Drunken kids, probably."

But Devon knows the thing driving that car was no kid.

"Well, here we are," Rolfe tells him. "Home sweet home."

He swings the car on to a small dirt road that leads to the edge of the cliff. On the very precipice stands a small cottage with the glow of a fire reflecting in its windows. The fragrance of pine wafts down from the smoke from the chimney. They step out of the car and Rolfe opens the door to the cottage, inviting Devon inside.

A woman is there, dressed in a gold satin blouse and black jeans, reading through some papers at a table. She's striking, like a supermodel: black skin, long legs, intense golden eyes. "Rolfe," she says, then looks over at Devon. "Hello, young man."

She doesn't seem to be surprised to see him. "Roxanne, this is Devon March," Rolfe says, adding pointedly, "from Ravenscliff."

"Hello, Devon March," the woman says, offering her hand. Devon shakes it. "Hello."

"We'll be down in the study," Rolfe tells her, and she nods.

Devon follows Rolfe down a small spiral staircase that leads to a room seemingly built into the side of the cliff, with one wall nearly all glass, facing out on to the sea. The other three walls are covered from floor to ceiling with bookshelves. There are books everywhere, in fact, and interspersed among them Devon spies crystal balls, a couple of skulls, and at least one shrunken head. Just like the parlor of Ravenscliff.

"Awesome room," Devon says.

"You like it? I spend most of my time here." Rolfe gestures around. "And who wouldn't, with that view?" He sighs. "But mostly it's because of my father's books. They're very comforting to have around me."

He withdraws a bottle of red wine from the small bar in the center of the room. He uncorks it, and pours two glasses. He hands one to Devon, who looks at it funny.

"Go ahead, Devon. A little wine doesn't hurt. In France, boys far younger than you drink wine the way most kids here drink Coca Cola."

Devon takes a sip. He's snuck beer before, but never wine. At first it tastes bitter to him, warm and dry. But after a few more sips he begins to like it: thick and soothing, rich and fruity.

They sit on opposite sofas, facing each other. Below them the waves crash against the rocks as the sun drops lower in the sky. Devon's not sure where to begin, and the wine suddenly makes him feel a little fuzzy, as if he can't quite remember why he came to visit Rolfe Montaigne.

"To ghosts and other dangers," Rolfe toasts, holding up his glass of wine. "So tell me what it's been like these past few weeks."

"Intense." Devon tries to think through his words. "I feel I'm really close to finding out stuff about myself."

"Yourself? Say more."

"Finding out my past. Who I am."

Rolfe nods. "Ah, yes. Your father's deathbed revelation of your adoption. So what are you finding?"

Devon looks at him intently. "You said you saw your share of ghosts when you lived at Ravenscliff."

Rolfe shrugs. "Anyone who spends any amount of time there eventually does."

"What do you know about Jackson Muir?"

"That he was an evil man. And that his evil did not die with him."

Devon can tell he's being deadly serious. As if to punctuate his words, the first flickering of silent lightning appears on the horizon over the sea.

"I can vouch for that," Devon agrees. "I've seen him. Several times."

"Where?"

"In the cemetery. In the East Wing. And other places, too. . ."

"Amanda's a fool," Rolfe says, more to himself than Devon.

Suddenly Devon's aware of the woman from upstairs, Roxanne. She's come down with a platter of strawberries, sliced pears, French bread, and cheese. She looks into Devon's eyes.

"You're hungry," she says.

He *is*. But how did she know?

"Thank you, Roxanne," Rolfe says.

She smiles.

"Yeah," echoes Devon. "Thanks."

She nods, the fire reflecting against her skin and dancing in her strangely golden eyes. She moves soundlessly back up the stairs.

"It's like she could read my mind," Devon says, popping a strawberry in his mouth.

"Roxanne's very perceptive," Rolfe tells him, smiling after her.

Devon slices a wedge of cheese and breaks off a piece of the French bread. "So getting back to what we were talking about," he says, mouth full, "why do you say Mrs Crandall is a fool?"

Rolfe sips his wine. "She should never have brought you, an innocent kid, into that house." He moves to stand before the glass, looking out at the roiling sea below. In the distance a very low tremble of thunder rolls across the waves.

He can be trusted, the Voice tells him. Any fear, any apprehension Devon may have felt earlier about this strange man, vanishes. He can tell that Rolfe not only has answers, but that he's being straight enough with him that he might just share some of them. Finally — someone being straight with him.

Devon approaches him, biting into a pear slice. "Why is the East Wing closed off?"

Rolfe looks over at him. "Devon, you're a good kid. But you need to go to Amanda—"

"I *have*. I've *tried*. She won't say anything. She won't admit what she knows."

Rolfe finishes his wine, shaking his head.

"Look," Devon says. "I am *entitled* to this knowledge. This is my *past*, my *history*."

Rolfe studies him. "Why do you think it's *yours*, Devon? We're talking two separate things here: what Amanda may or may not know about your real parents, and what she's not saying about the ghosts of Ravenscliff."

"I think they're connected," Devon says plainly.

"Why do you think that?"

"Rolfe, that car that tried to run us off the cliff on the way over here — that was no *kid* behind the wheel."

He can see in his eyes that Rolfe knew this bit of information as well, that he'd been shielding it, thinking Devon blind to it.

Rolfe's studying him. "How do you know that?"

"I'm not as innocent as you might think," Devon tells him. He finishes off the last of the strawberries. "You know about the demons, *don't* you, Rolfe? You know about the bolted door in the East Wing."

Rolfe's eyes narrow as they lock on to Devon's. "*Who are you?*" he asks very softly.

"That's what I want to find out."

Rolfe just looks at him.

Show him, comes the Voice.

Devon lifts his left arm, gesturing with his hand. He has a pretty good sense his powers will work. And sure enough: a book lifts off of Rolfe's shelf and glides smoothly through the air into Devon's grasp. Rolfe is watching all along, expressionless.

"*Registry of the Guardians of the Portal*," Devon reads, looking down at the title. "There's another copy of this book in the East Wing."

"Yes," Rolfe says, taking the book from him. "Yes, indeed there is." He hasn't taken his eyes off Devon. "Let's go sit by the fire, shall we?"

They settle down into two large overstuffed chairs. The fire snaps in the fireplace. Outside the rain pecks hesitantly against the window panes, as if loathe to disturb them. The thunder grumbles, but it's still miles away.

"You've known others with powers like mine, haven't you, Rolfe?"

"I have."The older man is still studying him, as if trying to understand. "How long have you known of your abilities? And who else knows you have them?"

"I've known ever since I was a kid," Devon tells him. "And so far, besides you, only Cecily knows for sure. Some of the kids at Gio's saw me wrestle a demon, but they think it was just adrenaline."

"They saw you *wrestle a demon?*"

"Well, punch it out, really. I had to. It had attacked a guy."

Rolfe's face goes pale. "Then they've returned," he says quietly. "I've sensed it. Tonight, that car cinched it for me. But if what you say is true, there are more than I imagined. If they're randomly attacking kids——"

"I don't think it was random. It spoke to me. It was trying to draw me out. I was its real target. But *why*, Rolfe? That's what I want to know. All my life, these things have been trying to get at me. My dad did his best, but a couple times they got through. And since coming here, I've been fighting them off right and left."

"And apparently winning, if you're sitting here," Rolfe observes, admiration in his voice.

"Yeah." Devon feels some pride himself. "Yeah, I've done OK."

"You know what you are, don't you, Devon? Your father *must* have explained it to you."

The boy sits forward in his chair. "That's just it, Rolfe. I *don't* know. My father never told me, except to say that I was stronger than anything out there, and that I shouldn't be afraid."

Rolfe makes a face. "That's odd. I assume your father was

a Guardian, and it's a Guardian's job to teach." He seems to consider something briefly. "Your real parents must have entrusted you to his care. Given that he was a Guardian, he'd understand your powers. But why they wouldn't want you to know of your heritage, I can't imagine. It's a proud heritage, noble—"

"*Whoa*. Can we do a little rewinding here? My heritage? Guardian?" He looks at Rolfe with eyes wide. "Can you start from the beginning? *Please?*"

Rolfe smiles a little. He looks down at the book on his lap.

"Your father must be in here, isn't he?" he asks. "In this book?"

Devon nods. "Only it can't be my dad. It was a different name, and the picture was from more than a hundred years ago."

"Point him out to me," Rolfe says, handing the book across to Devon.

Devon flips through the old musty pages. He finds Thaddeus Underwood. He holds the book open facing Rolfe and points. "This one," he says.

Rolfe's eyes widen. "Thaddeus was your father?"

"You knew him?"

Rolfe looks from the book up to Devon's face, then back again.

"Oh, yes," he says, "I knew him." He stands, pouring himself another glass of wine. The rain comes harder now, rat-a-tat-tatting against the glass. Lightning flashes on the horizon. Another Misery Point storm is under way.

"But this can't be my father," says Devon. "It's from another century."

"Guardians live a long time. They have to. They teach and train and protect generations. How old did your father say he was?"

"When he died he was fifty-seven."

"Add at least a couple hundred to that, my boy," Rolfe says, grinning.

"That's impossible," Devon says, sputtering.

Rolfe's grin widens. "As impossible as your levitating that book from the shelf? As impossible as wrestling a demon at a pizza joint?"

Devon tries to comprehend this new information about his father. "Then *March* wasn't my father's real last name," he muses out loud. "He probably took it because it was the month I was born." He looks suddenly back over at the other man. "How can a Guardian — whatever that is — live to be so old? My dad was *human*. He *had* to be."

Rolfe sighs. "He *was* human, Devon. All Guardians are. But their bloodline is ancient . . . dating back to the early days of sorcery, when they were given special gifts. And in turn, they teach, train, protect. . ."

"Teach *who*, Rolfe?"

Rolfe seems not to hear him. His eyes are far away, remembering. "When I was a boy, Thaddeus Underwood was the greatest Guardian in the Americas. I *worshiped* him. He was like a grandfather to me — a wise, generous, kind old grandfather. My own father thought the sun rose and set around him." He pauses. "We all loved Thaddeus. Mr Muir. Edward. Amanda."

"He was *here*? My father was at *Ravenscliff*?"

"Yes. For a time. He had come to train *my* father. You see, my father was a Guardian, too." Rolfe looks at Devon, as if trying to see something there, something he might recognize. "Though I can't imagine for the life of me who your parents could have been. I know of no one who might have placed you with Thaddeus as a Guardian."

"They had to have been *here*, in Misery Point," Devon insists. "Why else would Dad send me here after he died? And why didn't he ever tell me anything about all this?"

"I don't know the answers to those questions. But Thaddeus Underwood never did anything without a reason. He was far too sharp for that. Yes, I'm quite sure he wanted you to discover your heritage here – but I can't fathom his reasoning for keeping it from you himself. There are no Guardians here any longer, no one left who could teach you in the way he could. . ."

Devon has stood to face Rolfe near the windows again. "Rolfe, I'm confused. I don't understand what a Guardian is. Guardians of the Portal . . . what's a Portal? Is it like that door in the East Wing?"

"Very perceptive, Devon. Yes, exactly like that door." He smiles a little sardonically. "In more common language, they're referred to as Hellholes."

"Yes," Devon says. "Like my closet back home. Hellholes."

Rolfe looks at him compassionately. "They took root in your closet? You poor kid."

"But *why*, Rolfe? That's what I want to know. Why *me*?"

Rolfe studies him sadly. "You really *don't* know, do you?"

"No," Devon tells him, his voice imploring the truth.

Rolfe sets down his wine glass on the window seat. He places his hands on Devon's shoulders and looks him square in the eyes.

"Devon March, you come from a long and ancient line, a proud and noble heritage," he tells him. "Devon March, you are a necromancer – a sorcerer – of the Order of the Nightwing."

The thunder comes then, fittingly.

* * *

"The — the *Nightwing?*"

It's taken Devon several seconds to respond. The word has sent chills up his spine. He feels his skin tingle from his toes to the tips of his ears.

"The Order of the Nightwing," Rolfe repeats.

In his mind Devon sees again those books in the East Wing of Ravenscliff. The word had given him pause then, too. *Nightwing.* He knows without even asking that the Muirs are Nightwing as well: he recalls the ravens, black as night, that had once lived in their house.

"Nightwing," Devon breathes. "Sorcerer — warlock! Just like Jackson Muir."

Rolfe looks angry. "Oh, no. Not like him. Jackson Muir defiled the ancient honorable tradition of the Nightwing. The tradition taught to him by his father, the great Horatio Muir. Jackson used his powers for evil. That made him an Apostate — a renegade sorcerer, shunned by all Nightwing around the globe."

It sounds like the stuff of fairy tales to Devon — stuff he might read about in comic books. It's hard to fathom, yet it's oddly reassuring too. Whatever this Nightwing is, he's a *part* of it — one of them. For the first time in his life, he feels connected to something bigger than he is.

"So there are more of these — these — Nightwing people?"

Rolfe smiles. "Oh, yes. The Nightwing can be found all over the world. Their history dates back to ancient days, when the first Nightwing learned the secrets of the old elemental Knowledge — and tapped the power of the demons for their own use, for good."

Devon laughs. "This is just too freaky."

"I thought so, too, once. But I can remember, as a boy, watching my father and old Mr Muir corral a demon in the courtyard at Ravenscliff. I watched as Mr Muir twisted it and pummeled it, all without ever even using his hands, only his mind. I watched as the filthy thing was sent back to its Hellhole — and I knew then that I was witnessing greatness, that I had been given a great privilege, to see in action the magic of the Nightwing."

"So the Muirs — all of them — *are* part of it," Devon says. "The *whole family*. I was reading about them, about Horatio —" He looks over at Rolfe. "So Mrs Crandall *has* to know this?"

"Of course she knows. But —" Rolfe makes a face, clearly troubled by a memory. "It was a long time ago. Terrible things happened. Sorcery and magic were banned from that house."

"Because of Jackson, right?"

Rolfe nods. "He was known as the Madman."

Devon shivers at the word. "The accounts say he left Ravenscliff for Europe. . ."

"Yes. He had broken with his father, begun using his powers for his own gain."

"So he was considered an Apo— What was it you said?"

"An Apostate. A member of the Nightwing order who rejects the power of good. Who harnesses the power of the demons for his own gain."

Devon's having a hard time keeping up. He steadies himself against the table. "But Jackson came back to Ravenscliff," he says. "He came back and married Emily. . ."

"Yes, he did. He convinced his brother he'd reformed. Oh, Jackson was very canny. Shrewd. Poor old Randolph Muir learned too late how shrewd Jackson was."

Devon remembers the clipping of Emily's death. "I saw your father's name in an article about Emily Muir's death. Is it true that she jumped? Because of Jackson?"

Rolfe folds his arms across his chest. "You *have* been doing your homework. I was quite young when Emily Muir died. But

I remember her as a sweet, sad young woman. When she failed to get pregnant, Jackson began cheating on her. It sent her into a deep depression."

"So she killed herself."

Rolfe nods.

"But Jackson grieved for her," Devon says. "That's what Cecily told me. He erected that monument to her. So he couldn't be all bad – not if he loved her."

Rolfe laughs. "Well, aren't we the young romantic. But believe me, Devon, there was nothing but evil in the heart of Jackson Muir."

Devon looks off at the furious sea. "Why was he so keen on having a kid?"

"Isn't it obvious? So his line could take back Ravenscliff. His evil would have lived on in another generation. A child of Jackson's would have guaranteed the destruction of Randolph's line. Amanda, Edward, Cecily, Alexander . . . none would be here today."

Devon thinks of something. "Did he have a kid with some-body *else* then, other than his wife? With whoever he was cheating with?"

"No. Jackson died without an heir."

"Are you sure?"

"Yes, Devon, I'm sure."

The boy has walked over to the bookcase. He touches a skull that stares out at him from the shelves. He feels a little electric shock.

He turns back to Rolfe. "Why did Jackson want to be Master of Ravenscliff so bad?"

"Horatio Muir built the house on one of the largest Hellholes in the Western hemisphere. He drew his power from a vast and powerful resource. Jackson wanted control of the house and the portal — which, as the eldest son, he believed was his birthright."

"So that's where a Nightwing gets his power — from the Hellhole?"

Rolfe manages a smile. "Listen, Devon. This is all too complex for me just to sum up quickly for you. Maybe in one of my father's books. . ."

"But I've *got* to know. Does Jackson control the demons? Is he the one who's been sending them against me?"

Rolfe sighs. "Perhaps Jackson is in league with some of them, but I don't fully know the answer. There are many Hellholes, Devon. Some have been sealed over. Some are under the control of Nightwing — and some are open. 'Earth's gaping wounds,' Thaddeus used to call them. From them many creatures have escaped over the centuries, and these things walk among us. Some are crafty. Some are just plain stupid. But all have one intent: to release their brethren and once again be permitted free rein upon the earth."

Devon nods. "That's what the creep at the pizza joint said."

"Of course, Jackson would use them to his own advantage, as I imagine he's doing now. Being dead is only a minor in-convenience for him . . . especially now that there's a new Nightwing at Ravenscliff."

Devon looks up at Rolfe. "He's got Alexander in his power now."

"What do you mean?"

"At first I just thought it was Alexander being the malicious kid everybody said he was. But not any more. Now I know Jackson's working through him. I saw him, on this weird TV show Alexander watches—"

"*TV show?*" Rolfe barks. He rushes over to Devon and grabs his shirt. "*What* TV show?"

"Hey, take it easy," Devon says. "It's called *Major Musick*. . ."

"Dear God," Rolfe breathes. "Not again."

"What do you mean, not again?"

Rolfe glares at him. "When I was a teenager, the Madman tried the same thing. It was a few years after his death. We discovered this television show one day, and became hooked. Only later did we realize that it was a televised version of the magic show Jackson used to put on for us in the parlor when we were kids." He looks sternly at Devon. "Have you seen this program? Have you *watched* it?"

"A little," Devon admits.

"*Don't.* And you've got to prevent Alexander from doing so ever again."

"It's too late for that. He's already in Jackson's power."

Rolfe shakes his head. "If Alexander's still here, it's not too late."

"What do you mean?"

"If he's *physically* still here. The Madman's plan is to bring him inside."

Devon looks astonished. "Inside the TV? How crazy is that?"

"Inside the *Hellhole*, Devon. The TV screen is just like a monitor into the depths of hell."

"*Whoaaa*. . ."

"Yeah, whoa all right." Rolfe bites his lower lip, contemplating something. "I'll tell you a story, Devon. I imagine Thaddeus never told you he had another son — a son of his own."

"No," Devon says.

"His name was Francis. We called him Frankie. He was about my age. He came to Ravenscliff with Thaddeus. We all hung out together, Eddie Muir, Frankie, and I. It was the three of us who started watching *Major Musick*. Every day we watched it faithfully, and none of the adults suspected a thing. None of the adults who were always on the lookout for the Madman's return — Mr Muir, my father, Thaddeus. They just saw three boys watching a clown. How innocent was that?" He pauses. "How devious of Jackson Muir."

"What happened?"

"One day Frankie disappeared. We searched everywhere for him but he wasn't found. Poor Thaddeus was so distraught."

Devon thinks of his father with another son. There's a small twang of jealousy, but it dissolves under the realization of the pain Dad must have felt. Devon remembers once when he got lost in a department store. He was maybe five or six. Dad had been far more upset than Devon, throwing his arms around the little boy when he spotted him, saying over and over again, "Thank God you're all right! Thank God!"

He understands now why his father had been so distraught. He'd been through it before.

"Was Frankie ever found?" asks Devon.

"Oh, yes, he was found." Rolfe pauses. "Do you know where?"

Devon swallows. "Tell me," he says, dry-mouthed.

"Sitting in the bleachers of *The Major Musick Show*. There he was, just sitting there. Blank-eyed and vacant. I remember sitting in front of the TV and recognizing him. Just a slight kid, covered with freckles. . ."

Devon feels as if a cold hand has just touched him on the shoulder. "I've seen him!" he shouts. "I've seen him on the show!"

Rolfe grimaces, running his hand through his hair. "Poor Frankie. All this time in the Hellhole."

Devon still feels the icy grip. "That's what he wants to do to Alexander? Bring him in there? *Why*, Rolfe?"

"Because he wants *you* to come in and try to save him," he says.

"*Me?* He wants me to go – in there? Through the bolted door?"

Rolfe nods. "Just as poor old Mr Muir was forced to do. The last of the Nightwing." He looks sadly at Devon. "He never came out."

"Mrs Crandall's father? He died in the Hellhole?"

Rolfe sighs. This is clearly dredging up long-ago, painful memories. "And he wasn't the only one who died in that struggle."

"Your father, too?" Devon ventures.

Rolfe nods, his eyes shining with tears now. "The Madman won. Which is why sorcery became forbidden at Ravenscliff. Why the spells were cast to renounce their Nightwing heritage. The ravens left one bright afternoon, flying up into the air all at once, obscuring the sun for several seconds before disappearing."

"But Jackson has returned," Devon says.

"Yes, and I suspect you *were* the catalyst. He sensed another Nightwing had arrived. He wants that portal opened, Devon. He wants the demons released so he can harness their power."

Devon runs his hands over his face. He feels staggered by all this information. "Rolfe, it's just so hard to . . . make sense of it all. . ."

Rolfe frowns. "I understand, Devon. There's so much you need to know, so much you need to learn, and I'm not a Guardian. I was meant to be, but my father died too young to teach me everything he knew."

"I need to know about the Nightwing, Rolfe. What I *am*."

"Yes, Devon, you deserve to know your own history, the heritage of the Nightwing." Rolfe shakes his head. "But not now. We don't have time for all that. We have to move quickly if we're to save Alexander."

Devon looks at him with some alarm. "What do you mean?"

"We need to go to Ravenscliff and confront Amanda."

"Why? Confront her *how*?"

Rolfe sighs. "I'm not sure how much she knew about the specifics of that television program. Her father kept a good deal from her. But she was *there*. She certainly remembers Frankie's disappearance, and what happened to her father and mine as a consequence of it." His jaw sets in determination. "No matter our own personal antagonism, she's got to listen to me when I tell her Alexander is in danger."

"Well, she insisted to me he *wasn't*," Devon says.

"She thinks they're protected from the Madman. She thinks because they've renounced their family's heritage that Jackson is gone for good." Rolfe looks at Devon. "Perhaps because she doesn't know of your powers. If she did, she might be more wary."

"Should I tell her?"

"I don't know," he says. "I'll try talking to her first. Come on. Who knows how much time we have left to save the boy?"

Devon considers something. "Rolfe, I think it'd be better if we don't show up together. It might antagonize Mrs Crandall to see us arrive in the same car."

Rolfe nods. "You're a sharp kid. OK, I'll drop you back at Stormy Harbor." He laughs. "Reminds me of the night I brought you in from the train station."

How long ago now that seems to Devon. And how much more he now knew. Not that he *understands* all of it fully—

His mind is spinning. So much information in such a short time. It seems utterly fantastic, and yet so *right* somehow. As if he already knew everything that Rolfe had told him, somewhere deep down within his soul. As if the knowledge had been embedded in his psyche, in his genes.

They head back up the spiral staircase. Roxanne is at the table, still going over old manuscripts. She and Rolfe just exchange knowing smiles as Rolfe grabs his coat from the rack and heads outside. Devon wonders what their relationship is.

"Goodbye, Devon March," Roxanne says.

"See ya later," he says, managing a smile. "And thanks again for the food."

He and Rolfe speak very little in the car heading back to the village. What could they say? Devon feels talked out. His head struggles to absorb all the new information.

I'm a Sorcerer of the Order of the Nightwing, he repeats, over and over again to himself. *And Dad was a Guardian. . .*

Over two hundred years old. . .

He waves so long to Rolfe as the Porsche crunches the gravel driving out of the Stormy Harbor lot. Then Devon sighs, looking up at the dark sky, grateful that the rain has eased for his climb back up the hill to Ravenscliff.

"I can't *believe* you, Devon," comes a voice.

It's Cecily. She's standing next to DJ's car, parked a few yards away.

"Cecily," he says. "What's the matter?"

"I saw you get out of Rolfe Montaigne's car," she says.

"I had to talk to him——"

She's furious. "Devon, I've *tried* to understand you. I really have. I know you want to find out why you are the way you are. But you've gone too far, Devon."

He approaches her, extends his hand, tries to touch her face. But she recoils from him.

"I know Rolfe can be cool," she says. "I don't hate him the way Mother does. But the fact remains that he wants to hurt my family, and there you are sneaking off to meet with him. I'm telling you, Devon, in your search for the truth, you've gone too far. Alexander's not possessed, he's just a brat. And Rolfe isn't your friend, he's just using you to get at my mother!"

"That's not true, Cecily. If you knew the stuff I've just found out—"

"I don't want to hear any more of it. It's madness!"

She turns away sharply, her hair flying, rushing to the other side of the car and sliding in beside DJ. Devon hears the engine kick in.

"Cecily!"

He runs after the car as it starts to move. DJ looks out from the driver's window.

"Hey man, she's mine now," DJ says.

The car accelerates. And in that last instant before the Camaro guns out of the parking lot, Devon sees DJ grin — shiny pointed fangs in the dark, flashing a thumbs-up sign with a hooked, yellow talon.

11
The Light in the Tower

"Cecily!" Devon shouts — but the car screeches off down the road.

Hey man, she's mine now.

A demon posing as DJ. The same one, he thinks, that had assumed the shape of the boy at Gio's. What would it do to Cecily?

Flo's red tail lights are vanishing in the darkness.

I've got to save her. I've got to—

Without even consciously willing it, Devon finds himself airborne — thrust forward in a single leap at a speed that leaves him gasping for breath. Within seconds he's on top of the Camaro, looking down through the glass T-top at the two figures within.

The demon looks up and roars, now exposing its true face.

Cecily screams.

A taloned hand comes crashing up through the glass trying to grab Devon. He darts out of the way, managing to stay attached to the car as if he's got suction cups on his hands. The Camaro swerves across the road into the oncoming lane. A tractor trailer barrels toward them.

"Yikes!" Devon shouts.

The truck leans on its horn. The demon is driving the Camaro with one claw, its other still trying to grab hold of Devon's legs through the smashed roof. It's laughing maniacally now, the same laughter Devon had heard when the thing tried to run him and Rolfe off the road.

Devon concentrates on Flo's steering wheel. With his mind he wrests control of it from the creature who's driving, managing to turn the wheel abruptly. The car swerves out of the truck's path and off the road into a grassy embankment. It comes to a resounding thud against a tree.

"Hope you remembered to buckle up," Devon calls, jumping off the roof of the car and opening the passenger-side door.

Cecily had, indeed: she's dazed, but unhurt.

"Cecily, get out," Devon commands, unhooking her seat belt. Meanwhile the demon, still dressed in DJ's clothes but looking like its true self – scaly, reptilian, hissing smoke through its flaring nostrils – has jumped out of the other side. It laughs at them over the hood of the car.

Cecily blinks. "Devon – that *thing*. . ."

"Get out!" he commands again, and she does, running into the woods on the side of the road just as the demon leaps, landing on Devon, pushing him down into the mud.

You should have just opened that door, the creature hisses in Devon's mind. *You should have just let them out. Such power you'd have then. . .*

"I have power *now*," Devon bellows, thrusting the thing off him. It flies through the air, landing on its back not far from Cecily, splashing her with mud. She screams.

"I'm stronger than you," Devon shouts at it, but it pays him no heed, getting back on its feet and leaping again, its face now a snoutful of fangs.

You will be ours, the demon tells him. *You will come over to our side.*

"A doubtful scenario, I think," Devon cries, hauling off and socking the thing smack in the face. It recovers quickly, its long arms swinging at him. Talons make contact with his skin, cutting him across his face.

"Listen, ugly," he cracks, "you keep this up and you're gonna really start hurting my feelings." Without even knowing he can do it, Devon throws himself feet first into the thing's belly, toppling it over. It roars in pain.

He stands over it. "I send you *back* to your Hellhole," he utters in a voice that seems alien — a deep, strong, adult voice. The thing on the ground quivers, then screams. Suddenly it's whisked away, as if by some giant unseen vacuum, across the night sky.

Devon just stands there, breathing heavily, in and out, for several seconds.

"Devon?" comes Cecily's little voice behind him.

"Are you OK?" he asks, turning to her.

"Am *I* OK?" She touches the wound on Devon's cheek, which stretches across the bridge of his nose. "Are *you* OK?"

He flinches a little at her touch, then reaches up to examine the wound himself. "Damn thing drew blood," he snarls. "I hate that."

"Devon, what the hell is happening?"

She begins to cry. And shake uncontrollably. He wraps his arms around her.

"It's OK, Cecily. It's gone."

She looks up at him. "I'm sorry I didn't believe you. I'm sorry for everything. I'll believe *anything* you say now."

He smiles a little, kissing her forehead.

"Oh, Devon," she cries. "It's like I always knew something would happen. Something would force the truth to come out." She manages a small laugh. "Not that I could have expected anything quite like this. But I knew *something* – something was out there."

"It's OK," he soothes her.

She buries her face against his chest. "Ever since I was little, I've known it. I've seen the lights in the tower, too, Devon. I've heard the sounds, seen the figures, felt the presences. All of my mother's reassurances couldn't push away the truth."

"Look, we can talk more later. Right now we've got to get back into town." Devon looks over at the Camaro with its fender mangled up against the tree. "Poor Flo. Poor DJ."

"Yeah," agrees Cecily. "Who's gonna tell him?"

Devon realizes something. "You know, if that stinking thing was masquerading as DJ, then where's the real one?"

Cecily looks at him dumbstruck.

"Where did you meet up with ugly?" Devon asks.

"At Stormy Harbor. I went down there looking for you. I saw DJ sitting in his car – what I *thought* was DJ anyway. A few minutes later you showed up."

Devon nods. "Then the real DJ is probably back there somewhere, and he may be hurt. We've got to go find him."

They look at each other. True enough – but just how are they going to get there? They're at least a couple miles out of town.

"I'm pretty sure I won't be able to repeat the stunt I pulled getting here," Devon says.

Cecily looks over at Flo. "Think she's still drivable?"

"Maybe." He grins sheepishly. "But Cecily, even if she is, I don't know how . . . to. . ."

She smirks. "Oh, so you can fight off demons but you don't know how to drive a car? Well, I didn't necessarily mean *you*, Indiana Jones. I'm not just a helpless female cowering in the woods, you know."

She slides in behind the wheel. "Jeez, the thing sure left a stink in here," she says, scrunching up her face. She turns the ignition. The engine kicks in. "Ah," she says, grinning. "Flo's still got some life left in her."

Devon gets in the passenger side, careful of the glass showered all over the interior. "But you're too young to have a driver's license," he says.

"For a kid who can wrestle down demons, you're pretty naive, Devon." She puts the car in reverse, backs it up on to the shoulder of the road. "DJ taught me a long time ago. And when you're Cecily Crandall, the police don't pull you over."

She speeds back into town, skidding into the parking lot of Stormy Harbor. "He was parked over there," Cecily says, pointing to the far end of the lot.

Sure enough, when they investigate, they find DJ, behind a clump of bushes, just in his underwear, bound and gagged and shivering – but otherwise OK.

They untie him.

"You should've seen it, man," he says as soon as the gag is removed. "Claws and fangs—"

"We know, DJ," Cecily says.

"You OK, buddy?" Devon asks.

The other boy realizes his near-nakedness in front of Cecily. "Uh, Devon," he murmurs.

Devon doffs his coat and throws it to DJ, who speedily wraps himself in it.

"Yeah, I'm OK," he says. "But that thing, man. It took my *car*."

Devon looks at Cecily. "You fill him in, OK? I've got to get back up to Ravenscliff."

She nods, helping DJ stand.

"Hey, man," DJ says, looking at Devon's bloody face. "What happened to you?"

"Tell you later. Just be on your guard, OK? Things may not be as they seem. Don't trust *anybody*." He winks at Cecily. "See ya at the big house."

He bounds off toward the road. Within minutes he's at the cliffside staircase. He takes three steps at a time. He emerges into the cemetery cautious, feeling quite certain Jackson Muir will be once again standing in the tall grass. But there's nothing there except the moonlight on the gravestones. He passes the flat stone marked "Clarissa" and realizes he hadn't had a chance to ask Rolfe about that name, or about the marker called "Devon." There's so much he hadn't had a chance to ask, so much he still doesn't understand.

But he knows one thing: their time grows short to save Alexander Muir.

He rushes into the foyer, out of breath. Ahead of him in the parlor he can see Mrs Crandall sitting in her chair in front of the fire, with Rolfe Montaigne standing over her.

They both look up at him as he enters.

"Devon!" Rolfe exclaims. "What happened to you?"

"I – had a little run-in," he says, sitting down on the couch.

"Dear God," Mrs Crandall is saying, on her feet now, looking at the boy's face. "Simon!"

The servant seems to appear from nowhere at the door to the parlor.

"Bring me a bowl of warm water, a cloth, some disinfectant, and some bandages. Quickly!"

She stoops down in front of Devon, inspecting his wound. "It's not too deep," she says. "If we clean it, bandage it, and keep using vitamin E, it'll heal quickly and not leave a scar."

Rolfe is looking down at him intently.

"Did you tell her?" Devon asks. "Did you tell her about Alexander?"

"Yes, he told me," Mrs Crandall says, but Devon can't tell what emotion lies behind her words. Anger? Gratitude? Indifference?

Simon has arrived with the first aid. Mrs Crandall takes the cloth, dampens it, and begins patting Devon's face. "Does it hurt, Devon?" she asks.

"A little."

He sits there and allows her to tend to him. It's a side of her he hasn't seen before: caring, nurturing, compassionate.

Dare he say *maternal*?

And the thought strikes him, as Mrs Crandall tenderly treats his wound, gently reassuring him — *could this woman be my mother?*

The idea startles him. It would make sense — more sense than her husband being his father. His powers, inherited through her, through Horatio Muir. After all, Mrs Crandall is Nightwing — just like him.

That's why my father sent me here. Because Mrs Crandall is my mother!

And then — Cecily — Cecily really is my sister!

He tries to get the Voice to confirm the idea — to tell him whether it's true or not. But the Voice remains stubbornly silent.

Devon looks at Mrs Crandall as she sits back to observe his bandaged face. "There, Devon. You'll be all right now."

Such concern in her voice. Is it possible, this crazy idea?

Cecily. . .

"You can fill me in later on the details of your little run-in, Devon," Rolfe says. "In the meantime, I think we've got things under control here for now."

Devon pushes aside the thoughts about Mrs Crandall. They're too much to consider right now. Way too much. He'd rather think about demons and Jackson Muir masquerading as that crazy clown than think about Cecily being his sister.

"So," he asks. "Alexander's OK?"

"We just came downstairs from talking with him," Rolfe says. "He's spitting mad, but he's OK."

Mrs Crandall has stood, resuming her more usual air of chilly grandeur. "Rolfe has some silly idea that watching television is dangerous for Alexander. While I agree about the harmfulness of TV, I think we're talking about different things."

"*Very* different," Devon says.

"Amanda *did*, however, see the wisdom of removing the televisions from both the playroom and Alexander's bedroom," Rolfe says.

Mrs Crandall looks at him icily. "And now that all that is settled, I thank you for your concern, Rolfe, and I'll show you to the door."

"Wait," Devon says, standing up. "That's not the end of it. I mean, Jackson Muir is still out there. He's not going to go away so easily."

Mrs Crandall sighs. "Devon, this talk about Jackson Muir has gone far enough."

Devon looks over at Rolfe. "Is she still denying it? Even after everything you told her?"

"I'm not denying anything, Devon," she says coldly. "There are just things I will *not* have discussed in this house. And certainly not with Mr Montaigne present."

Rolfe laughs. "You're an ostrich, Amanda. As vain and as obtuse." He's putting his coat back on. "You have three young lives under your care. Think about their safety, if not your own."

She bristles. "If I were *you*, Mr Montaigne, I wouldn't lecture *anyone* about putting young lives in jeopardy."

What Devon sees next startles him, causes him to gasp: Rolfe, in a sudden rage, bounds toward Mrs Crandall, gets right up in her face. She shrinks back in fear, and there's a part of Devon that thoroughly enjoys seeing her composure broken, even for a moment.

"I've told you this before, Amanda, and I'll tell you this again," Rolfe seethes. "I will find a way to prove my innocence – and then I'll make you pay dearly for the five years you stole out of my life."

"Get *out*," she spits.

Rolfe turns to Devon. "Remember," he says, "you're stronger than any of them."

With that, he turns and stalks out of the house, slamming the door behind him.

The seconds after Rolfe leaves feel like minutes – long, drawn-out minutes. Devon at first says nothing, then finally ventures over to the woman glaring out of the windows at the sea.

"Mrs Crandall?"

"What is it?"

"I don't want you to be angry with me. I want you to *under-stand*."

She turns to face him. "What am I to understand?"

"Rolfe told me about this family's legacy. I know about the Nightwing."

"He had no right."

Devon sighs. "Maybe not. But he did. So I know that these

things that have been happening aren't just my imagination."

"Listen to me, Devon. I am your guardian." She smiles. "Lower case. Guardian with a small 'g.' And with the legal admonition to watch out for your welfare. I am telling you only what you need to know. Anything else you must simply trust me about."

She pulls herself up to her full height, looking down at him. "And I assure you that no matter what frightens you in this house, *nothing* will hurt you. I have seen to that."

"That's what you always told *me*, Mother," comes the voice of her daughter.

They both turn. Cecily stands in the doorway.

"But it's not *true*," she says calmly, never taking her eyes from her mother. She walks into the parlor, approaching them. "I was almost *killed* earlier tonight. If it wasn't for Devon, I'd be dead."

"*Killed!*" Mrs Crandall grasps her daughter's face in both her hands. "Cecily! Are you all right?"

"I told you, thanks to Devon."

Mrs Crandall looks over at her young ward. "Devon. . ."

He pats his bandages. "You never asked how I got the wound. It was as if you didn't want to know."

She seems as if she might break then – as if her body is on the verge of trembling, collapsing, her emotions ready to shatter into uncontrollable tears. But she doesn't, and Devon marvels at the woman's control. He can see her struggle quite clearly, the yearning to surrender – but he can also see the invincibility that ultimately forbids it. She takes hold of the back of her chair to steady herself, drawing in and then exhaling a very long breath.

"Long ago," she says, "terrible things happened in this house. Maybe your friend Rolfe told you about them. Whether he did or not, it suffices for me to remember them only in their terror, not in their specifics." She looks off toward the fire. "Why do you think my brother wanders the globe? Why do you think my mother cannot bear to leave her room? Because they are trying, each in their way, to cope with the past. As I am. As I must raise the three of you to do."

Devon walks up to face her plainly. "But how can we do that if we don't know what that past *is*? Especially *me*, Mrs Crandall. I'm not a Muir. I never even knew such a place as Ravenscliff existed until a *month* ago. And suddenly here I am, dropped down in the middle of it, and you expect me not to ask questions, not to demand answers!"

She looks at him sadly. "I know it's difficult, Devon. But that's all I can say for now."

"No, you can say something else," Devon says. "You can tell me what you know of my parents. My *real* parents. You can tell me who I am and how I fit into all of this."

She sighs. "I've *told* you, Devon. I can't help you there. I don't know. . ."

"You *knew* my father. He lived here under the name Thaddeus Underwood. He was a Guardian here, teaching you and your brother in the art of the Nightwing."

"The Nightwing?" Cecily asks.

Devon keeps interrogating her mother. "Why did my father change his name? Why did he take me to New York to raise me?"

Mrs Crandall claps her hands to her ears. "I don't know, Devon! Stop badgering me with these questions. I don't know why he changed his name! I had no contact with him after he left Ravenscliff. I have no idea why he moved to New York or why he adopted you or why he sent you here!"

The face nearly cracks, but she pulls back again. She closes her eyes, sighing heavily, dropping her hands again to the back of the chair for support.

"Mother," Cecily says, near tears, "I'm frightened."

Devon sees the maternal love emanate from Mrs Crandall's eyes. She lets go of the chair, approaches Cecily, clutches her daughter to her bosom. Devon watches them, and feels very alone. He's never known a mother's love. As a young boy he used to dream about his mother. She was an angel, with golden hair and a long flowing white dress. She was the most beautiful creature he'd ever seen, lithe and lovely and ethereal. In his dreams, she'd sing to him, and hold him the way Mrs Crandall now holds Cecily.

If she's my mother, he thinks sadly, *she has no interest in consoling me*.

Mrs Crandall takes Cecily's cheeks in her hands again, looking at her. "I promise you, Cecily, as I promised you when you were a little girl. I will not allow anything in this house to harm you. I promise you I will redouble my efforts in keeping you safe."

Redouble her efforts? Devon wonders what she could mean by that.

"But Mother," Cecily adds, "it wasn't in this house that I was almost killed. It was on the village road."

Mrs Crandall lets her go. She draws herself up again. "Let us speak no more of it. No more mention of such things in this house."

"But, Mrs Crandall—" Devon insists.

She holds up a hand to silence him. "That's my final word, Devon. I don't know why such things are happening again, but I will do my best to put an end to them."

Devon considers revealing his powers to her – after all, that might help explain the *why* – but for some reason the Voice cautions him. It might be wise to keep one last card up his sleeve in dealing with her.

But she has another hand to deal herself. She levels her gaze at Devon. "One other instruction," she tells him. "One that I expect to be followed completely. Under no circumstance are you to have any further interaction with Rolfe Montaigne. As your guardian, I forbid it. Is that understood?"

"Mrs Crandall—"

"*Is that understood?*"

It's no use fighting her here and now. "Yes, ma'am, it's understood."

"Classic example of major denial," Cecily comments after her mother has swept out of the room.

Devon has filled her in briefly about what he's learned from Rolfe, as much about the Nightwing and the demons and the Hellholes as he can in the space of a few minutes.

"No doubt about it," he agrees. "But if her father died fighting Jackson Muir in the Hellhole, I guess maybe I can understand her reluctance to bring it all up again."

"*I* can't, not if it puts us in danger." Cecily sits down in front of the fire. "Like, how can I concentrate on my algebra homework *now?*"

Devon grins. "Oh yeah. Forgot about that."

They get out their books and work their way through a few problems. But Cecily's right: it's not easy to concentrate.

"You know what really makes me wonder?" Devon asks suddenly. "How she said she'd redouble her efforts."

"Yeah," Cecily says. "She said she'd do her best to put an end to all this." A thought seems to strike her. "Do you think my mother still has the powers of the Nightwing?"

Devon shrugs. "Rolfe told me the family renounced

all their powers, their whole Nightwing heritage."

"We've got to learn more about all this," Cecily says.

Devon nods. "I've *got* to talk with Rolfe again. There's so much I still need to know."

"Mother will *atomize* you if she finds out."

He smirks. "Or maybe cast a spell on me."

"Turn you into a toad. Hey, can you do that?"

He laughs. "Never tried. And don't think I will right now either." He considers something. "You know, if I can't get to Rolfe, I've got to get back into the East Wing. There are books there."

She shudders. "Yeah, and that *door*."

"And the portrait that looks like me."

It's all too confusing. They manage to get through their homework and wolf down a little dinner: Simon's prepared roast ham and butternut squash. After that, Cecily heads off to bed, though she admits she isn't likely to sleep much.

She goes to kiss Devon goodnight. He stops her.

"What?" she asks, bewildered.

"It's just . . . there's too much weirdness right now," he says.

"I know what you're thinking, Devon," she tells him, rolling her eyes.

He looks at her. "Well, you gotta wonder about it."

She frowns. "What does that Voice thing of yours say about it? Wouldn't that *tell* you if we were brother and sister?"

"It doesn't *always* tell me stuff. I think it only speaks up when it thinks I can handle it."

She sighs. "Well, we don't look *anything* alike." She winks. "Anyway, thanks for saving me earlier, Spider-Man."

Devon watches her close her door. He wishes he could have kissed her. In the midst of all this craziness, he admits to himself that he's really started liking her. A lot. He's never felt this way about a girl before. He and Suze might have held hands in the movies, but they were more like buds than boyfriend-girlfriend. They were twelve, thirteen. Except for the hand-holding, everything he did with Suze he could have done with Tommy. He remembers Dad saying that things would start changing now that he was fourteen. He'd start to feel differently. He'd see girls in a whole new way.

Well, they have, and he does.

He knows he won't be able to sleep right away. He decides to pay a visit to Alexander who, sulking about the lack of TV, had refused to come down for dinner.

He's not in the playroom. Not in his room either. Devon worries at first that the boy might be in East Wing, but the Voice tells him otherwise.

Try the basement, it says.

He spies Alexander in the cold, damp darkness, behind a forlorn dressmaker's dummy and several trunks plastered with stickers from foreign countries. The boy is crying.

"Hey," Devon says gently, approaching him.

Alexander doesn't look up. In the dim light from the overhead bulb, Devon makes out that the boy is holding something – *cradling* it, in fact – in his lap. Devon's eyes strain to make out what it is, and then he sees.

It's a television set. An old, vintage 1970 portable set, probably black and white. Devon makes out the reason for Alexander's tears. The television's cord snakes off along the floor like the tail of a dead animal, ending in a splay of wires. Its plug had been snipped off long ago, for forgotten reasons.

Except, as Devon suddenly remembers, there was another time in this house when the television proved a danger to little boys. . .

He sits down beside Alexander and puts his arm around

the chubby kid's shoulder. He feels terribly sad for the boy, as if he were some addict needing a fix, only to find his supply shut off. The analogy, he realizes, isn't far from accurate.

"It's OK, buddy," Devon whispers. "It's going to be OK."

"No, it's not," Alexander whimpers in a soft, pathetic little voice. "It's never going to be OK again. They took away all the TVs and this one is broke."

"It's for your own good," Devon tells him. "I know that's easy for me to say, but it's true."

The boy stiffens. "Yeah, that's what adults are always telling me. That it's for my own good. They say they know I don't understand, but it's for the best. Except it never feels that way. It never *feels* for the best."

"What do you mean, Alexander?"

The little boy hugs the television set. "I remember my father saying I couldn't see my mother any more, that it was for the best. But it felt *yucky*. I haven't seen her since." He heaves a little, catching his breath. "Then my father said I couldn't stay with him any more, that sending me away to school was for my *own good*. But I *hated* that place. Then, even there, the headmaster sent me away, cuz he said it was *for the best*."

Devon smiles sadly. "And it hasn't turned out that way, huh?"

Alexander shakes his head. He starts crying again.

Devon pulls the boy in close to him. This was a different Alexander Muir, down here in the damp shadows of the basement. Away from the ghosts, away from his own demons, the boy is just what he is: a small, terrified, lonely eight year old.

"Alexander," Devon tells him, "let me tell you something. I can relate to a lot of what you say. They took me away from my mother, too. I never knew her. I used to look at other boys with their mothers and wish I had one, real bad. You know, like the mothers on television. I always wanted a mother who would make me a lunch and pick me up after school and do all that sort of stuff."

The boy just sniffles against Devon's chest.

"But, see, I was lucky in one regard. I had a really good dad. He taught me something really important, and that's that you've got to let kids know they're loved. And safe. And all that."

"My father never did that for me," Alexander says.

"Hey, I'm sure your dad loves you a lot. He's just busy." Devon looks down at the top of the boy's blonde head. His hair is matted, sweaty. "But maybe *we* can hang out, Alexander. Maybe we can be friends after all."

Alexander caresses the television set in his lap. "But I found a new father," he says quietly, dreamily.

"No, Alexander. He wasn't real. He wasn't a father at all."

The boy pulls his head away from Devon's chest to glare up at him. "He was, too! What do you know? Major Musick was the best friend I ever had!"

"Listen to me, Alexander. Major Musick is *bad*. He wants to hurt you. And me. And everyone in this house." Devon pauses. "But I won't let him."

The boy makes a face, as if he might cry again. Instead, he just yanks the cord up to his lap and fingers the loose wires where the plug once was.

"Come on," Alexander says gently. "Let's go up to your room and talk some more. It's cold down here."

The boy says nothing, but puts the TV down on the concrete floor and follows Devon up the stairs. Once in bed, Alexander merely listens as Devon sits on the edge and describes what they might do the next day: take a walk along the cliff, go into town, play some video games. When Devon notices the boy's eyelids getting heavy, he tells him to sleep well, that he's safe now. And when he leans across to the switch off the light, Alexander Muir reaches up and embraces him, taking Devon by surprise.

Devon hugs him back.

The house settles into an uneasy quiet over the next few days, but Devon doesn't trust it. He knows Jackson Muir is just biding his time.

At school, DJ looks at him with even more awe. Devon swears his friend to secrecy, and feels confident he can trust him.

They whisper outside the cafeteria. "Man, this is some truly bizarreness going down," DJ says. "What's up with that thing that took my car? What's it got against you?"

"I can't explain everything now, and certainly not here." Devon looks around as kids pass by in the corridor, many of them looking over at him. He's already got a reputation as a mystery man, the bandage across the middle of his face only adding to that image. "Just be on guard, OK?"

"No problem there, dude. But why do you think it didn't just take me out? You know, instead of going to the trouble of tying me up and stealing my clothes?"

"As near as I can figure, it probably wants to keep its options open. You're my friend. It may want to disguise itself as you again. That's why I'm telling you to be on guard."

DJ shakes his head. "Freaky, man."

"To say the least."

He looks over at Devon. "Look. I know you and Cecily like each other. I'm not gonna try and come between you or anything. Just — just don't let any of this get to her, you know?"

Devon smiles wanly. "Believe me, I'm trying." He sighs. "Hey, I'm sorry about Flo."

DJ shrugs. "Mostly fender damage. The glass tops are the biggest hassle."

"I'll find a way to pay to replace them."

"Don't worry about it, man. I got some friends down at Sonny's Autobody. They can hunt me down some new ones. I was thinking of getting all the glass tinted anyway."

Devon smiles. "You're a good friend, Deej. There's got to be some kind of spell a Nightwing uses to protect his friends. I promise I'll look into it."

DJ gives him a jaunty salute. "Rock on."

But how can he look into *anything* if Mrs Crandall keeps him away from Rolfe? He had to trust that Rolfe would find a way to get in contact with him. And in the meantime, he had to find a way into the East Wing.

He keeps his promise to Alexander. For the next few days they do hang out. The boy, while quiet, seems to be coming around, no longer the nasty little precocious brat he was when Devon first met him. Devon takes him into town, buys him a handful of comic books at Adams' Pharmacy. They carve jack o'lanterns from the pumpkins Simon brought in from the garden, and Devon promises to take the boy trick-or-treating in the village on Halloween, something Alexander has never done in his life.

And every night Devon talks with him before he goes to sleep, sitting on the side of Alexander's bed like Dad used to do with Devon.

"Can I ask you something?" Alexander says, after Devon has stood, getting ready to turn out the light.

Devon looks down at him. "Sure."

"You're not going to go away or anything on me, are you?"

Devon smiles. "No way, buddy," he assures the boy. "I'm not going anywhere."

By the fourth day – with things still quiet and peaceful and Alexander blossoming more and more – Devon begins to wonder if maybe he was wrong. Maybe, in fact, the ditching of the television sets *did* stop the Madman in his ghostly tracks, and the whole nightmare is over.

Yet it *can't* be, Devon reasons: Jackson didn't need a dumb old TV screen to appear to them. Still, Devon thinks, maybe the malevolent Nightwing was frustrated in not being able to claim Alexander, and so he'd retreated.

Dream on, the Voice tells him.

Devon pulls back the sheets to his bed and slips inside, telling himself he should really be trying to memorize those English kings for his history quiz tomorrow, not attempting to figure out the motives and machinations of Jackson Muir. He closes his eyes. "William the First," he whispers to himself. "William the Second. Henry the First. Stephen. . ."

He's asleep before he can get to the Plantagenets. He dreams of the books in the East Wing. He's sitting before a fire, with the books piled high beside him.

"Of these enchanters," Devon is reading aloud, "the most noble, powerful, and feared have always been the Sorcerers of the Order of the Nightwing. Only the Nightwing have discovered the secret of how to open the Portals between this world and the one below. For nearly three thousand years, the Nightwing have been a proud and honorable clan, using their powers for good. They have jealously guarded the secret of the Portals, which, in common parlance, have come to be known as Hellholes."

"Devon," comes a voice.

He looks up from the book in his lap. In the swirling distance is a woman. Who she is, he's not quite sure, but she's definitely familiar. . .

"Devon," she calls again.

"Who are you?" he asks.

But she doesn't answer. She just beckons to him.

Is it Emily Muir?

"Devon," she calls again.

Or the spirit he saw in the cemetery . . . the woman crying over that mysterious grave. . .

"Devon."

"Who are you?"

"I am your mother, Devon."

He wakes up with a start. His heart thuds in his chest.

My mother.

Yet even awake he can still hear the woman calling his name in the night — soft and almost musical. The wind has risen outside, and it whistles through the eaves. Just below it, the lilting voice of the woman from his dream continues to call to him.

"Devon . . . Devon. . ."

He sits up. Yes, it's there, all right. He's not imagining it.

"Devon. . ."

He throws off the blankets and places his feet against the floor.

"*Devvonnn. . .*"

Like music.

It's coming from outside.

He pads across the floor to the window. Through the gauzy curtains he can see the light burning once again in the tower room. He unlatches the window and pushes it open.

There, looking back at him from the open tower window, is a woman — and she is indeed calling his name.

12
The Demon's Grave

Devon stares over at her, just as the light goes out behind her, and she disappears.

There's a soft knock at his door.

"Who – who is it?" he asks.

"Cecily."

He opens the door. She's in her nightgown.

"I heard someone calling you," she tells him.

"You heard it too," he says.

She nods. "I'm not going to just pretend I don't see and hear things in this house any more. I couldn't sleep – I haven't been able to sleep since that thing in the car – and I was *certain* I heard a woman's voice calling your name."

Devon nods, looking back out his window. "It was coming from the tower. I saw her."

"Who was it?"

"I don't know."

"What did she look like?"

"It was hard to tell. Just a woman – in white, I think. Long blonde – or maybe gray – hair."

"It must have been *Emily Muir*," Cecily reasons. "She's

trying to warn you about Jackson."

"Possibly." It's as good a scenario as any, but Devon's not sure. "I saw someone in the tower when I went in there before. I'm sure it was a woman." He sighs. "But investigating the tower again won't do us any good. It'll either be locked or else Simon will take a pick-axe to the back of my head."

"What are you going to do?"

"Nothing. Until I can learn more about this Nightwing stuff, I'm through investigating. Because I have a feeling, Cecily, that once I have the Knowledge, no one will be able to hide anything from me ever again."

Her eyes twinkle. "Do you mind if I kiss you goodnight, Mr Wizard?"

He looks at her. He's missed kissing her. Is this what falling in love feels like? That in spite of everything else, you can still feel anxious and flushed taking a certain person into your arms? He grins, and Cecily moves into his embrace. They do kiss, for several minutes, until the wind knocks a shutter loose, startling them.

"You'd better go back to your room," Devon tells her huskily.

She looks into his eyes dreamily. "Why is that, Devon?"

He smiles awkwardly. "Because I think our budding hormones are itching to do some damage, and I'm just trying to contain the fallout."

Cecily giggles. "Haven't you ever been in love before, Devon?"

He shakes his head. "Not really. Have you?"

"Oh, sure." She's trying to seem far more worldly than Devon. "Freshman year I was in love with an older guy."

"Who? Joey Potts?"

Cecily laughs. "Oh, Devon. Really, now. Are you still jealous of him?"

He can feel himself start to seethe. "Tell me, Cecily. Did you have a crush on him?"

She shrugs. "Does it matter? He's *far* too old for me to date. He's *nineteen*."

"Yeah. And he's a cop." Devon folds his arms across his chest. "He should know better than to flirt with a fourteen year old."

Cecily purrs up against him. "But *you*, Devon, on the other hand, are exactly my age."

He looks at her. *And maybe I'm your brother, too*, he thinks. That, more than anything else, is what caused him to push her away, however gently. It can't be true: If it was, wouldn't the Voice have warned him against falling for Cecily? The idea that they're brother and sister is simply crazy, impossible.

But after Cecily kisses him goodnight and heads back to her room, Devon lies awake for a long time, rolling the possibility over and over in his mind. "Crazy," he mumbles, drifting off to sleep. "Impossible."

That night he dreams of Joey Potts caught in a private Hellhole designed just for him. It actually gives Devon the best night's rest he's had in weeks.

The next day he even aces his history quiz, and for the first time, has a truly good day in school. He feels caught up. He feels he fits in. Even the seniors nod in the corridor to him. In the caf, Jessica Milardo, one of the cheerleaders, invites Devon and the gang to a Halloween party at her house later in the week. DJ agrees to drive; he's getting Flo's glass tops replaced this afternoon.

"What are you going as?" Ana asks Cecily.

"I don't know, but it won't be anything geeky like I'm sure you'll wear."

"I'm going as a harem girl," Ana sniffs. "I hardly think *that'll* be geeky."

Cecily smirks. "Harem girl? Cheerleader? And the difference between them is. . .?"

Marcus snorts. "You're supposed to go dressed as something *scary*."

"Then just go as you are then," DJ cracks.

Marcus lands a mock blow to DJ's gut. "The scariest thing is driving over there with *you*."

Oh, no, Devon thinks, allowing a small smile to play with his lips. *There are a lot scarier things than that.*

"What are *you* going as, Devon?" Cecily asks.

"Hadn't really given it much thought," Devon says.

"I know just the place we can look for ideas," she tells him.

When they get back to Ravenscliff, they head up to the attic — one place in the house Devon's never been. There's a narrow staircase leading up from a small door at the end of the upstairs corridor. Inside it's warm and stale, with Devon choking back dust. Parting cobwebs, Cecily leads him to a couple of old trunks against a far wall. "The Muirs have always been such pack rats," she says. "They never threw away *anything*. We're sure to find costumes in here."

They open the first trunk, and are nearly knocked over by the heavy odor of mothballs. Inside they find women's clothes: late nineteenth-century dresses, bonnets, corsets, gloves. In the next trunk, there are military uniforms from World War II.

"I could go as a Newport belle and you as her Army captain suitor," Cecily gushes, batting her eyelashes ridiculously.

Devon grimaces. He's never much liked playing war; he hated GI Joe as a kid. He wonders if that has something to do with his Nightwing blood: maybe the Sorcerers of the Order of the Nightwing only fought to defend themselves, always in the cause of good. *Damn*, he needs to read those books.

As Cecily pulls out lacy dresses and pantaloons, holding them up against her, Devon wanders through the attic. Against the far wall, just below where the roof comes to a point, he spies an armoire.

Look inside, the Voice tells him.

He approaches it. He expects the knob to be hot, but it isn't. He turns it, and peers inside the armoire.

There are several dark suits hanging there. The shoulders look a little mildewed. He touches one, feels along the length of the material. *It's a cape*, he realizes.

He takes a hold of the hanger and lifts the cape out. Hanging with it are black wool pants striped up the side in blue. The cape is lined with red satin. Looking back into the armoire he spots tall black leather boots, still shiny under the blotches of mildew.

"What's that?" Cecily asks, coming up behind him.

"My costume," he tells her.

"But what is it?"

He lifts the cape and feels it between his fingers. "It's the ceremonial dress of the Nightwing," he says, not knowing *how* he knows this, but certain it's the truth. "It's what *I'm* going to wear."

They spend the rest of the evening cleaning the clothes. Devon buffs the boots to a high polish. Cecily has to pin the dress she's chosen to make it fit, but Devon's suit could have been tailor-made for him. Whose suit could it have been? Edward Muir's? Or did it belong to Mrs Crandall's father when he was a boy? Or — Devon's hands tremble just a bit thinking it — might it have been worn by Jackson Muir himself?

He fits into the pants and white lace-up shirt perfectly, and the boots slide on with ease.

The cape is the *pièce de résistance*, and he looks at himself in the mirror with a slightly embarrassing sense of awe.

"It's you," Cecily assesses.

Yes, Devon thinks. *It is.*

After school the next day, he tells Cecily he's got to see Rolfe. Finding the costume had cinched it for him. "I've *got* to know about my heritage," he says. "It's *time*. I need to learn the truth of the Nightwing."

"But Devon, the danger's passed. Alexander is OK."

He shakes his head forcefully. "Cecily, I don't believe for a minute that Jackson's gone for good. He's just biding his time."

She sighs. "I'm past the point of doubting you, Devon."

"Cover for me?" he asks. Cecily nods. He sneaks off down the cliffside staircase and hurries into town.

He recognizes Roxanne at the front desk at Fibber McGee's. "Good afternoon, Mr March," she says, her voice warm like syrup.

"Hi," he says. Her golden eyes seem to glow. Devon wonders exactly what her story is: Rolfe had hinted she was something special. And not just on account of her awesome body, which is right now encased in a form-fitting gold satin dress. Devon's mouth goes a little dry. "Is . . . is Rolfe here?"

"He's at the house," she tells him.

Devon sighs. It's too far to walk.

"That doesn't matter, not to you," Roxanne says.

He looks at her oddly. "What do you mean, it doesn't matter?"

She smiles. Her eyes glow. "That it's too far to walk."

Devon's astounded. "How — how did you know I was thinking that?"

Roxanne laughs gently. "Just click your heels, Devon March," she says, the cadence of the islands in her voice. "Isn't that how the fairy tale goes in your culture? Click your heels three times and you will go where you want to go."

He doesn't know what to think. But he knows he can do it. He knows he has the power. He remembers how he'd leapt on to DJ's car as the demon drove it off down the road. Rolfe's house was much farther away — three, four miles — but that doesn't matter.

"Not to you, Devon March," Roxanne repeats.

He looks up at her. She smiles. Then he closes his eyes.

When he opens them he's in Rolfe's den, the late afternoon sunlight slanting through the glass. Rolfe's sitting in a wing chair with a book in his lap. He looks up at Devon without much surprise.

"Getting the hang of this sorcery stuff, huh?"

Devon blinks. "Guess so," he says, then looks down at himself, dissolving into laughter, "OK, that was *totally* awesome!"

"I was wondering when you'd pop by," Rolfe says, closing the book. "I figured sooner or later you'd appear."

"Can I do that all the time?" Devon asks excitedly. "Heck, I won't need to get my driver's license!"

Rolfe smiles. "I'd still sign up with the Big-A Driving School over in Newport if I were you. Leaping around through time and space isn't exactly the best way to take a girl out on a date."

"Oh, I don't know," Devon says, grinning. "I think Cecily would be mighty impressed."

Rolfe raises his eyebrows. "That's just it, Devon. It's not about impressing anyone."

Devon remembers how embarrassed he was when he'd tried to show off his powers to Suze back home. He sighs, approaching Rolfe. "There's just so much I gotta know."

The older man nods. "That's why I've been reading through all of my father's books again. But words on paper simply can't tell you everything."

Devon sits down in the chair opposite Rolfe. "But can they tell me about what I am? I mean, what *is* a Nightwing? Like, is my blood the same as everyone else's? My bones?"

"You're the same as anybody else, Devon. Except you have something special."

"But how is it passed? Through the genes?"

Rolfe smiles. "Good question. I'm not sure science could explain it. But it *is* passed from generation to generation. And has been, for almost three thousand years."

Devon sits down opposite him, rapt. "The Nightwing have been around that long, huh?"

"Oh, yes. There's so much history in these books – ancient Rome, ancient Egypt, Celtic Britain, the Crusades, even Japan and China – the Nightwing sure got around."

"And no other warlock or sorcerer has powers as strong as a Nightwing?"

"That's right. The powers of the Nightwing are unique, though if one chooses, they may share their abilities with a spouse or a close comrade. Sometimes this is temporary; other times, with great ritual, the sharing of power is made permanent. Often, when a Nightwing marries, he or she will give their spouse the power as well."

"But Jackson didn't give Emily any powers," Devon says.

"Oh, no. He was far too selfish to do that. But his brother gave them to *his* wife."

"Old Mrs Muir? *She* has powers?"

Rolfe sighs. "She *did*. Remember that sorcery and magic was repudiated at Ravenscliff."

"Yeah. Now I'm the only one left with it. Which I think is too bad, because I don't know if I can stop Jackson all on my own."

Rolfe raises an eyebrow. "I don't think he's gone, either, Devon."

"If I'm going to fight him, I need to know everything about what I am." He pauses. "About the Nightwing."

Rolfe stands and walks over to his bookshelves as lightning crackles over the white caps of the crashing waves below. *Funny how it always starts to storm when I'm here*, Devon thinks.

"There are books here you should read," he says. "They'll tell you more than I can." He slides one in particular out from the rest. It's covered in gold leaf. Devon recognizes it from the room in the East Wing.

"*This*," Rolfe says, "is the sacred text of the Nightwing. It's called *The Book of Enlightenment*. It has been passed down for centuries, begun by Sargon the Great himself."

"Sargon the Great?"

Rolfe nods. "The first Nightwing of all. Nearly three thousand years ago."

Devon remembers suddenly the children's books in the basement at Ravenscliff. "I saw that name. Sargon the Great. It was a kid's book — Sargon and some other guys. Vortigar. Brutus. Wilhelm." Strange how he can remember the names. "And a girl, too. Diana."

Rolfe smiles. "All great Nightwing of the past. All part of your heritage, Devon." He laughs. "Those books were mine. I can remember reading about all their exploits. Brutus sailing to ancient Britannia, finding a Hellhole in the middle of the ocean, slaying the sea demons. . ."

"*Cool*," Devon says.

"But greatest of all was Sargon, the founder of the Nightwing. So great was he that the gods decreed that no Nightwing would again have such unlimited power until a hundred generations had passed." Rolfe looks at Devon solemnly. "The hundredth generation, I suspect, has arrived with *you*, Devon."

"Me?" he asks in a little voice.

"Actually, I'm certain of it. It's an event that has long been awaited. It was anticipated that the hundredth generation would be born sometime in the late twentieth century, and shortly before he left, Thaddeus told me he had received word that finally a child of that generation had arrived. He must have meant *you*."

"Me," Devon whispers.

"Great is your destiny," Rolfe says, handing him *The Book of Enlightenment*.

Devon feels the electricity in his hands as holds the book. It must weigh ten pounds. "I'm supposed to read all of this?" he asks.

"Eventually," Rolfe says. "But for now, since we're pressed for time — " He takes the book from Devon and settles it on to the table. "Tell me, Devon. Did Thaddeus ever wear a ring? With a white crystal embedded in it?"

Devon thinks. "No," he says. "I don't remember ever seeing one."

Rolfe nods. "It's not surprising. He was trying, for whatever reason, to keep all knowledge of your heritage from you. But every Guardian has a crystal. The Crystal of Knowledge. The Guardian's crystal holds within it all the ancient alchemy and history of the Nightwing. In its center is the knowledge that you need to learn. I remember Thaddeus wore his in a ring. But what he did with that ring after he left here, I don't know. "

Devon feels desperate. "So without his crystal, what can I do?"

Rolfe smiles. "You're forgetting, Devon. *My* father was also a Guardian."

"So he had a crystal ring, too?"

"Not a ring. My father was a gardener. He kept his crystal on a stone pedestal, surrounded by tall flowers. I remember as a very young boy being mesmerized by it. How it shone in the sun, the spectrum of color that reflected off it. I remember birds that would hover above it, seemingly caught by its magnetic pull. Butterflies, too. Hummingbirds."

He turns, withdrawing from a shelf a gleaming white crystal, about the shape and size of a baseball. Devon blinks, as if the crystal were emitting a powerful light. But it isn't: at least, not a light that he can physically see.

"The Guardian's crystal holds immense power," Rolfe is telling him. "It will give you the answers you seek. But it might be a little – well, *intense*."

Devon smirks. "So, in other words, it might sting a little."

"Or something," Rolfe says, smiling.

Devon laughs. "Like I should be afraid of a rock when I've had demons at my throat?" He holds out his hands. "Hand 'er over."

"Hold it in your hands, Devon," Rolfe says, placing the crystal into the boy's palms. "Hold it and *see*."

He feels its cold smoothness roll against his palms. He looks down at it. Nothing happens. "Is there any spell you have to say?" Devon asks. "Any incantation?"

"Not that I know of," Rolfe tells him.

"Too bad," Devon says. "I was hoping for a little hocus-pocus."

"Oh, I think you'll get it," Rolfe says.

Devon looks down again at the crystal. He's about to say something else when, all of a sudden, he's no longer there — no longer in the room, no longer in Misery Point, no longer anywhere he recognizes. Devon senses he's not even in the same time or place, maybe not even the same planet, as he was just moments ago. He's surrounded by blue light, just as was in the East Wing. And the man he'd seen there — the white-haired man in the flowing, star-studded purple robe — is speaking to him again:

"Know this, that the world is far older than anyone can imagine. Once, well before the coming of the Great Ice, the world was inhabited by Creatures of Light and Creatures of Darkness, battling each other for eons for dominion. Their masters were the elemental gods — of fire, of wind, of sea, of earth — omnipotent rulers of nature, neither good nor evil. It was left to their shifting, roiling creatures to forge the battle lines. As the ages passed, and the time of the Creatures fades farther and farther into the dim recesses of time, they have come to be known as angels and demons."

"Angels . . . and *demons?*" Devon asks, his voice small and faraway, not even seeming to come from his own throat.

"Yes, child." The man bears down upon him. He looks old, terribly old, but his eyes burn with a blue fire. "But these are not the creatures of your Sunday school catechism. Their shape was inconsistent, their powers various, and their allegiances to many and diverse gods and devils."

Devon pulls back. "But what do they have to do with me?"

The man's eyes grow wide. "Came destruction from the sky in the form of fiery rain, and then the Great Ice moved across the globe. The masters had grown tired of their battling Creatures, and banished them to a realm of lower vibration.

There, without the interference of the elemental gods, the demons quickly bested the angels, and created the kingdom of hell!"

"Hellholes," Devon whispers.

"Every culture that has evolved since has recognized the existence of this place in its religions and mythology – the underworld of the damned." The strange old man looms over Devon, his blue eyes blazing. "While the Demons there reign supreme, they still seethe in fury over their loss of Empire in the world above. The world of man."

"They want to get it back," Devon says.

"Yet as man evolved, some came in touch with the old elemental Knowledge. These mortals came to be known by many names in many cultures: wizards, medicine men, shamen, priests, witches, necromancers, alchemists. Through the old Knowledge, they were able to manufacture some semblance of the powers once wielded by the Creatures. Such powers they used for their own ends, both for good and for evil."

Devon feels himself being drawn away, but he struggles to listen to the last of the old man's words.

"Of these enchanters, the most noble, powerful and feared have always been the Sorcerers of the Order of the Nightwing. Only the Nightwing have discovered the secret of how to open the Portals between this world and the one below, the realm of the demons."

The blue light obliterates everything else. Devon feels himself being whisked as if down a long chute, every fiber of his body pulled by an unseen force, a giant vacuum through time and space. He can't catch his breath. He feels as if he might suffocate, and starts to panic—

And then he lands, with a thud, on a grassy plain.

He can breathe again. But he has no time to think: above

him roars an enormous demon, scaly and dripping wet. It raises its head on a long dinosaur neck, flaring its gigantic nostrils. It opens its mouth and belches a spear of fire.

"Slay it! Slay the dragon!" come the chants from the crowd watching him.

Devon realizes he has a sword in his hands. He thrusts it upward, into the belly of the demon. Scalding hot orange blood gushes out all over his hands. The crowd cheers.

The images around him disintegrate, like a television losing its picture.

Falling again.

"It's not difficult when the thing is as primitive as that," someone is saying to him.

Devon struggles to see and to regain his balance. He finds solid ground, steadying himself, breathing heavily. He opens his eyes. A man stands in front of him, someone he thinks he recognizes, but isn't sure.

"The ignorant ones are blundering and obvious," the man tells him. "Defeating them is no test of a Nightwing's strength."

Devon stares at the man. He's wearing a tunic and sandals, with long reddish hair and a beard. A sword is sheathed at his side.

"Can you not spy the demon now, child? Can you not see it? You, of my hundredth generation?"

"You're *Sargon*," Devon breathes in awe. "Sargon the Great."

"The epithet came only after the fact, after proving myself a sorcerer of dexterity, strength and cunning." Sargon levels his gaze at the boy, Devon shrinking back from its intensity. "What will they call *you*, Devon March? The Blind? The Muddled? The Daft?"

Devon stiffens. Great founder or not, there's no reason for him to get nasty. "What do you want me to *do?*"

"Send the demon back to hell," Sargon says plainly. "Can you not *see* it?"

Devon looks around. For the first time he takes in his surroundings. They're in a meadow that stretches off to the horizon for miles unbroken by any trees or structures. Only tall grass and wild flowers sway in the slight breeze. The sun is bright, the sky an unbroken dome of blue. Devon sees no demon, senses no filthy thing crawling in the grass. He concentrates, but feels no heat, no pressure. He turns his eyes back to Sargon.

"There's no demon here," he tells him.

The great master turns from him in contempt. "A Nightwing should never use only one or two of his senses at a time. You disappoint me, Devon March."

Devon stares after him. What does the guy want? *I'm new at this*, he thinks defensively.

Prove him wrong, comes the Voice. *He's daring you to prove him wrong.*

OK, Devon tells himself. *So don't just base it on sight or feel. How else can I detect a demon?*

He listens. No thrum, no vibration, no scuttling of hellish feet. He stands there in the meadow a few yards from Sargon, the first Nightwing of all, and hears no demon presence. None of his senses indicate one is nearby.

Except—

That smell.

They stink, Devon realizes. *That's right: they stink. And I can smell the putrid thing somewhere. But where?*

He looks around. He sees nothing. Nothing except the tall grass.

And Sargon the Great.

Suddenly Devon knows. Faster than he's ever moved before, he lunges at the great founder of the Order of the Nightwing, tackling him down into the grass. Sargon's eyes flash surprise at first, then fury. His eye sockets turn yellow, his fangs ripping through the flesh of his face. A claw twice the size of Devon's head grips him around the middle and lifts him high in the air, holding him over the demon's mouth.

"Let — me — go!" Devon commands.

But the thing simply tightens its grip around Devon's waist, drawing him down closer to its mouth. A whole snout of fangs has pushed through the mask of Sargon the Great, dripping with blood and saliva. Devon can smell its horrid breath, feel the heat of its body. In seconds his face is going to be lunch for the snapping jaws of the thing.

"Back!" comes a voice. "Back to your Hellhole!"

The demon twists under Devon, releasing its hold and shuddering uncontrollably. Devon topples to the grass, while his attacker is suddenly seized as if by an unseen giant hand and flung through the sky. It disappears into the air.

Devon looks up. Sargon the Great is standing over him.

"You passed your first test, Devon the Abecedarian. But failed your second."

"I tried to send him back," Devon tells him. "It's worked before."

"Your fear was too great. These things feed off fear. They become more powerful the more fearful you are."

Devon sits up, rubbing his elbow where he banged it falling back to the ground. If this is a dream or simply taking place inside his head, it's all too real. He looks over at Sargon.

"Listen, back home I'm fighting off a Nightwing gone bad

– what do you call them? An Apostate. Any suggestions on how I might —?"

But Sargon is gone. So is the field, the very ground Devon was sitting on. All there is is a strange gray mist, and as it gradually clears he begins to make out Rolfe's room, and realizes he's still standing there, in the same place, holding the crystal.

"Devon, are you OK?"

"Yeah, I – uh—"

But he's falling again. Back through time and space. He flails his arms wildly, trying to grab on to something, anything. For below him he can see a gaping hole in the earth, growing wider and larger and more terrifying as he approaches. He knows what is.

A Hellhole.

"Rolfe!" he screams. "Get the crystal out of my hands!"

He keeps plummeting toward the Hellhole. He hears a voice, laughing at him.

"*Why do you fear the Portal, Devon? It is the source of your power.*"

Everything goes black. He is no longer falling, merely floating. The temperature begins to rise. Thick humidity presses in around him.

Am I – am I in the Hellhole?

Laughter again. Raspy and insane.

"*Didn't you think you might find me here?*"

That voice. Devon knows it.

He is no longer floating, and the heat is gone. He's in a cold, dark, confined place. He tries to look down at his body, but he can't see a thing. The darkness is total. He can't move. He shivers. It's as cold as a tomb—

Devon gasps.

He knows where he is.

Who he is.

"That's right," comes the voice inside his head. It's the raspy voice of Major Musick. "You're in my grave. G-R-A-V-E. Can you spell it, boys and girls?"

The chalk-white face of the clown appears in the dark.

"Yes sirree, boys and girls, Devon is in the grave of Jackson Muir, in the cemetery out by the cliff, under the statue of the broken angel! Hee hee heee!"

Mocking laughter fills his ears.

Devon still cannot move. After much struggle all he manages to do is to lift his head. His nose touches something solid above him. Wood. He realizes he is prone.

In a coffin.

I'm buried alive!

No, he tries to tell himself. *I'm standing in Rolfe's den.*

But the crystal was meant to give him knowledge of the Nightwing, information on his heritage. Why is he then *inside the rotting corpse of Jackson Muir?*

"Isn't that obvious?" rasps the voice of the Madman inside his head. "You want answers as to who you are. You are a Nightwing — like me!"

No, not like you. I am no Apostate!

"How can you be so sure, Devon? You, who know nothing of what you are?"

I know that our power must be used for good. You used it for your own ends, and died because of it!

"We are the same, Devon March. The sooner you acknowledge that, the sooner we shall both have the power to rule the world!"

The Madman's laughter rumbles inside his head. Devon

can smell the decay now, a sickening odor that threatens to overwhelm him.

"Go ahead, try and break free," Jackson taunts him. "What if you never move from this spot? What if I've brought you here for ever? What if you can never break free of me?"

Devon feels terror clutch his throat.

The laughter again.

Could it be possible? Devon begins to panic. *Might I really be trapped here?*

"All too possible," comes the voice of the Madman. "Prepare to spend eternity with me, Devon March — in my grave!"

13
Halloween

This can't be happening . . . can't be real.

Devon struggles to unclasp the bony rotted fingers from across his – Jackson's – chest. He moves the hands down the sides of his body – his *corpse* – and feels the edges of the coffin. Moldy, decaying satin. He can hear a sloshing sound as he shifts in his place.

It can't be, he thinks. *This can't be happening.*

"Devon March, you are mine now. You thought you had won. That you had defeated me! But you were wrong!"

Devon makes a little sound of terror through his rotting skull.

"*Wrong!*" the Madman exults. "Can we spell that, boys and girls! W-R-O-N-G! What's it spell? *Wrong!*"

His laughter threatens to trip Devon over into insanity.

He suddenly remembers the words of Sargon the Great.

Your fear was too great. These things feed off fear. They become more powerful the more fearful you are.

That's right. He's fearful. *Terrified.* But he's got to control his fear. It's the only way.

For some reason, Devon all at once sees Roxanne in his

mind — Roxanne, Rolfe's friend. The woman with the golden eyes. He recalls something she said to him.

"Just click your heels, Devon March. Isn't that how the fairy tale goes in your culture? Click your heels three times and you will go where you want to go."

He tries. He manages to move what he knows are the skeletal feet of Jackson Muir. He brings them together once, then twice, then three times.

It will work, he says, and he believes it. The fear ratchets down.

And suddenly he's back, standing in Rolfe's den, holding the crystal in his palms.

"Get this thing away from me!" Devon shouts, thrusting the crystal as far as he can.

Rolfe tries to catch it but misses. He watches helplessly as his father's prized gem shatters into several pieces on the floor.

"I'm sorry," Devon says. "But I was in Jackson's grave — I was in his *body*!"

Rolfe gingerly picks up the pieces. "It's all right. It retains its power no matter its form."

Devon's panting for breath. "That was worse than anything I've dealt with before," he says. "I *was* Jackson. I was his decomposing *corpse*!"

"Take it easy, Devon." Rolfe places the crystals on the table. "Did the Madman speak to you?"

"Yeah. He wanted me to acknowledge I was like him. But I'm *not*." He looks intently at Rolfe. "Right?"

Rolfe tries to smile. "Not if you don't use the powers you have for evil. But what I don't understand is why the crystal brought you to him. The goal was to give you knowledge about your heritage as a Nightwing."

"It started out that way," Devon says. "I met – Sargon the Great!"

Rolfe's eyes widen in wonder.

Devon manages a small smile. "He was testing me. He asked me to find the demon, but I couldn't see any. So I tackled him."

Rolfe blinks his eyes. *"You tackled Sargon the Great?"*

"Yeah. I passed the test. The demon was masquerading as him." Devon sighs. "But I was unable to defeat the demon because I was scared. That's the thing I have to learn to control."

Devon rubs his head. He's still a little grossed out by being in that coffin. He imagines he can still smell the decay on his clothes.

"But then I remembered something Roxanne said to me," he tells Rolfe. "Reminded me I had the power to get out of there."

Rolfe grins. "You are stronger than any of them."

"Yeah," Devon says. "That's what my dad always said."

"But the fact that the Madman came to you," Rolfe says, clearly alarmed, "merely confirms our fears."

"He's still around," Devon agrees.

The older man sighs. "If he can appear to you, he may still find a way to appear to Alexander."

Devon nods. Thinking of Alexander reminds him of Ravenscliff: he'd better get back soon. Mrs Crandall will start suspecting something's up if he misses dinner. "Rolfe, thanks for all this. I got a lot out of it. Though I'm sorry about break-ing your dad's crystal."

"It's OK, Devon."

He thinks of something. "Hey, Rolfe. Would you give me a ride back to town? Somehow I don't think my little trick in getting out here will work on the way back. I don't think the gods care much about things like curfews or being late to dinner."

"Sure thing, buddy."

"Oh – and what does *abecedarian* mean? Sargon called me that."

Rolfe suppresses a smile. "It means novice. Amateur."

"*Amateur?*" Devon's blood rises. "I'll show *him*." Then he laughs. "Well, I guess there still is a lot I need to learn." He sighs, looking over at the pieces of crystal on the table. "Though maybe I'll wait a while before trying that again. Being trapped in a coffin was a little more than I expected to deal with today."

They climb the stairs and head outside. They're about to get into Rolfe's car when Devon pauses. "*Halloween*," he breathes, as if just realizing something.

"What about it?"

"It's in a couple days," Devon says. "And it's the anniversary of Emily Muir's death."

Rolfe nods. "A day to be on guard, I imagine."

"Yeah," Devon agrees. "We'd better be. Just in case anything goes wrong."

The first thing that goes wrong on Halloween is that Devon forgets his promise to Alexander.

"Oh, *no*," he says, done up in his Nightwing best, scrunched into the backseat of the Camaro between Ana and Marcus, with Cecily in the passenger seat up front. "I was supposed to take Alexander trick-or-treating in the village."

"Like, *groan*," says Ana.

"What was he going as, Freddy Krueger's younger brother?" DJ asks.

Devon ignores them. "Aw, man, I feel terrible." He wants to kick himself. "I didn't see him all day, so I forgot. He was supposed to tell me what he wanted to go as, but he never did."

"He'll get over it," Cecily says. "Besides, Devon, you couldn't do that *and* go to Jessica's party. Believe me, this will be much more fun than hanging with that little monster."

"It's just that he was starting to trust me," Devon laments.

Marcus looks over sympathetically at him. "Sounds like you feel responsible for him somehow."

"Yeah, kinda," Devon admits. "He's never really had good role models."

He feels terrible. He feels as if he's failed yet another test, that if Sargon the Great were around he'd call him an abecedarian, or worse. *A Nightwing shouldn't forget promises*, Devon tells himself. *And little kids should be out having fun on Halloween, not holed up by themselves reading comic books.*

Devon's just glad the TV is still off limits.

As Cecily predicted, the party is a lot of fun. Some of the kids are so done up you can't even recognize them. Jessica herself is an old witch, with a huge putty nose and mounds of warts. Marcus gets the lion's share of applause for his highly detailed Frankenstein's monster, complete with electrodes, scars, and enormous elevated boots, but Ana's harem girl gets plenty of attention, too – especially her exposed belly and her heretofore secret navel ring. Cecily, garbed in layers of crinoline and lace, fumes a bit, but consoles herself with the fact that Devon rarely leaves her side.

The best part of the party is the "haunted house" Jessica's dad set up in the garage, with creepy music playing and Mr Milardo himself costumed as a monster who lunges out at them from behind doors and corners. It's good for a couple scares and a lot of laughs before they head into the house to eat pizza delivered from Gio's.

But Jessica's parents insisted from the start that the party would end precisely at ten o'clock. They begin hauling away the punch bowl and taking down the crepe paper even as their daughter has just popped in another CD. "Aw, Mom," she whines. "Daaaaddy."

But it's to no avail. They begin wrapping up the brownies and turning on the lights, splitting up couples liplocked on the couch.

Outside the exiled kids gather around the cars of upper-classmen. Cecily, determined the night will not end so soon, whips out her cell phone and calls her mother. A muttered conversation, and she snaps it off in triumph. "Mother said I could have a few kids back to Ravenscliff," she exults to DJ and Devon. "Spread the word."

In all, three cars head back to the great house on the cliffs of Misery Point. The kids are psyched; few have ever been up to the old mansion before. They honk and call out from their car windows as they pass each other on the street. Devon suspects the kids in one car — seniors — are high, and worries that the impromptu party might get out of hand.

"Cecily, get real, OK?" he says, as one of the guys moons them from another car. "How many kids did your mother say you could have over?"

"A few."

"How many's a few?"

"Look, Devon. She's up with Grandmama. She won't even hear us if we stay in the parlor."

He narrows his eyes at her. "She said like no more than five or six, right?"

Cecily smirks. "Try three or four."

"Oh, *great*, Cecily. We've got two whole cars following us and some of them we don't even *know*. A couple of the seniors are pretty messed up, too."

"Stop worrying, Devon."

Devon sighs. He doesn't want to come off as a drag, but something doesn't feel right in his gut. This is, after all, the anniversary of Emily Muir's death, and a bunch of kids are coming to party at Ravenscliff – where there's only a mad ghost and a Hellhole full of demons to worry about.

Why can't I just have a normal life? Devon wishes, not for the first time.

Inside the house, they're greeted by a giant jack-o-lantern placed on a table in the foyer, a candle flickering inside. Cecily insists everyone keep their voices down, but most can't help whooping over the exotic trinkets in the parlor. "Check out this suit of armor," gushes one of the seniors, his eyes spacey and bloodshot. "Awesome. . ." He lifts the visor. "Can I try it on?"

"No," Devon says forcefully, shutting the visor. "Why don't you just go sit down on the sofa? Take a load off your feet."

"Not a bad idea, man," he agrees, shuffling off.

"Look at those dudes," DJ says. "They're already higher than King Kong on the Empire State."

That's for sure. Devon watches as the two seniors, both dressed as vampires, make out with two junior girls dressed as Barbie dolls. The others milling about he doesn't even recognize: two kids, one in a lizard mask and the others looking like the thing from *Alien*, are inspecting the shrunken heads in the bookcases. A couple of guys dressed as cowboys light up cigarettes and use the eye sockets of a skull as their ashtray.

"No smoking in the house," Devon complains, pushing them out on to the terrace.

He turns to see Cecily and Marcus dancing – a freaky

sight, given that they look like Scarlett O'Hara and Boris Karloff. Ana jacks up the volume on the CD; rap music incongruously fills the parlor – a place where Devon imagines Horatio Muir once sat listening to Mendelssohn or Wagner.

He stalks over to Cecily, his Sorcerer's cape swinging majestically behind him. "Excuse me, but don't you think this is getting the least bit out of control?"

"Devon, can't we just be shiny, happy people for a change?" she says, dismissing him with her hand. "Do you know how *long* I've wanted to have a party here? How *awesome* it is to hear music – *real* music – in this house?"

"Cecily, if your mother comes down here—"

"*Eeeeeewwwwww!*"

They turn. Even over the thud-thud-thud of the music, they can hear Ana's cry of revulsion. She's standing in front of the bookcase, scrunching her face as the kid in the lizard mask sticks out his tongue.

"That was *so* gross," she's saying. "Do it again."

The kid complies, sticking out a long, slithery, pointed pink tongue from the snout of his mask. "*Eeeewww,*" Ana says again, laughing and recoiling at the same time.

Another girl has walked up to see it too. "How do you *do* that?" she asks. "Is it curled up inside there?" She taps the mask.

Out darts the tongue again.

"Who *is* he?" the girl asks Ana, cracking up.

Ana giggles, looking up at the lizard. "Do we even *know* you?"

Devon's watching intently. It's like a movie in slow motion, the rap music soundtrack fading off in his mind. It's replaced with a high-pitched vibration, matched at that very moment with an overpowering gust of heat.

"Ana!" Devon calls — but his voice sounds muffled and distant to his ears.

The girls begin to turn their heads in his direction — he sees everything in slow motion still — and he tries to run toward them. But his feet feel leaden, the gravity under his feet magnified a hundredfold.

Behind the girls, the kid in the lizard mask opens his mouth, revealing fangs that are all too real.

Cecily sees it too. She screams.

Devon breaks free from whatever force was trying to hold him in place. Cape flying, he lunges at the lizard kid, who's now got his arms around Ana. She turns and looks up into his face, realizing it's no mask, that the tongue and the teeth are real. She screams.

Devon lands a punch into the demon's side. It bellows, dropping Ana to the floor. It turns savagely to snarl at Devon, its long tongue darting in and out of its mouth.

"Come on, ugly, come on," Devon taunts. "Give me your best shot."

"Devon!" Cecily shouts. "Behind you!"

Out of the corner of his eye he can see the kid in the *Alien* make-up. The long talons are real. He slashes them against each other like blades.

"Oh, no, you don't," Devon calls out, trusting once more that his limbs will respond instinctively. They don't fail. His right leg shoots up in a swift kick, slamming his polished Sorcerer's boot right under the Alien's chin, sending him crashing into the sofa. The kids who were making out there yell in terror now, scrambling over to huddle together in a corner of the room.

Meanwhile, the lizard thing is poised on its haunches, ready to spring. "Think again, Godzilla," DJ shouts, tackling the creature before it can strike.

But there are others: the two cowboys pull their claws out of their dungarees and make for the girls.

"Cecily!" Devon shouts. "Just *go* for it! Believe you can and you *will!*"

She looks at him in terror, then back at the approaching cowboys, one of whom licks his lips. His hands are like bear paws: furry and enormous, with claws bared.

"I guess you're not aware who I am," Cecily says, her voice trembling. "I'm Cecily Crandall, and no one – I repeat – *no one* messes with me."

Let her do it, Devon thinks, concentrating.

Cecily lunges, crinoline and ruffles flying, kicking up hard with her knee into the cowboy's groin. He howls in pain and collapses to the floor.

"*Atta girl!*" Devon yells. "Everybody! Just *believe* you can fight them off, and you will have the power to do so!"

The terrified seniors, however, don't try. Instead they run out into the foyer. Looking back just once, they scream and bolt outside. That leaves just the five friends to fight off the four demons.

"We've still got 'em outnumbered," Devon says.

But the demons have them contained. At that moment the double doors of the parlor swing shut, and Devon can hear the lock slide into place. The demon cowboys laugh.

"No one panic," Devon says. "We can do this."

The lizard swishes its long powerful tail, toppling over a table, smashing an antique lamp to pieces.

"Hey," barks Cecily, "that was my mother's favorite."

She's cocky now, swinging her leg around like Wonder Woman on a good day, bashing the thing upside its head. It roars as it falls to the floor.

One of the cowboys hisses, baring his fangs as he prepares

to defend his fallen comrade. "I don't think so," Marcus says, landing a swift flat Frankenstein-boot kick against the creature's back, sending it flying towards DJ, who catches it.

"Hey," DJ says. "I recognize you. You're the one who stole my car!" He grins malevolently. "And you're gonna pay for what you did to Flo!"

He hauls off and punches the beast so hard it flies backward, crashing up against the fireplace.

But the Alien has grabbed Ana. He holds her in front of him, his long sharp fingers ready to slit her throat. It makes all of them pause.

"I'll let her go if you open the Portal," it speaks.

It's the first time that Devon has actually heard a demon speak with a physical voice. It's low, guttural, the sound of stone against stone.

"*Never*," Devon says, facing it. "I'll *never* open that door!"

"Devon!" Ana screams. "Do what he says! *Please!* He's going to kill me!"

"No, he won't." Devon stands firm in front of them. "He *can't* — because I forbid it."

How he knows that for sure is as yet unclear. Maybe the Voice has insisted it's so, and in all the commotion he didn't consciously hear it. But Devon feels confident that he can claim power over these things.

I'm stronger than all of them. I am the one-hundredth generation descendant of Sargon the Great.

His eyes lock on to the eyes of the demon, and he calmly stands his ground.

"I *forbid* it," he repeats.

The thing lets out a long, low growl from deep within its body.

"Let her *go*," Devon commands.

The demon suddenly lifts its face to the ceiling and howls in obvious frustration. It thrusts Ana away from its body. She tumbles into Devon's arms, shaking uncontrollably.

"Now all of you," Devon commands, in a voice barely recognizable as his own. "*Back to your Hellhole! Now!*"

All four of the demons scream then. They fly up into the air and disappear.

". . . Wow," DJ breathes.

"What *were* they?" Ana asks, still quaking in Devon's arms.

Marcus has walked up to Devon and is staring at him in wonder. "How did you do that? How did we all get so *strong*?"

"And what's a Hellhole?" Ana asks.

"I don't have time to explain." Devon turns to Cecily. "We've got to go check on Alexander."

Her face shows sudden fear. "You think they've gone after him?"

"Not them. The Madman."

But just the doors to the parlor open. Mrs Crandall stands there, her eyes wide in outrage.

"Cecily! Devon! What is going on here?"

"Mother, we—"

She's aghast at the sight of the room.

"All the way up in the West Wing we could hear commotion. Your grandmother is *very* upset. She's shaking as if. . ."

She looks around. Devon senses that even beyond the loud music and smashed lamp and the books scattered along the floor she can tell what went on here. She turns her eyes to bear down on Devon.

"I've got to go check on Alexander," he tells her forcefully.

She says nothing.

He turns to DJ. "Fill in these guys as best as you can for

now," he says, nodding over at Marcus and Ana who are still wide-eyed and terrified. "And tell those wimps who ran out of here that it was a Halloween prank. Something we rigged up."

"Yeah," Cecily adds. "Like Jessica's dad did." She pauses. "Only way more realistic."

"Way," Devon agrees.

DJ manages a grin. "They were so messed up they'll believe anything."

Devon and Cecily prepare to head upstairs but Mrs Crandall stops them in the foyer.

"I demand you tell me what went on here tonight," she says, only the slightest quiver betraying her voice.

Devon looks at her hard. "I think you know, Mrs Crandall," he tells her plainly. "I think you know."

She says nothing more, just stands there, the terror stark upon her face, as Devon and Cecily race upstairs.

Alexander's not in his room.

"If only I hadn't forgotten about the trick-or-treating," Devon says.

"Let's look in the playroom," Cecily says.

Devon feels a terrible sensation deep in his gut. Even before they arrive at the door, he can hear the sound of the television.

Tinny laughter, a raspy song.

"Dear God, no," he says, running down the carpeted corridor.

Blue light and silver shadows dance against the wall of the playroom. There, in front of Alexander's beanbag chair, is the old portable TV set from the basement.

"But that's impossible," Devon says, his eyes trailing along its cord. "It was *broken*."

"Not any more, apparently," Cecily observes.

Someone had *fixed* it. Devon's eyes latch on to the black electrical tape wrapped around the cord, securing a new plug to its end. It's now firmly attached to the socket on the wall.

"Alexander!" Devon shouts. "Alexander! Get away from there!"

But when they run up in front of the television set, Alexander's not in his beanbag. They turn to anxiously face the TV. On the screen, Major Musick is saying, "The letter for today, boys and girls, is D."

"Where's Alexander?" Cecily asks frantically, near tears. "Devon, where could he *be*?"

"Deee," Major Musick intones. "And an Eeee, and a Veee, and an Ohhhh, and an ennN."

The camera moves in for a tight close-up. Devon watches, transfixed.

"What's it *spell*?" the chalk-white face of Jackson Muir asks, a maggot crawling from his between his lips.

"*Devon!*" call the children in the bleachers behind them.

"*Devon!*" the demon clown repeats, and he laughs.

Devon watches as the camera moves over to pan across the children. There they sit, in monochrome black and white now, three rows of vacant-eyed kids. There's poor, freckle-faced Frankie Underwood, who Devon knows was his father's first son, who's been sitting there now for decades, staring into eternity.

And there, beside Frankie, at the very end of the row, his deadened eyes staring out accusingly from the screen, is the boy they seek.

Jackson Muir has won. He's taken Alexander Muir into the Hellhole.

14
Into the Hellhole

"I have to go . . . *in there*," Devon says, dazedly.

"In *where*, Devon?" Cecily asks.

He looks at her. "Into the Hellhole." He looks back at the TV screen. "It's the only way to save Alexander."

"Not so fast," comes a new voice.

They both look up. Rolfe Montaigne has entered the playroom. His face is solemn. He looks at Devon intently.

"Rolfe," Devon says. "He's *won*. Jackson Muir has *won*."

Rolfe joins them to look down at the TV set. His face grimaces upon seeing Alexander sitting there, staring blank-eyed out at them. Beside him on the bleachers sits Frankie, Rolfe's childhood friend — as young as he was when Rolfe last saw him, twenty-five years ago.

"Our new letter, boys and girls, is *aaaR*," Major Musick taunts. "As in Rolfe. . ."

"Damn you!" Rolfe shouts, and kicks the TV with his foot, smashing the picture tube and sending the box flying across the floor, smoking and popping.

Devon looks up at the older man. He glimpses the fury beneath Rolfe's suave facade. He's seen it before, in the rage that had erupted at Mrs Crandall, the pent-up anger of having lost five years of his life for a crime he doesn't believe he committed. Anger, too, for losing his father to the demons of this house – demons Rolfe fails to distinguish much from Ravenscliff's living inhabitants.

"Rolfe," Devon tells him, "I have to *try*. You said it was the only way. We can't leave Alexander in there."

Rolfe spins on him. "You have no idea what you're suggesting. You have no idea what going in there entails. I was here when it was tried once before. I saw what happened. I *heard!* Randolph Muir's screams echoed throughout this house. We *all* heard it. We waited and waited and hoped for the best, but neither Frankie Underwood nor Randolph Muir ever emerged from the portal again!"

Cecily begins to cry. Devon just swallows.

"If so powerful and experienced a Nightwing as Randolph Muir could not survive the Hellhole, how can you? A boy who only a few days ago didn't even know what he was? Who even just using the crystal to gain knowledge found himself at the mercy of the Madman? How can you hope to make it back out alive?"

Devon feels dizzy. He tries to focus on Rolfe, to listen to his words, but it's difficult. He looks over at the smashed television set, its guts still smoldering. He follows the cord to where it's plugged into the wall, his eyes resting again on the electrical tape that mended it. Did Jackson do that as well? A ghost who can do electrical work?

Suddenly he feels as if he's not in the playroom, and with him are not Rolfe and Cecily, but rather Dad – and they're in the garage of their old house. Dad is fixing the engine of a neighbor's Buick; his hands are black and grimy, and across his cheek there's a slash of oil, where he must have wiped his face.

Devon is eight, maybe nine — about Alexander's age, leaning up against the car, peering into the engine to watch his father work.

"Dad," he says, "how come you're fixing Mrs Williams's car?"

"She asked me to, Devon."

"But how come you're doing it here, not down at the shop?"

"Because I'm just doing it as a favor for her."

"She's not paying you?"

His father smiles. "No, I haven't asked for any payment."

"You're just doin' it to be nice?"

His father is tightening a nut and bolt. "Not so much being nice, Devon. Just doing what I feel I should."

"But we hardly know her," Devon says.

Now his father straightens up to look him in the eye. "Let me tell you something, Devon. In this world, we're given gifts. One of mine happens to be fixing cars. Well, I believe if we're given gifts, they don't come free. We're given them not to just hide them to ourselves. With any great gift comes responsibility."

Dad reaches over a blackened hand to place it on Devon's shoulder. "You have your own gifts, Devon. Remember, *always* remember, the responsibility that comes with them."

"Devon?"

He blinks, and it's Rolfe standing in front of him again.

"Rolfe," Devon says, "I might not know much about my heritage, but I do know one thing." He pauses, looking up into the older man's green eyes. "The Nightwing believe that with great power comes great responsibility."

"But, Devon——"

"I can't just look away from what I'm called to do." As

much as it terrifies him. "Maybe," he says, "maybe that's my destiny — what I've been hoping to find — the reason why my father sent me here."

Rolfe says nothing. There's nothing more he can say.

Cecily just begins to cry harder, and comes around to embrace Devon around his neck. He just holds her, saying nothing, *thinking* nothing — just feeling her warmth and smelling the sweetness of her hair.

"It can't be happening," Mrs Crandall is saying. "Not again."

"It *is,* Amanda," Rolfe tells her coldly. "I suggest you go sit with your mother for the duration."

She bristles. "This is *my* house, Mr Montaigne. I'll not take orders from *you*."

They're in the parlor. Rolfe has informed her of Alexander's abduction and Devon's decision. She has yet to look over at Devon, who has gone to sit with his friends by the window overlooking the cliffs. Mrs Crandall, while disturbed that they are witnessing this, nonetheless has not yet permitted them to leave the house, apparently fearful of what they might say to others.

"This can't be real," Ana whispers. "All of this can't be happening."

"It is," Cecily assures her.

"How were we able to fight like we did?" DJ asks.

"A Nightwing can share power with comrades in times of a crisis." Devon looks at the faces of his friends. "So long as they *believe*. And all of you did."

"What did Rolfe mean that you were going through a door?" Marcus wants to know.

"Dude," DJ says. "You don't mean that door you told me about — the one that the demons want opened?"

"Yes, that's the one," Devon says, without any emotion. As the minutes tick by, he feels more and more light-headed – as if gravity no longer exists, as if he might just float away. He realizes he's trembling. Cecily reaches over and takes his cold hands into hers.

"This is just too bizarre," Ana says, shivering in her harem-girl's costume. "I want to go home."

"And you will," says Mrs Crandall, approaching them, a forced, artificial smile on her face. "Enough of these Halloween games. My, didn't Devon and Mr Montaigne put on quite the show? I think they should win Academy Awards for their performances, don't you?"

The teens just look up at her as if she's certifiably loony. Which a few of them have thought for some time now.

"Such high-tech gimmicks, too," she's saying. "I hope you all weren't too frightened. Now run along home. Cecily, Devon, it's getting late. You should start getting ready for bed."

Cecily stands and smirks at her mother, hands on her hips. "And will we have some milk and cookies before beddy-bye, Mommy?"

Mrs Crandall glowers at her.

"You guys probably *should* go," Devon says to his friends.

"I don't think so," Marcus tells him. "I'm not leaving you alone for all this."

"No way we're leaving the D-man," says DJ, echoed by Ana.

Devon smiles. "You're good friends. But you have no idea what's going to go down." He laughs. "Actually, neither do I."

"Dude," DJ tells him, "we're stationary till you get back. Deal with it."

Mrs Crandall looms over them. "I'm *telling* you, all of you will have to go home now."

"Amanda," Rolfe calls over to her. "Your mother is no doubt already getting agitated."

She looks over at him significantly.

"And you may want to *be* with her," he adds.

She seems to consider something, then turns to Cecily. "You and your friends are not to leave the parlor. Do you *understand?*"

"They won't leave this room, Mrs Crandall," Devon assures her. "You have my word."

She looks at him now fully, for the first time. There's emotion in her face — feelings tightly coiled for decades. They barely break the surface, but in her eyes Devon can see the pain, the fear, the concern. She reaches over, cupping his cheek in her hand. She says nothing, but her eyes hold his. Then she turns and sweeps out of the room.

"So she knows," Devon asks, as he approaches Rolfe. "She knew all along about my powers."

"I don't know how long she knew about them," Rolfe says. "But she asked no questions when I said you were the only one who could try to save Alexander."

"And she wasn't surprised? She didn't seem at *all* surprised that I was Nightwing?"

"Not in the least."

"Then she *has* to know who my parents are!"

Yet that mystery fades into the horrifying immediacy of the present. Rolfe holds a book open in his palm, and he is reading intently. Devon's not sure what it is, but he recognizes it as one of the volumes Rolfe had said belonged to his father.

"Devon," comes Cecily's voice behind him.

He turns to face her. Her mascara drips down her face. She stands there in her ancient gown, a forlorn belle of Newport.

She can't seem to find the words to fit her feelings. Neither can he. He just embraces her. Crinoline crinkles between them. "Oh, Devon," she finally says. "Please be careful. Please come back to me."

"I will," he says, and they kiss briefly. She's crying too hard to remain in his embrace. Ana is behind her, gently taking her away.

Devon looks back at his friends. He's only known them a short time, but already they feel like old, trusted comrades. He remembers the pentagram he had seen on Marcus' face. Would he ever know what it meant? Would he ever know the answers to so many mysteries?

Or is this it? Is this as much as he'll ever know before being lost in the Hellhole for ever?

"Devon," Rolfe says. "Are you ready?"

He manages a smile. "Let's go."

DJ gives him a high-five. "Go whup some demon butt."

Devon grins.

Rolfe has the key to the East Wing door. He unlocks it, and the door creaks open in his grip. They pass the steps leading up to the tower, Devon wondering only for a moment about yet another mystery hidden there, and head down the corridor, finding the dusty old back stairs. They brush aside cobwebs as they climb. At the top of the stairs, they emerge into the upper corridor of the East Wing that Devon had explored with Alexander. He remembers the dead gas fixtures on the walls, the faded swans of the wallpaper. Ahead the moonlight barely reveals the stained glass of God casting Lucifer into hell. Devon allows himself a moment to muse on the irony, then casts the thought away.

"Devon," Rolfe says huskily, as his flashlight cuts a hole through the darkness, "I wouldn't blame you if you backed out. There's still time."

"I wouldn't be much of a Nightwing then, or you much of a Guardian," he says.

Rolfe looks down at him. In the back glow of the flashlight, Devon can see Rolfe's powerful green eyes. "We're both new at these roles, Devon. My father wasn't able to teach me very much. I'm afraid it's true that I'm not much of a Guardian. I wish I knew more, could give you advice on what to do, what you might find."

Devon grins. "You're all I've got."

"And you're all Alexander has," Rolfe says seriously.

They've entered the old upstairs parlor now. They pass through to the inner chamber. They stand before the door to the windowless room: the heat here is almost unbearable, burning their faces like a sunlamp. Devon can see Rolfe recoil from it too.

"Rolfe," Devon says, suddenly thinking of something. "What made you come to Ravenscliff tonight? What made you show up when you did?"

Rolfe looks at him. "I had a visitor," he says plainly.

"Who?" Devon asks.

"Never mind that now." He opens the door. Heat rushes at them as if from an oven. They both cringe but push on.

Inside the flashlight's beam reveals the room as Devon remembers it: pitch-black and coated in a thick layer of dust. The beam falls upon the books, the rolltop desk, the portrait that looks so much like Devon.

"You see?" he whispers. "It could be me."

Rolfe studies it, moving the flashlight to illuminate first the face, then the neck, then the hands, and then the face again. "Yes," he agrees. "It certainly could be."

"Rolfe," Devon says, "if I don't make it out of there, promise me you'll still try to find out who I was. Where I came from. Somehow, I feel if *you* find out, *I'll* know too."

Rolfe looks down sadly at the boy. "I promise, Devon."

"And tell Cecily. . ." He chokes up. "Tell her that I . . . that I . . ."

Rolfe smiles. "I think she already knows, Devon." He pauses. "But I'll tell her anyway."

The flashlight beam falls on the bolted door.

There's not much time, but Rolfe slides several old volumes out of the bookcase. He blows off the accumulated dust and holds the flashlight over them. He commences to read:

"Once, well before the coming of the Great Ice, the world was inherited by Creatures of Light and Darkness, battling each other for aeons for domination. Their masters were the elemental gods — of fire, of wind, of sea, of earth — omnipotent rulers of nature, neither good nor evil. It was left to their shifting, roiling, restless creatures to forge the battle lines."

Devon listens, but it's difficult to concentrate. Is he learning finally about who and what he is — only to march into his doom?

Rolfe has turned several pages and is scanning them with the flashlight. "'While the Creatures are immortal, the world around them teemed with mortal life, blooming and fading with the seasons. Such life became the pawns in the struggle between the Creatures. The Demons claimed the plants of poison and thorn, the beasts who ate flesh, and the snakes of the grass; the angels held sway over the herbivores and the flowers, the birds of the air and the trees of life-giving fruit.'"

"Rolfe," Devon says. "All that, I'm sure, will make for fascinating reading some rainy day when I've got a fire going and a cup of Nestlé Quik in my hands. But right now I need some practical how-tos, cuz I'm pretty clueless about jumping into Hellholes and rescuing little boys."

Rolfe sighs. He puts down the book and looks into the bookcase with his flashlight. "Here," he says, pulling out another book. "All right, listen to this. 'A Sorcerer derives his power from the Creatures of the other realms, but the source of *their* power remains with the neutral gods of the elemental universe. Anything that upsets the balance of the world upsets the distribution of power between good and evil: that is, the selfish claiming of power or the usage of sorcery for one's own gain. Such action tips the scales away from the universal equilibrium.'"

Devon's getting impatient. "Translation, *please*, Rolfe."

"Good is more powerful than evil," Rolfe tells him plainly. "A creature like Jackson Muir disrupts the balance of power that keeps everything ticking."

Devon remembers his father's words. *All power comes from good*, he'd said. *All truth. Trust in the truth, Devon, and you will always win.*

"The *truth*," Devon says dreamily.

"The *truth*, my friend," Rolfe echoes, "is that you *will* return, and you'll return with Alexander."

Devon swallows. Terror has him by the throat now; he can barely breathe. He knows fear is his downfall, but how can he deny it? Words are impossible. He stares at the metal door in front of him. He can hear them now, scuttering and scampering behind it.

Let us out. Open the door. Let us out.

"But, Rolfe, if I open the door to get *in*, the demons will get *out*," he says.

"No. The book explains that the Nightwing can enter a Portal without allowing anything to escape. It opens only for you, not for them."

Devon just stands there. He's not sure what to do next. Does he attempt to slide back the bolt? He knows he can't do it with his hands. . .

"There's one more thing, Devon," Rolfe is saying. "Something I remember both my father and yours saying, and saying often. A Nightwing must believe utterly in his power. You must *believe*, Devon, if you are to succeed. Remember your confidence against the demons. Remember what you did down in the parlor tonight."

"But that was on *my* turf," he manages to croak, his mouth as dry as the desert. "Now I'm on *their* side of the fence."

Rolfe bears down at him. "You must *believe*, Devon."

Does he? He thinks of the way he ordered the demon to release Ana. The way he's been able to send each and every one of the things that have attacked him back to their Hellholes. The way he'd even been able to empower his friends.

But he'd been powerless against Jackson Muir before.

Remember, Devon, you are stronger than any of them.

Any of them.

ANY OF THEM!

He stands tall in his Sorcerer's boots. In his pants pocket he grasps the St Anthony medal, which he'd been sure to bring along.

He turns to Rolfe. "I believe," he says firmly.

"Then concentrate on the door." Rolfe pulls back a little. "That's as far as I can counsel you, my friend. I wish you Godspeed."

Devon looks at the door. So heavy. Its large bolt so secure. He imagines it being sealed magically by the benevolent power of Horatio Muir. He visualizes the demons behind it. He sees Alexander among them. And suddenly he remembers the boy's words.

You're not going to go away or anything on me, are you?

"I'm coming for you, Alexander!" Devon shouts. "Do you hear me? I'm coming to get you and bring you home!"

The bolt on the door trembles.

This is it, then, he thinks. *What I came to find.*

He knows now his entire life has been pointing toward this moment. Every encounter with the demons in his room, every lesson taught by his father, every flex of his power had been in preparation for this. All those nights lying awake in his bed, staring at the ceiling, wondering why he was the way he was — here, now, is the answer. *This is why.* This is the destiny his father had sent him to Ravenscliff to find. Here, behind a locked door in a secret room in a forgotten part of a mysterious old house. After all these years, *here* is his answer.

He feels subsumed by his power then, as if his heart had suddenly ceased pumping blood and instead replaced it with raw energy — a passion, a magic, that flows vigorously through every one of his veins and arteries. He stands up tall, takes in a long, deep breath — and the bolt on the door slides easily and smoothly from its place.

The metal door creaks open to reveal the blackness within.

The heat.

For several seconds that's all Devon is aware of — the staggering heat, like none he's ever felt before. An old memory resurfaces: as a little boy, opening his closet and tossing in his teddy bear, only to see it disappear into nothingness. Try as he might, he couldn't find Teddy among his shoes and sneakers. Not until several days later did Teddy turn up, far back in the corner of the closet, as if spit up by the demons of the nether regions. Teddy was burnt to a crisp, his fur nearly gone, one scorched button eye staring up at Devon.

"The heat will not burn me," Devon says now, but his voice sounds odd, displaced.

He tries to look around, but sees nothing. The room is gone; Rolfe is gone. There is only darkness, horrible and complete.

He is walking, but there is nothing beneath his feet, nothing solid. For a second he recognizes panic, brewing somewhere down deep inside him, but he's able to suppress a mutiny by his thoughts. He keeps moving forward into the heat.

Now he can hear them. And smell them, too – rancid and rotting. "Take me with you," something whispers in his ear. "Such power you'll have then. I can give you so much!"

"No, not him! Me!" comes another voice. Devon can feel its bony body pressing against him, so cold despite the heat. "Take *me* with you, master!"

His eyes have become gradually accustomed to the dark. He can make out vague images of the creatures that assault him. One is bloated and pulpy, with the hideous bulging eyes of a malformed reptile. The other is nothing but wings and bones, the skeleton of a gargoyle.

He brushes both of them aside. There's a light up ahead. He seems to make out a door: a door he recognizes. He reaches it, places his hand on the knob.

"Devon," comes a voice from the other side.

He opens the door. He's back in his old house in Coles Junction, the house where he grew up. The door leads into Dad's room, where Devon finds him in bed. Everything's as it was just before Dad died: the bedside table with the pills and the empty bottles of ginger ale; the radio playing classical music softly in the background; Dad propped up with pillows, shirtless and gray.

"Dad," Devon says in a small voice.

"Devon," his father rasps. "Devon, come to me."

He does. He nearly falls at his father's bedside, grabbing the old man's hands in his own and staring up into his eyes.

"Why are you here, Dad? Why are you in the Hellhole?"

"Oh, Devon," his father says. "How disappointed I am in you."

The words stab him as surely as a knife in his gut. "Why, Dad? *Why?* I've tried so hard. . ."

"But you've *failed*, Devon. You *failed* me. The boy . . . the little boy . . . the Madman has taken him. You should have prevented it."

Devon looks pleadingly at his father. "I'm trying to, Dad! I'm trying to save Alexander."

"Bah!" His father withdraws his hand. "You are a *failure*, Devon. Your powers are *nothing*."

Devon begins to tremble. This is his worst fear, always lurking down deep in his thoughts. *I won't live up to what Dad hoped. I won't discover what he sent me here to find.*

"Dad, please. I'm trying. . ."

His father scowls. "How you've disappointed me, Devon. I had hoped for so much more from you. But you are not nearly as strong as Jackson Muir."

Devon feels the tears well in his eyes. *What point is there in going on now? If even Dad feels I'm not strong enough. . .*

He suddenly looks up at his father. "Dad, you always said I was stronger than any of them. . ."

"You're *not*, Devon! *He's* stronger than you!"

His voice. Something about Dad's voice.

Devon stands up. "You're *not* my father!" he charges.

The eyes of the sick old man in the bed begin to glow.

"You're not my father!" Devon shouts. "My father always believed in me! He still does! He still does!"

The creature in the bed begins to transform. He throws his head back, laughing, revealing his fangs. Devon watches as the room around him begins to dissolve. The floor beneath him disappears, and he finds himself falling, his cape billowing up around him. He drops through a burning nothingness, the velocity of his fall increasing. If he hits anything solid, he'll die — splattered to bits on the surface of this Hellhole.

But there is no surface here — it is all an illusion, he tells himself. *Even this fall. . .*

"You need to believe in yourself," he hears Rolfe say.

I am not falling, Devon says. *I am stable, strong. In control.*

Immediately the sensation of falling is gone. Devon stands on what feels to be solid ground. But it is still dark, utterly black. He feels the medal in his pocket through his pants.

Give me light, Devon commands.

All at once he can see. There are giant arc lamps hanging above him. He looks around. He appears to be on a soundstage of sorts; there are cameras and monitors and electrical wires. A frayed red velvet curtain separates the backstage area, where he appears to be, from someplace else.

A place he suspects he's seen before.

He hears the music then, indistinct at first, but gradually becoming more familiar.

The theme from *The Major Musick Show*.

"Welcome, boys and girls," comes the gravelly voice of the unseen clown as Devon steps through the curtain on to a wooden floor. He looks around. An unmanned television camera rolls threateningly towards him, as if to record a close-up. Above, the arc lamps hum as they pulsate blinding light on to the set.

Devon's eyes scan across the room. He sees the bleachers, with their rows of blank-eyed children. Devon tries to make out Alexander, but he's suddenly distracted by a hand on his shoulder. A hand cracking with cakey white make-up.

He turns to stare face to face with Major Musick.

"Today's guest star is Devon March," the creature croaks. "Won't you all join me in welcoming him?"

The children in the bleachers begin to clap their hands emotionlessly. Devon looks up into the two television monitors overhead. In one, he can see himself standing with the clown on the set. In the second, he sees Rolfe, Cecily, DJ, Marcus, and Ana, all huddled together, looking in.

They're watching me, Devon realizes. *On one of the TV sets Mrs Crandall had hidden from Alexander.*

The clown's repulsive breath is in Devon's face.

"The word for today, boys and girls, is *Devon's death!*" He cackles wildly. "Oh! That's *two* words, isn't it! Silly old clown am I!"

Devon glares at him. "Two words you're not going to ever say again!"

He lunges, grabbing the filthy thing around its waist and toppling him into the camera. It crashes with shuddering force beneath them. But as soon as they've hit the floor there's nothing in Devon's arms but the clown's tattered white robe. Devon spins around and looks up.

Looming over him is Jackson Muir.

"Such a rash young fellow," the ghost speaks.

Devon cannot move. It's the first time Jackson has spoken in his own voice. It's a deep, commanding voice, with the arrogance dripping like warm syrup from his lips. He towers over Devon's fallen form, an enormously tall man with blazing black eyes and raven hair. He's dressed all in black, a red carnation in his lapel.

"Look at you," Jackson Muir booms. "Wearing my old

clothes. The clothes of the Nightwing. Did you think they would make you more powerful? That somehow they'd frighten *me* – the most powerful Nightwing of all time?"

Jackson Muir leans back and laughs. His laughter echoes throughout the hellish soundstage, rising to the rafters. While Jackson's chin is raised in his own mirth, Devon has time to look around. The rope to the frayed red curtain is coiled near his hand. With one nod of his head, Devon pulls the rope, and the heavy velvet curtain comes crashing down on to Jackson Muir.

It surprises him for just an instant, but it's an instant Devon uses to slip out from under him.

"What a naughty boy you are!" Jackson says, grinning widely, as if he's actually enjoying their encounter.

Maybe he is, Devon thinks. *It's been a long time since he's tangled with anyone who could give him a real run for his money.*

"I've come for Alexander," Devon says. "I'm taking him back with me."

He can feel the power flowing from his hands. He can almost *see* it hurl through the air, like a torrent of knives, like the blast of a ray-gun, aimed at Jackson Muir.

But with one casual flick of his wrist, Jackson diverts Devon's power, sending it cannonballing into a far wall. There it burns a hole into the blackness outside.

"Really, my boy, your Guardian has not taught you very well," Jackson says, approaching him now. "If it were up to me, I'd hand him his walking papers."

"He taught me enough to know that I was stronger than *you*," Devon spits.

"Stronger than *me*?" Jackson Muir laughs again. "I thought we'd already moved on from that foolish notion."

He raises himself to an enormous height. Eight feet now,

then nine, and getting taller. "*Do you have any idea who I am?*" he bellows. "What I have *done?*"

"I know you killed your own family," Devon tells him. "Starting with your wife!"

The demon's face twists into rage. "How *dare* you mention my wife?"

"This is the anniversary of Emily's death," Devon shouts up at him.

"I forbid you to say any more!"

"You can't forbid me to do anything! I know you grieved for Emily! I know somewhere down deep you still have a soul! You loved her, Jackson! But you killed her!"

The demon shrieks in rage.

"Tell me who Clarissa was, Jackson! Why would Emily cry over her grave?"

"You know nothing," Jackson spits down at him.

"I know you might as well have pushed Emily off Devil's Rock yourself! You drove her there! You *killed* her!"

Jackson Muir roars. Suddenly everything changes: the mirage of the television soundstage is gone, and they are in the center of the Hellhole. But its darkness has been replaced by a fierce, harsh, cruel yellow light. Devon can see all of the creatures around him clearly: filthy, slimy, slithering things, moving like worms over and under and around each other. Their bloodshot eyes blink against the light. Their skin is pallid from eons spent in the darkness. They are like creatures under a rock suddenly exposed to the sun: terrifying and terrified.

But the demons' terror turns to fury as they recognize Devon. Their eyes burn, their yellowed talons claw their air. Nearby, one reptilian thing hisses, its forked tongue slapping Devon across his face, its breath reeking like old rotting fish.

"They will devour you as they devoured my fool brother,"

comes the voice of Jackson Muir. "They will consume you into the very bowels of hell."

The things surround Devon, pressing against him from all sides. He tries with all his might to push them away but it is useless. Tentacles wrap around his neck from behind. A talon rips his shirt and claws his chest. He can feel sharp skeletal teeth puncturing the skin of his thigh.

This is it, Devon thinks, just before he loses consciousness. *I really have failed. They are eating me alive.*

15
The Demon Lives

You are stronger than any of them.

"Dad?"

The Nightwing must believe utterly in his power.

"But I've tried . . . failed." The tentacles wrap around Devon's face, leaving him in blackness. "I tried to stand up to Jackson, but he was stronger." He can feel warm blood on his legs where a demon is eating away his flesh. He feels teeth strike bone.

Believe, Devon. Believe. . .

There is nothing left.

"Devon," comes a voice, very small.

The tentacles begin to squeeze his head. *My skull will crack, my brains will ooze out. . .*

"Devon, help me!"

Alexander. It's Alexander.

"You must *believe*, Devon."

Dad! I've got to help Alexander!

"Then you must believe you can," comes his father's voice, as clear as if he were there in the slithering, slimy mass with him.

And maybe he is.

The very thought sparks the last flickering hope deep within Devon's soul. He moves his hand down his leg, pushing past the scaly, squirming monsters that have gripped his body. Through his pants he feels the outline of the St Anthony medal. Dad's medal. His charm.

Devon opens his mouth, tasting the salty pus of the thing that's wrapped itself around his face, and shouts.

"Get off of me, you filthy hellspawn!"

The tentacles disappear. He can see again. He looks down. A stupid-looking creature, hairy with fangs, is gnawing away just above his knee.

"Hey, *you!*" Devon shouts. "No more free lunch!"

And he kicks, sending the thing sprawling into the tangle of beastly bodies around them.

"All of you – out of my face!" Devon commands.

And instantly, they're gone.

He's alone.

The pain finds him then: everywhere, but especially his leg where the thing had been munching away.

I can't give in to it, Devon tells himself. *I have to find Alexander and get out of here.*

Simply by articulating his goal he finds himself back on the soundstage. Major Musick is nowhere to be seen. But the children remain motionless in the bleachers.

"Alexander!" Devon calls.

He can see the boy now, at the end of the row, beside Frankie Underwood. Devon begins to run toward him, his leg burning with pain.

"Alexander!" he calls again.

But the boy remains impassive, staring straight ahead. Devon stands at the edge of the bleachers. His face is about even with Alexander's.

"Alexander, it's me. *Devon*. Come on, buddy. We're blowing this joint."

Still no response from Alexander.

"Come *on*, kid!" Devon shouts. "We haven't got much time!"

He encircles the boy's waist, attempting to pull him off the bleachers. But suddenly there's a hand stopping him, reaching around from the other side to keep Alexander where he is.

It's Frankie Underwood.

"Hey!" Devon shouts. "I'm trying to *save* him!"

Frankie Underwood's eyes belie the immortal youthfulness of his body. They are old eyes, ancient — weary from decades of staring into space.

"Look, Frankie," Devon says. "I know who you are. In fact, you're kind of my *brother*. Your father was Thaddeus Underwood, and he was my father, too. Come with us, Frankie. I can save you, too."

Something flickers in Frankie's eyes for a second. Something shines: a tear, maybe? But he only tightens his grip on Alexander's waist.

"All right, Frankie. I'm sorry to do this to you, but I have no choice."

Devon concentrates. All at once Frankie's arm releases Alexander, and he falls backward into the girl on the other side of him. He makes no sound; he just topples into the girl, who topples into another. The whole row goes down like dominoes. Devon grabs hold of Alexander and scoots him off the bleachers.

"Going so soon?" booms a voice.

A great torrent blows across the stage, sending both Devon and Alexander facedown on to the floor.

"I wouldn't *hear* of it. Why, my little party has just begun!"

Jackson Muir, towering now twenty feet tall, lumbers into view. His every footstep quakes the ground.

"I could crush you like roaches under my foot," he roars.

Alexander pulls himself out of Devon's grasp and runs now toward the demon giant, his arms outstretched.

"You see?" Jackson laughs. "The boy wants me."

"You want to claim him, so you'll finally be master of Ravenscliff," Devon says.

"My rightful heritage," Jackson says, and without Devon even noticing the change, the Madman becomes human-sized again, wrapping Alexander in his arms.

"Come with us, Devon," Jackson says, holding out a hand to him. "It can be *your* heritage, too."

His eyes dazzle. Devon looks away. *I mustn't look at him,* he tells himself. *If I don't look, I will remain stronger . . . than any of them. . .*

"Look at me, Devon." Jackson's voice is softer now, gentle, even kind.

"No!"

"Don't you want it, Devon? It's your birthright. The *power,* Devon. Can't you *feel* it? Come. Join us—"

"Alexander!" Devon calls, still averting his eyes from the Madman. "Listen to me. It's up to you. Make the choice. It's him or me."

Jackson Muir laughs. "He's already made the choice. Now *you* choose, Devon. Life or death. Power or nothingness. I told you before, Devon. We are the same. You and I."

"Alexander!" Devon shouts, ignoring the Madman. "I am *not* like him! I am your friend! He is not! You know that!"

Still not looking at Jackson, Devon manages to see the boy. His passive expression has changed. Devon can see the conflict there.

"I came here to *save* you, Alexander. I came into the Hellhole to find you. To bring you back. He just wants to *use* you. To keep you here for his own power."

The child looks at him. "You forgot me," he says in a tiny voice. "You forgot a promise to me. You said you wouldn't go away but you did."

"And I *am* sorry, Alexander," Devon says. "You will never know how sorry I am. All I can say is — if you come with me now, I will never forget a promise to you ever again."

Jackson Muir is laughing. "Here, Devon. Look. You see?" He opens his arms, lets Alexander stand free. "He is free to go, but he stays. It is his decision to stay with me. Now why don't you join me, too."

Devon keeps his eyes on Alexander. The boy looks at him, then back up at Jackson.

"Alexander, it's up to you," Devon says softly.

The boy looks between the two again.

Then he trembles a little.

And bolts toward Devon, who is nearly knocked over in the impact.

"You've done it, Alexander!" Devon exults. "We've won!"

"*No!*" roars Jackson, who grows to gargantuan size again. He smashes through the roof of the soundstage, and in the resulting chaos, all light ceases. There is an explosion, and debris bombards Devon as he tries to shield Alexander in his arms. There is the sensation of flying through the air, then a sudden collision with something solid.

Then nothing. Nothing at all.

"Devon?"

It's Rolfe's voice.

"Where . . . am I?"

He sits up. He's back in the secret room. Alexander is slumped beside him.

"You did it, Devon!" Rolfe exclaims. "You brought him back!"

Cecily is there, too. "Oh my God! Your leg!" she cries.

Devon, still breathing heavily, looks down at himself. Above his right knee where the thing had been chewing there's a large wound. His black pants are soaked with blood. A puddle is collecting on the floor beneath him.

Cecily immediately tears off her blouse and wraps it around Devon's leg, using it to cauterize the wound. All she's wearing underneath is a brassiere. Black.

"Sweet," he manages to say, smiling.

"Rolfe, push his eyes back into his head, will you?" she says.

Rolfe lifts Alexander. The boy is groggy, but is waking up. "Hey, kiddo. You OK?"

Devon turns to look at the metal door. The bolt is secure again.

And one thing more, he notices:

The heat is gone.

Cecily helps him to bed, and Doc Lamb, long the Muir family practitioner, is called. Devon says he was attacked by an animal in the woods — a "vicious dog," he thinks. He clenches his teeth as the wounds on his chest and leg are cleaned and bandaged. The doctor finishes up by giving him a rabies vaccination. Devon smiles to himself, wondering if antibiotics can protect against viruses spread by things from Hellholes.

Doc Lamb checks out Alexander, too, and proclaims him fine. The boy seems to remember nothing after settling down in the playroom to watch the television.

One by one the crew comes up to visit Devon at his

bedside. DJ, then Ana, then Marcus, and finally the whole gang lines the side of his bed. "We've called a meeting for after school tomorrow," Marcus tells him. "You and Cecily need to fill us in. On *everything*, man."

"We took a pledge," DJ adds. "Not to reveal anything about tonight. But we need to know some answers."

Devon smiles. "I *know* about looking for answers, guys. All right. You'll get them."

They leave so that Devon can rest. Cecily remains, stroking Devon's hair. Rolfe comes back into the room.

"You proved yourself tonight," he tells him.

Devon smiles. "I guess I did." He looks up at Cecily then back at Rolfe. "But there's still so much I don't know, Rolfe. Those guys say they want answers. Well, I'm not sure how much I can tell them, cuz I still don't know *why* I am the way I am."

Rolfe shrugs. "I guess that will just have to remain on the horizon. But I can help you with some things, Devon. There are books we can read together. And there are other people out there we can find."

"Other people?"

"Guardians. Maybe we can track down some who can give us more of what we need to know."

Devon realizes the one person who hasn't come to see him is Mrs Crandall. "Your mother, Cecily," he says. "I still think *she* knows more than she's letting on."

She nods. "Maybe all this will force her into telling her secrets."

Rolfe laughs. "Don't count on it. Your mother has spent her life safeguarding secrets." He looks at Devon. "She was relieved to know you and Alexander were all right. She's with Alexander now. I expect she'll come in to see you next."

Devon can feel sleep overtaking him. He's exhausted beyond words.

"Rolfe," he manages to ask, "do you think Jackson Muir is gone for good?"

"Hard to say. Once before, we thought he was. But you've shown you're stronger than he is. You brought back the boy, which even Randolph Muir was unable to do."

Devon lifts his heavy lids. "I *saw* him. Frankie Underwood, I mean."

A sad expression clouds Rolfe's face.

"I tried to save him," Devon says. "But he wouldn't come."

"Maybe he couldn't. Maybe it's been too long for him."

They're all quiet a moment, thinking of the freckle-faced little boy who had once played happily in this house, now for ever lost.

"Rolfe," Devon says, his voice hoarse. "I've been wanting to ask you. I put the question to Jackson, and he became enraged. Who was Clarissa?"

Rolfe's reaction surprises him. If the mention of Frankie had made Rolfe sad, this name seems to unsettle him even more. His face tightens. "Why do you ask about her, Devon?"

"Because the ghost of Emily Muir led me to her grave. Who *was* she, Rolfe?"

The older man's eyes glisten. "She was the girl in my car, Devon. The girl whose body was washed out to sea."

Devon suddenly feels terrible for raising such a memory. "I'm sorry, Rolfe," he says.

Rolfe tousles his hair. "It's OK. You couldn't have known."

"But what connection does she have? Why would Emily. . .?"

"No connection that I know of, my friend." Rolfe takes a deep breath. "Clarissa Jones was just a girl who worked at

Ravenscliff, the daughter of a servant. A spirited, happy girl." His voice cracks. "One whose death I carry around with me, every day of my life."

They're quiet. Devon tries to imagine where Clarissa might fit in to all of this, but he can't. He's too sleepy to figure out much right now anyway.

"We'll talk more in the morning," Rolfe assures him. "You need to rest now."

"Wait, Rolfe," Devon asks, once again fighting back sleep. "Please. One more thing. You said you had a visitor earlier tonight. Someone who told you what was going down here at Ravenscliff."

Rolfe brightens, smiling again. "Yes, Devon, I did have a visitor." He places his hand on Devon's shoulder. "It was Thaddeus Underwood. Your father."

"My – father!"

Rolfe nods. "You weren't alone in there, Devon. A good Guardian is never far from your side."

Devon had known this. He had *felt* his father with him, heard his voice.

"Did you see him, Rolfe? Actually see him?"

"At first I wasn't certain, but then I found something left behind on the floor that made me positive it was Thaddeus." He reaches into his pocket and hands Devon something. "It was his ring. The one I told you about. The ring with the crystal."

Devon holds it. A plain golden band, worn smooth where Dad wore it for hundreds of years. On one side there's a small white crystal embedded into the gold. Devon knows the ring contains answers for him, more information about his heritage as a Nightwing. But he's too tired to go there now. He sets the ring on his side table, beside Dad's St Anthony medal, which made it to Hell and back with him.

Are you proud, Dad? Did I make you proud?

He doesn't need even the Voice to answer him on this one. Devon knows the truth. He closes his eyes, content at last, and finally allows sleep to take him away.

The storm begins about three-fifteen. And Devon quickly learns the terror is not over. Not yet.

"Foolish boy," comes the voice in the night. "You will not keep him from becoming master of this house!"

Devon sits up in bed. Lightning crashes and illuminates the room. He can see a figure dart into the shadows.

"Who's there?" Devon asks.

No answer. Just the howling of the storm outside. Thunder shakes the great house.

Devon swings his legs out of bed. His right thigh still aches, and the painkiller the doctor gave him makes his head buzzy. But he manages to put his feet on the floor and stand. He pushes the button to turn the light on beside his bed. The lamp stays dark.

Another Misery Point power outage.

"Great," he murmurs, feeling for the candle and matches. He lights the wick and holds the candle in front of him. He sees nothing in his room but shadows.

He pads out into the corridor. He's wearing just his flannel pajama top and boxers. The house feels terribly cold, the wind sneaking in between the eaves. Yet that very chill reassures him: surely if there were demons lurking, he'd feel their heat.

He pauses to look out of the window.

Yes, just as he expected: candle light in the tower.

I am stronger than you, he tells Jackson Muir in his mind. *I will banish you once and for all from this house.*

Downstairs the only light is the dancing flame from the

jack o'lantern, casting weird moving shapes against the walls. Devon wonders why the candle hadn't been extinguished. Or maybe it had been lit again, just to unnerve him?

Thunder rattles the chandelier in the parlor, sending a tinkling sound echoing through the house. The shapes on the wall twist and shift. Devon finds the door to the East Wing unlocked, and beyond it, the entrance to the tower wide open – seemingly left that way to beckon him to enter. He holds his candle high and begins his climb. At the second landing, the door to the room where he'd seen the light is locked. He tries it, but is quickly distracted by motion still higher up. Someone has just moved through the door to the roof of the tower.

That's where I saw Jackson the night I arrived, Devon remembers. *Standing outside on the top of the tower, looking down at me.*

He resumes his ascent. At the top of the stairs the door leading out to the roof stands ajar. Devon steps outside. His candle is quickly snuffed out by the wind and the rain. The deep purple sky above roils as fiercely as the sea below. Sharp lightning slices through the air down at him, as if drawn to the magnet of this house, to the slight figure of the teenager walking along its roof.

There is someone else out here, too, he thinks. Devon can see him now, at the other side of the tower.

But it's not Jackson Muir.

Not nearly so tall. . .

A flash of lightning reveals the figure's identity.

There, in the brief luminescence, is the hideously contorted face of Simon Gooch.

"Simon!" Devon shouts.

The gnomish caretaker grimaces. "You were supposed to be his way back," he rasps. "His way back to reclaim his rightful place!"

Simon's hands are outstretched towards Devon. The boy backs up, looking down over the parapet to some twenty feet below.

"I've been waiting so long for his return!" Simon shouts into the wind. "Such power he promised me! I have known many Nightwing, but none so powerful as he!" Simon has reached Devon, staring up now into the boy's face. "A mere teenager will not be strong enough to stop him!"

Devon stands defiant. "I'm no mere teenager, Simon, and I think you've known that all along. I'm the one-hundredth generation of Nightwing, and I *have* stopped the Madman. I *have* stopped him!"

Thunder roars across the house. The wind buffets them.

Simon only grins. From his pocket he withdraws a small pistol. But it's not the pistol that interests Devon so much as what else falls from his pocket.

A roll of black electrical tape.

"It was *you*," Devon says. "*You* fixed the television set so Alexander could watch. You *wanted* Jackson to get him!"

"Yes," he grunts, sticking the barrel of the gun into Devon's stomach. "It was part of his plan to come back. The boy. You. You were *both* part of his plan."

"You're crazy," Devon says.

Simon grins again, revealing those eerily perfect teeth in his profoundly imperfect face. "I haven't been a Guardian for three hundred years not to know my path to true power. Your arrival here was the sign I'd been waiting for. For *thirty years* I waited." He grunts. "You were *supposed* to be more cooperative."

"Sorry to let you down," Devon quips.

"You were the key. What he's been waiting for ever since they drove the ravens away. The return of the Nightwing to

Ravenscliff! You had the power to bring him back – and still do!"

"Then why did you try to kill me?"

"Just wanted to overpower you – get you to see who was boss. I wanted to get you to do what he wanted. But I'll kill you now, boy, I swear I will – unless you do what must be done. Bring him back! You can still bring him back!" Simon cocks the gun, ready to pull the trigger.

"I don't *think* so," Devon says, and instantly the gun becomes scalding hot. Simon drops it, screaming out.

Devon tackles the little man to the ground. But Simon is strong: stronger than is humanly possible. Devon looks down into the caretaker's face, and he realizes it's not just Simon he's fighting. In the man's beady little eyes Devon can see Jackson Muir staring back at him.

"Listen to me, Jackson Muir," Devon demands. "I don't know what connection there is between you and me, but I'll tell you one thing: *I'm stronger than you!*"

"No," the beast within Simon's body growls. "You are a foolish child!"

Devon pins him down by his wrists. "Why am I the key to bringing you back? Tell me! *Tell me who I am!*"

But Simon roars, sending Devon flying across the tower. Only the stone parapet on the other side keeps him from falling off and smashing to the ground three stories below. The little man staggers to his feet and limps over to where Devon lies. The boy looks up at him.

"Don't you see?" the voice of Jackson Muir booms through the sky, as loud as the thunder. "We are the *same*, you and I! Join me – taste the power I offer you – join me and we both will live supreme!"

"*No!*" comes a new voice. "He is not the same as you, Apostate!"

Devon looks to find its source. This is a voice he has never heard. A woman's voice. Old and broken, but nonetheless powerful.

There, in the doorway leading back down the tower steps, he sees standing an old woman, her long gray hair wild in the wind. She wears a long black robe and her bony fingers point accusingly at Simon.

"You will not have this house! It is not yours!" she commands, and Devon watches transfixed as a bolt of lightning leaps from her forefinger and crashes into Simon's chest.

He screams, grabbing his heart. He staggers, then falls backward – over the parapet of the tower, screaming long and wild until his horrible impact with the earth silences him forever.

Devon stands. He looks down. Simon's crumpled body lies on the driveway of Ravenscliff, only a few yards from the front door.

He spins around. The woman is gone. But there are footsteps coming up the stairs now: Mrs Crandall, wide-eyed and breathless, emerges from the doorway. She looks at Devon, then over the edge of the tower. She recoils in horror.

The rain comes down heavier now.

"He tried to kill me," Devon says plainly, shivering in his pajama top and boxers.

She just looks at him. Then – in the last move Devon would ever have expected her to make – she reaches over and pulls the boy close to her chest. She holds him there, tightly, for several long moments, as the rain comes down fiercely around them, drenching them both from head to foot.

The next morning Devon meets the woman he believes rescued him.

"Mrs Muir," he says.

But the old woman in the bed just looks at him with uncomprehending eyes, smacking her toothless gums. She curls her long gray hair around a finger twisted with arthritis, blinking her eyes as she looks at Devon.

"I *told* Mama I can't see any beaus today," Mrs Muir says coquettishly. "How *naughty* of you to sneak up here."

Mrs Crandall stands behind him. "Her mind comes and goes, Devon," she tells him. "That's why I felt it better you not meet her right away."

But this morning he'd *insisted* he meet her, certain that it must have been she who saved him the night before on the tower. What other old woman lived in this house? What other woman could have the power of the Nightwing?

And seeing her now – well, he's quite certain it's the same woman. She *must* be. Isn't she? The same long gray hair, the same bony hands – but how *frail* this woman is. How . . . *confused* . . .

"Mother hasn't been out of bed in *weeks*, Devon – and it's been *years* since she's left her rooms." Mrs Crandall smiles at Devon's befuddlement. "There's certainly *no way* she could have ever climbed those tower stairs."

"It was *her*," Devon says. "It *had* to be."

Mrs Crandall just smiles again.

He thinks of something. "I've seen her there in the tower before, too." Devon looks from Mrs Crandall back at the old woman, who now softly croons some old ditty to herself. "One night she called me – by name – from the tower window."

"Those tower rooms are locked, Devon. Mother doesn't have a key. And even if she *had* been able to manage the stairs, and manage to find her way into a room – she didn't know your name. She didn't know you were even *in* this house." She looks over at her mother sadly. "Still doesn't, I'm afraid."

"Who are you?" the old woman asks her daughter, her rheumy eyes trying to focus. "Are you the new maid?"

"Mother, I'm Amanda. Now just close your eyes. I'll be back soon."

"Goodbye, my beau," she calls out to Devon, waving her gnarled, veined hand. "Next time I'll wear my prettiest pinafore! You'll see!"

Cecily confirms that her grandmother does indeed slip in and out of rationality, and that it's highly unlikely she could have made it up those tower steps. She also can't imagine that it was she who called to Devon that night. Cecily insists it was the ghost of Emily Muir.

"I don't know *what* to believe," Devon admits.

They're sitting in the parlor, waiting for Mrs Crandall. She's allowed both of them to take the day off from school, given everything that happened last night. Devon hadn't slept after the episode with Simon on the tower. He'd waited with Mrs Crandall as she called the police. Soon the grounds were swarming with cops. That snotty little deputy Joey Potts had taken statements from them. Both Devon and Mrs Crandall swore that they'd heard a scream and, upon investigation, found Simon dead, an apparent accidental fall. Or a suicide?

Deputy Potts had looked suspiciously at Devon's wounded leg. "How'd you get *that?*" he asked.

"You can check with Doc Lamb," Devon told him. "Wild dog. Better track it down, Joey."

Sheriff Patterson, however, had seemed convinced Simon's death was an accident. Of course, they'd have to do a full inquiry. Mrs Crandall understood fully, and promised complete cooperation. Then Devon had watched solemnly as Simon's broken body was loaded into the ambulance and taken away.

After that, Mrs Crandall had refused to speak more until the morning. Now, after seeming to have disproven Devon's contention about the old woman's identity, she has told Devon and Cecily to wait for her in the parlor.

He looks around now at the skulls and crystal balls in the bookcases.

The Voice told me they were mine, the very first night I came here, Devon thinks, *Jackson Muir said he and I were one.*

"I can't stop thinking about that poor kid Frankie," Devon tells Cecily. "He's my *brother*. And he's still trapped in there."

She shudders. "You tried to help him, Devon. You said he wouldn't go with you."

Devon looks at her fiercely. "Someday, Cecily, I promise I'm going to get him out. I'm going to save him." He sighs. "I just need to know more about what I'm doing."

"Look, Devon," Cecily tells him. "Mother has finally promised to tell us everything. All our questions will be answered."

He doubts that. Mrs Crandall arrives as composed as ever, and as guarded. Still, Devon knows there are certain things she can no longer deny. He watches as she settles into her chair in front of the fire.

"Well, it's over now, and we can all breathe a long sigh of relief," Mrs Crandall says.

"Did you have any idea that Simon was working in league with Jackson Muir?" Devon asks her.

She shakes her head. "No, and I blame myself for that. I look back now over the years and see how fascinated Simon was with our family history. I should have suspected. But he had been a trusted family servant for so long, I didn't allow myself to question him."

"He said he was a Guardian."

This time she nods. "He had worked with many of the Nightwing before coming to Ravenscliff. But you see, Devon, when he came here, he professed a desire to leave that world behind. We had repudiated our past involvement in sorcery ourselves, so he seemed ideal to work for us. Unfortunately, he harbored other plans."

Devon leans forward looking at her. "*How* did you repudiate sorcery? Isn't it in your *blood*?"

She closes her eyes. "Rolfe told you of the horrible events that happened here in the past. How my father was killed. After that, spells were cast that ended our sorcery, divorced us from our Nightwing heritage, and took the sheen of magic off Ravenscliff."

"That's when the ravens disappeared," Devon says.

She opens her eyes. "After my father was killed, after the little boy Frankie was lost – those of us who were left determined our family would never again find ourselves at the mercy of Jackson Muir."

"But Jackson *returned*," Cecily says. "Mother, you always said the ghosts in this house would never harm us. But Jackson tried to *kill* Alexander."

Mrs Crandall doesn't look at her. She keeps her gaze fixed on Devon. "That's because *you* arrived, Devon."

"Me?"

"Jackson sensed that you were Nightwing. He determined you would be the conduit by which he returned to power. Your arrival here stirred back to life whatever mystical forces remain here. Your very presence counteracted the spells that had repudiated our sorcery."

She stands up and approaches him.

"We are all very grateful to you for saving Alexander. It was a courageous and noble deed." She pauses. "But the fact remains, Devon, that if you had not been practicing sorcery in the first place, Jackson would never have been able to return. *You* are responsible for the mystical disruptions that happened in this house."

"But he *had* to use his powers, Mother! There were things – demons – coming at him! And at me!"

"Be that as it may," Mrs Crandall says, still looking down at Devon, "they are gone now, and all practice of sorcery must cease. Do you *understand*, Devon?"

"I . . . I'm not sure I can promise that, Mrs Crandall."

"How can you *say* that? Would you risk bringing danger once again to this family?"

"Of course I wouldn't want that," Devon tells her. He seems to think of something. "Mrs Crandall, have you *really* surrendered all your powers? I mean, with a threat as great as Jackson, did you maybe just keep a few?"

She stiffens. "I told you. Sorcery and magic were repudiated here."

"Yeah, but I still remember what you said about redoubling your efforts to protect us from Jackson. What did you mean by that?"

She sniffs. "Simply that I would make sure no one got into the East Wing again."

"What about your mother, then? She must have kept her powers. I saw her last night on the tower! It *had* to be her! She shot lightning out of her fingers!"

"Devon, I thought your visit to my mother had convinced you that she's incapable of even remembering my *name*, let alone practicing sorcery."

"That much is true, Devon," Cecily says. "Grandmama really is bedridden."

Devon's not buying any of it. "All I know, Mrs Crandall, is that my father brought me up to respect my abilities. He promised that some day I would understand them."

She's rigid, unmoving. "If your father had wanted you to practice and develop your powers, why did he never tell you about the long tradition of the Nightwing? Why did he never share with you the secrets of the Guardians? Why did he never train you in the use of your powers?"

She raises herself to her full height as she's so prone to do whenever she attempts to intimidate him. She glares down at him.

"Thaddeus Underwood was a great Guardian," she says, "one of the most respected in all the world. Why then did he become just plain Ted March, raising his son to be just an ordinary boy?"

Devon stands up straight himself, raising his face to look at her directly. Her intimidations no longer work on him. "I don't know, Mrs Crandall," he says. "Why don't *you* tell *me*?"

She backs down, a little.

"All I know, Devon, is that for whatever reason Thaddeus adopted you, he chose to raise you without a knowledge of your heritage. He did not want you to be part of the Order of the Nightwing."

Devon can't answer. Maybe she's right. Dad never did tell him much . . . and he *could* have. He could have told him so much. But he didn't.

He looks over at her. "When he left here, Mrs Crandall, did he give any indication *why*? Or of any Nightwing who might have had a child? Namely, me? Rolfe told me that my father said he'd heard that the one-hundredth generation had been born. . ."

"No, Devon. Thaddeus did not give any indication why he was leaving or where he was going." She walks over to the fire and warms her hands. "In fact, I believe your father sent you here because he knew of our repudiation of sorcery. He knew we'd understand your abilities, but he also knew we would forbid you to use them."

"My father never forbade me to use them. In fact, he—"

"None of that matters," Mrs Crandall says severely, interrupting him, "because *I* do. I *forbid* you to use any magic, any sorcery, from here on in!"

Cecily just looks at Devon anxiously.

Again Devon's not sure what to say. He can't openly defy Mrs Crandall. It's her house, and she's his guardian. Lower case.

"Mrs Crandall," he says, after a moment's consideration, "I promise I won't use my powers except to protect myself or anyone else from demons or Jackson Muir. Is that fair?"

She looks at him warily. "I suppose so. For now." She brightens. "But I truly believe that such protection will no longer be necessary. Once more, we do not have to fear anything in this house."

"I hope you're right, Mrs Crandall."

"I *am*." She looks over at Devon. "And one other rule still stands, Devon. I do not want any further contact with Rolfe Montaigne."

"But, Mrs Crandall — he's the only one who can tell me more about my Nightwing heritage—"

She scowls. "If you are not practicing sorcery, you don't need to know." She seems exasperated. "*Devon*. For God's sake. You're a high school sophomore. Next semester you've said you want to join the track team. You have studies to think about. Algebra, trigonometry. And then college. A career. That's *plenty* for a young man."

"I have a right to know who I am," he tells her. "I believe my father wanted that much for me anyway."

"Then why did he never tell you?" She crosses the room, placing her hands on the knobs of the double doors of the parlor. "You've learned enough. There's no need to know anything more." She opens the doors to leave. "And be careful of how much you share with your friends. There are already too many legends of Ravenscliff out there. Let's not stir the pot any more than we already have."

Indeed, when they catch up with the gang at Gio's, Devon is unsure how much he should say, but he does manage to give them a bare-bones account of the episode with Simon, promising that as he learns more he'll fill them in.

"But, dude, if we're going to be doing any more fighting off demons," DJ says, "you got to promise to make us honorary Nightwing again."

Devon promises. He's glad to hear they've done a good job convincing the terrified seniors that the fight with the demons had been staged for their benefit. Devon knows he can trust these guys. In some ways, after just a month, they've become the best friends he's ever had.

It's Alexander he isn't so sure about. He hasn't been allowed to see him yet, and he half expects that when he does, the child will glare up at him with the same malevolence as ever in his round button eyes.

"Alexander?" Devon whispers that night, peering into the boy's bedroom.

"Devon!" Alexander calls happily.

"Hey, buddy. Feelin' better?"

Devon sits on the edge of the bed. Alexander's been reading the comic books they'd bought: Superman, Batman, Justice League.

"Yeah. I feel fine. But Aunt Amanda said I had to stay in bed all day, just to be sure I wasn't coming down with anything."

Devon looks at him. "You remember anything about last night?"

"No. The doctor said I fainted or something." Alexander tries to recall what happened. "I was waiting for you to go trick-or-treating, but you never showed up."

"And I'm real sorry for that, Alexander," he tells him.

"I know. I think I remember you telling me that at some point."

Devon smiles. "I did. But to make up for it, how about if we go into Newport this weekend and play some video games at the arcade?"

"Cool," Alexander says.

"We'll get you out of the house more often. Away from the old boob tube."

Alexander frowns. "I hate television," he says.

"Me, too, buddy." Devon tousles his hair. "I'm glad we're friends now."

"Me, too." Alexander looks over at Devon. "You still promise you're not going to go away?"

"Still promise, Alexander," Devon tells him. "You can count on that."

Epilogue
The Ravens

"Well, the most bizarre thing of all this is the change in that little monster," Cecily says as they stand on the terrace, looking out along the cliffs. At last, a peaceful, starry night over Misery Point. "You really *are* a master sorcerer, Devon."

He looks up toward the roof of the old house. He sees motion there, a flurry of wings in the moonlight.

"Cecily," he whispers, pointing. "Look."

Ravens.

They've returned.

The birds settle down, one by one, dozens of them, taking up their posts once more. Enormous, proud, fierce ravens with piercing, shining eyes.

They left when the Nightwing were gone from Ravenscliff. Devon smiles. *Now they've returned — because a Nightwing has come back as well.*

He beams. "If I'm such a sorcerer," he says, embracing Cecily, "maybe I've cast a spell on you."

She encircles his neck with her arms. "Only magic there is those hormones you talked about."

They kiss.

But Devon has become accustomed to doing everything with at least one eye open. With that eye he spots something else in the upper reaches of the great house.

A light in the tower.

"Cecily," he says again. "Look."

She sees it.

"Always that light," Devon says, shaking his head. "What does it mean?"

Then they *hear* something, too, from behind them.

The *sobbing*.

They step back into the parlor and listen as the long wailful cries echo across the marble of the great house.

"Some things don't change," Cecily says, sighing, running a hand through her hair.

Devon looks up into the sad eyes of the portrait of Emily Muir. There are still many secrets left to discover at Ravenscliff. Jackson is gone, but for how long? What does the story of his life – and the lives of all those who have lived here – have to do with the mystery of Devon's own past? Who was Clarissa Jones? Who is the boy in the portrait? Who is buried under the gravestone marked DEVON?

Simon had hinted at knowing some of those answers – and Jackson, too. But their secrets had gone back with them to their graves. Would Devon ever learn what they were?

And what of his Nightwing heritage? Forbidden access to Rolfe, how could Devon find out the history of his people? Dad's ring would tell him what it might, but he'd need help in understanding it. Would he forever be made to go behind Mrs Crandall's back to find out the truth?

He stares up into the oil-paint eyes of Emily Muir. There, a single glistening tear falls slowly, achingly, down the portrait's face.

CONTINUED IN BOOK TWO

ACKNOWLEDGMENTS

Gratitude goes to Judith Regan, for believing in this book from the start; to my smart and supportive editor, Cassie Jones; to my agent, Malaga Baldi, for her tireless determination; to James Rea, for creating such a phenomenal website (www.ravenscliff.com); and to T.D.H., for having faith in the power of the Nightwing.

To the readers: I want to hear from you. Write me at HuntingtonGeoff@aol.com.

– G.H.